Instruments of Darkness

Nancy Huston

Instruments of Darkness

Nancy Huston

LITTLE, BROWN AND COMPANY (CANADA) LIMITED
BOSTON • NEW YORK • TORONTO • LONDON

FIRST PRINTING

Canadian Cataloguing in Publication Data

Huston, Nancy, 1953 –
[Instruments des ténèbres]
Instruments of Darkness

ISBN 0-316-38020-2

I. Title. II Title: Instruments des ténèbres.

PS8565.U825515713   1997   C843'.54   C97-930103-3
PQ3919.2.H8715713   1997

Typesetting & Design by *MICHAEL P. CALLAGHAN*
Composed at *MOONS OF JUPITER, TORONTO*
Cover Design by *TANIA CRAAN*
Cover Photo by *BARBARA COLE*
Printed and bound in Canada by *BEST BOOK MANUFACTURERS*

The Walt Whitman quote appearing on page 23 is from
"Out of the Cradle Endlessly Rocking."

Several episodes of the *Resurrection Sonata* were inspired by
actual events related in André Alabergère, *Au temps des laboureurs
en Berry*, Cercle généalogique du Haut-Berry, 1993.

LITTLE, BROWN AND COMPANY (CANADA) LIMITED
148 YORKVILLE AVENUE,
TORONTO, ON, CANADA, M5R 1C2

10 9 8 7 6 5 4 3 2 1

for Ethel Gorham,
guardian devil

Table of Contents

"But 'tis strange,
And oftentimes to win us to our harm,
The instruments of darkness tell us truths ;
Win us with honest trifles, to betray's
In deepest consequence."

SHAKESPEARE, *Macbeth*

"The mind is its own place, and in itself
Can make a Heaven of Hell, a Hell of Heaven"

JOHN MILTON, *Paradise Lost*

"Nothing can
Quench the mind if the mind will be itself
And centre of surrounding things; 'tis made
To sway."

BYRON, *Cain*

"It's *the same life.*"

JOHN BERGER

The *Scordatura* Notebook

Lake House, August 31st

Late summer. I note this.

But add — I've never given a flying fuck about nature, never collected leaves, not even as a child, not even pebbles. I don't care whether it's spring or fall or winter; the miracle of life doesn't touch me — life budding, evolving, exploding, changing, buds swelling sexily and bursting into bloom — all of this leaves me cold (though I'm not a cold woman — not frigid — not at all). It has always baffled me that people like to garden, find it worthwhile to tell each other their tomatoes have come up, or to exclaim over flowers, flowers, every year the same flowers — hydrangea, for instance.

Hydrangea with their dowdy pastel puffs win first prize for my hatred. People who exclaim over hydrangea come in a close second.

No, I am exaggerating (I have a pronounced penchant for exaggeration). There are any number of things I hate more. Hatred is one of my sweet pulsating inner specialties, in my heart is an entire university that teaches nothing but hatred, offers graduate seminars in hatred, distributes Ph.D.'s in hatred.

Still, I am polite. When women in the neighbourhood point out to me their blue bursts of hydrangea and sigh in ecstasy, I do not slap them.

I've never wanted to know the names of plants and flowers and trees, this is a game, a silly game, we make up names for them and then we test each other's knowledge of these names, they have no names so why do we pretend?

Nature is silent.

I am the namer.

(Myself also I have named, or renamed. My parents called me Nadia and when it became clear to me that "I" did not exist, I cut it out. Now my name, pen name, pet name, only remaining name, is Nada. Nothingness. The initial N delights me. A nineteenth-century French author once wrote that this phoneme was particularly apt for expressing ideas of negation, annihilation and nothingness, and I tend to think — *Nil Nul Nix Niet* — that he was right. His own name was Nodier.)

Even here, in this dear small clapboard house to which I retreat when my nerves have been thoroughly jangled by the screaming sirens of Manhattan, I do not grab a basket as other women do and go out to gather blackberries. The fact that they're ripe in late August and not in early February is of no interest to me.

So much that is arbitrary people make a fuss about. And then these irrelevant details start taking up all the room. When one was born (whence: phases of life, sense of contemporaneity). Where one was born (whence: patriotism, baseball games, wars, dotdotdot). Time passes, yes, this is one of the raking relentless facts of life. It has passed through my child's body, making it the body of a woman, a body of adamant sterility, and soon it shall make of it a stiff, I don't see what there is to rejoice over, this is it, *amen*, the flat grim sordid, so-what truth. The God/damn truth. Personally I put little stock in truth — falsehoods are what fire me. My own falsehoods especially. Even as a child I loved to lie and ever since I started to write, lying has been my ruling passion.

Late forties now (forty-nine: how late can you get?) . . . Stella says you know you're getting old when people stop calling you wild and start calling you things like "peppy" or "plucky." But so far it seems to me that my beauty isn't fading, only steeping, growing steadily stronger and darker like good tea. How many men have visited my body? (I used to enjoy imagining that one day all the penises I've met would be lined up together, side by side — all, of course, in full tumescence — not for idiotic length comparison, simply for counting and inspection — would I recognize which was whose? Some circumcised and others not, this long pink slinky one, that swarthy chunky one, some thick-veined, others with hairy or violaceous testicles — a rather puerile fantasy, I admit.) How many men? Years since I stopped keeping track. Some, several, continue to come to my bed and pass over me, spilling their seed into a stomach they know will never stealthily transform it into a pudgy squaller. It's too late now anyway, of course. But always, all my life long, just like the beautiful witches who cavorted with Satan during Black Sabbath ceremonies, I've needed to know my pleasure would be sterile. Otherwise no pleasure.

Getting rid of my babies has moved me exactly as much as flushing down the toilet a beetle found on its back on the bathroom floor, flailing its legs in the air. A tiny distress; finished.

I don't care is my deepest opinion about the world of humans. This is what people bear most badly. One can be insensible to gardens provided one is interested in feminist politics, or vice versa. Both concerns, all concerns, all the things friends pour out their hearts to me about, worry about, lose sleep over, invest huge sums of money in, bore me to death. These are epiphenomena. Indifferent to me, in and of themselves. I cannot tell my friends this — it is the most silent of my silences, this knowledge, when it wells up in me in the midst of a conversation about day-care centres or computer programs or defence budgets or racial strife — I don't care.

I don't care about the world.

The world is a lost cause, meaningless.

Meaning is what I make.

Come with me.

Yes (instantly).

I always say yes to my muse, my fine invisible dæmon, the disincarnate voice who gives me access to the beyond, the otherworld, the underworld. The devils of Ivan Karamazov and Adrian Leverkühn have always made me scream with laughter, materializing as they do in the flesh, rigged up in mid-

dle-class pin stripe suits and pince-nez . . . oh no no
no no! *My* dæmon is a man but bodiless — the only
man who has never disappointed me, the only one
in whom I have perfect confidence. We fly together. When he decides to take me. It's up to him.

Fly with me.

Yes. I believe you. Yes.
We take off. We soar together, floating, gliding
through a sort of effluence. A non-concrete substance, flimsier than gossamer, more impalpable
than air. An im/material. There is no effort, no
wind, no atmospheric resistance, and though we
move quickly our motion has nothing to do with
speed, with measurable velocity, is it miles, is it
years, no matter, we can do it, do anything, fly
through not only time but space, endless space —
oh, not the cosmos, nothing as insipid as the cosmos — we are not soaring amidst the glitzy con-
stellations of the Universal Films logo — no, it is
flight without sight, over oceans and decades but
smoothly, soundlessly, without turbulence, or fric-
tion of any sort, in just exactly the time it takes to
say it, read it, think it, neither an instant more nor
an instant less . . .

Come with me.

Yes . . . through the soft ethereality . . .
There becoming *here*, arriving thus in another
continent, but still a part of this Earth, this same old

planet, and zeroing in towards the heart of that continent already known as Europe — zeroing in but gently, imagelessly, not in the blatant maudlin way of an airplane or a helicopter or a camera zoom, no, riding on the back of the idea of zeroing in, hunched upon the words zeroing in, towards the heart of the heart of that continent, not only France but the dead centre of France . . .

Then becoming *now*, flipping backwards through old photo albums, the colour gradually fading into black and white then sepia, sinking towards grey, back farther still, farther still, beyond the yellowing serrated edges of the oldest photographs of your grandparents, your great-grandparents, the onion-skin pages torn along their accidental folds, back beyond the invention of photography, daguerreotype, beyond the shimmering mists of memory, all the way to the year 1686, the year after the Sun King decided to revoke the unconscionably tolerant Edict of Nantes, thereby forcing Protestants to hide or convert or emigrate . . .

Now we are then, here we are there and — quickly now, close-up — the space can be covered in an instant or an hour, all is infinitely extensible, infinitely compressible, we are in control — yes, it is starting to happen . . .

Look, look.

I look . . . and out of nowhere, an image materializes, crystal clear.

The Resurrection Sonata

I - Nativity

A candle.

And then — a forest of candles of different lengths, burning, trembling, the flames flickering because there is so much rushing about in the room, the smell of fear in the air, women's long skirts swishing as they take fast, effective steps, silent peasant women with pursed, tightened lips, it is not only fear one smells in the air, no, it is death, the smell of death, and every few minutes the screams of the shepherd-girl who used to sing so beautifully rent the air, the screams of young Marthe Durand trying to give birth, the sound of it is enough to curdle your blood, turn your blood to ice, but her own blood is neither curdled nor frozen, her own blood is flooding out of her, the women have laid her down on a palliasse to absorb the vermilion liquid, they stare anxiously into the face of the poor girl in labour by the flickering candlelight, they know she is not going to make it, the little shepherdess with the silvery voice will not pull through, she's only seventeen years old and already her strength is ebbing away, her friends are fearful because the confirmed matron, herself ill and bedridden, was unable to come and none of them has the authority to pronounce the words of private baptism *in extremis,* soon they will have to go and waken the parish priest.

One of the women keeps an eye on a cauldron of boiling water suspended from the pot-hook in the fireplace, another holds up to the fire the linen that will receive the child but young Marthe is still struggling, still screaming, she strains with all her strength against the ungentle, unclean peasant hands that pin her down — screaming, she arches her body against them but the others press her back onto the palliasse, this must end soon, they are frightened, turning away from her they make the sign of the Cross, and then, furtively, covering their mouths with their hands, murmur words known to themselves alone, words that have nothing to do with the Virgin Mary or her Son the Baby Jesus — all the while knowing that whatever words, prayers or supplications they might now pronounce, it is already too late. Marthe's best friend Raymonde is holding her head on her lap, stroking her face with a clean cloth, gently wiping the sweat that trickles from her forehead and her neck, speaking to her softly all the while, telling her Don't worry, Marthe, you'll be fine, we're all here with you, we've all been through the same thing, it comes out fine in the end, calm down now dearie, calm down sweet friend, and meanwhile the other women continue to rush about, to pray and to despair.

At last Marthe's screams grow farther apart and begin to sound more and more like sighs, almost like sighs of happiness, yes it is almost as if she were humming with contentment in her sleep — again one can recognize, in an attenuated form, the pure melodious voice of the young shepherdess — and Raymonde, still holding her friend's head and stroking her brow, feels the sighs of contentment cease at the very instant the muscles of Marthe's neck go slack and her head abandons its full weight upon her lap.

Silence. Now is the time. They must make haste. All of them glance covertly at the eldest among them — the act is hers to perform.

And so, yes — with a nod of her head, the old woman tells Cécile, Marthe's younger sister, to run lickety-split and fetch Father Thomas in the nearby town of Torchay, and the terrified girl dashes out of the house without even thinking to take her cape, despite the icy penetrating humidity of the November night.

Cécile gone, the old woman crouches down next to the dead woman's bared stomach. The knife-point slides in under the breastbone and commences its descent, human flesh is so tender, tenderer still than pig flesh when one slits the hog open on slaughtering-day — there, too, from breast to groin, it is the same gesture only infinitely smoother in the present case, Marthe's flesh offers itself up to the knife-edge like the finest of roast meats, cooked to perfection and served up rutilant on the Sun King's dinner table, the knife's descent is swift, the flesh lips part and the blood streams forth; Marthe's friends stare wide-eyed at the scene, divided between curiosity and dread.

Suddenly the hovel door bursts open, letting in a gust of cold wind, the disgruntled priest, and little Cécile, panting, beside herself.

Naturally, good Father Thomas does not have his cassock on, and he is in a foul mood because Cécile's coming tore him from the most sensuous of dreams, he scarcely had time to grab his spectacles and boots and a flask of holy water — and now, his inner gaze still trained upon the imaginary breasts between which he had been rubbing his half-imaginary penis, he absent-mindedly begins to sprinkle water on the fetus the old woman has withdrawn from the cadaver, *In nomine patris et filii et spiritus sancti* — when, suddenly and in unison, the women utter a cry of surprise

it is not a child, no:

it is *two* children! Two of them, embraced, entwined, their limbs affectionately mingled in a tight hug — this is why their mother had been unable to expel them through the natural passageway, this is why their mother is dead.

When the women have managed to separate the babes, gently loosening their grip on one another, prying away tiny sticky fingers, pulling at minuscule arms and legs, severing the twisted braid of their umbilical cords, it turns out that the twins are boy and girl. The precious membrane of the caul is on the girl's head — the women murmur and grunt softly in approval as they clean and caress her, for it is a sign from Heaven, she will lead a long and felicitous life, a life of luck.

The names are chosen — expeditively, so that the priest can go back to bed, tomorrow he will commit all of this to writing in the parish register — the girl will be called Barbe, and the boy Barnabé. Good, now. It is done.

The *Scordatura* Notebook

Perry Street, September 13th

I must work fast, pen flying, phone off hook, long strand of hair in mouth, glasses slipping down nose, knees squeezed together, tension in shoulders, con/centr/ation (everything converging towards the centre) — quick, quick, before the putrefaction sets in. The sentences must slipslide through me without touching me. My contact infects them. Everything my dæmon says, thinks, does is sublime, pristine, suprahumanly beautiful. As soon as I intervene it is tainted, impoverished, rendered ill and banal . . .

Later

So here's the deal. You'll be given a thing called a body and the resulting restrictions on your freedom will be excruciating, almost intolerable: henceforth you shall be able to manifest your presence in only one place and one epoch at a time, and, moreover, these places must be geographically contiguous and the times chronologically linked in a compulsory forward direction.
Oh, no!
I've always thought that's how it must have happened. That's the real punishment, the real ban-

ishment from the real Eden. Imprisoning us in the here and now, how dare He? He, whoever. The One who lays down the law of reality and says there is no getting around it. I spend my time not only getting but dancing circles around it, prancing upon it, grinding it to dust beneath my heels. Fighting His dictates. And winning. Thanks to another He, who is not my enemy but my ally.

My lying ally.

Or allies. All lies. His name is legion.

"Except ye become as little children," the Son of God admonishes His followers, "ye shall not enter into the Kingdom of Heaven . . . " So let's make the hell sure we don't become as little children! Mine, mine, the othersaying lines of Walt Whitman:

Never more the cries of unsatisfied love be absent from me,
Never again leave me to be the peaceful child I was before what
*   there in the night,*
By the sea under the yellow and sagging moon,
The messenger there arous'd, the fire, the sweet hell within . . .

I love the sweet hell.

"Let your word be Yes, Yes; No, No; All the rest comes from the Devil," Jesus also says. "All the rest" is the only thing that has ever interested me.

God is literal-minded. He hates metaphors because they get you places. *Metaphor* means to carry over — and *diaballein* means to throw across. The devil throws us across, gets us from here to there. God just sits on His throne and aims His benevolent grave blank stare at us, He takes us nowhere because He's strictly from there Himself and He wants us to stay put. Satan is a born leader. And he leads us — not just anywhere — into temptation. Where else would we want to go?

God is One — whence His consummate dullness. Even when He's Three, He's One. The devil is the Other. *"L'Autre"*, the French also called him, for centuries. God is one long dangling beard and the devil is two up-pricked horns (to say nothing of his horny prick). Two-faced, yes, that too. A wily smiling face on his head; a grimacing face on his rear end which the Sabbath-goers ritually kissed. Even his hoofs are cloven!

They say God is all-knowing but in fact He doesn't know peanuts about humans. All He knows is the truth, which is only half the truth (and even that is stretching it). The devil — Prince of Lies, Father of Lies — is much smarter. He needs to be, because he's much weaker. (If you're omnipotent, what's the point in learning anything?) The words whispered by the snake into Eve's ear were the truth, the whole truth and nothing but the truth about humans — they love good food and they love to break the law.

God is pure, unadulterated, pitiless, unwavering Light, whereas the Prince of Darkness is named . . . Lucifer. Again the Devil is double, an oxymoron, a marriage of opposites. *Fourchu et fourbe.* I too need to be double, duplicitous, two-timing, I thrive on division and derision, I never cease to compare, contrive, seduce, betray, translate. My heart and brain are cloven like the devil's hoof. English, French. I am enamoured of all things French. (Save the people.)

While the contours of holiness are soft, smooth, symmetrical — long flowing robes, lofty verticality and glorious radiation, the devil and things devilish are pointed, warped, perverted, twisted out of shape (bass-ackwards, Father would have said, as in those terrible inverted-initial jokes he used to tell us and which shamed more than amused us, what's the difference between a goldfish and a mountain-goat, the goldfish mucks around the fountain) . . .

Dæmon in the good old days of Greece used to mean someone's spirit as in sprite, their genius as in genie — but as soon as the Christians got hold of it they reduced it to mean only evil, devil, impure spirit. Yes — it is spirit *per se* that is impure! Down with spirit and spiritedness! Up with sighing, moon-eyed "spirituality". Down with genies and geniuses, down with ghosts. The only Ghost to have survived the hecatomb was the Holy one, full of hot air, impregnator of virgins. (*My* ghost is an unholy one — he is my dirty-faced guardian angel, my djinn, my dragon, he breathes fiery wit into my ear. And I want there to be lots of ghosts in my story.)

The Holy Ghost is witless. Wit in English, like *esprit* in French, stretches its graceful arms into both wisdom and humour. God has neither, the Devil has both. He's a wise guy. He makes wise cracks, wise-ass jokes. And he laughs! If you don't know anything about *double entendre*, you can't get the joke! Did you ever see God giggle, snicker, throw back His head and roar with laughter?

Some said Socrates's *dæmon* was no more nor less than a sneeze; others claimed it was a voice. After weighing the evidence on the subject, Plutarch writes — oh this delights me, just think, this is a man from one thousand nine hundred years ago quoting *a being who appeared in the dream of someone else*, Timarchus, and here we have the dream being's exact words, I am copying them out again today, all these centuries later — ". . . From those other souls, which from their very beginning and birth are docile to the rein and obedient to their dæmon, comes the race of diviners and of men inspired. Among such souls you have doubtless heard of that of Hermodorus of Clazomenæ— how night and day it used to leave his body entirely and travel far and wide, returning after it had met with and witnessed many things said and done in remote places . . . The story as thus told is indeed not true: his soul did not leave his body, but gave its dæmon free play by always yielding to it and slackening the tie, permitting it to move about and roam at will, so that the dæmon could see and hear much that passed in the world outside and return with the report." (Plutarch, *Dæmon of Socrates*, para. 592)

This is so important. It is exactly what happened to the witches, those inspired women whose souls were so exceptionally docile that all they needed to do was rub their bodies with an ointment and they could fly away on broomsticks and dance and feast and make love with great strong tireless devils all night long

   — and it's exactly what happens in a novel.

Yes but this novel, Nada. This one, at this time. Why?

   I think because I need, now, at the age I have reached, more than "midway on life's journey," to come to terms with the death at birth of my twin brother, and the disaster of my parents' marriage.

The last thing I'm interested in is diminishing madness and suffering, you know.

   Yes I know. Besides which, you're far less expensive than a shrink — all you cost me is my soul. My twisted-strings soul . . .

   I remember the day Stella first explained *scordatura* to me. I must have been nine or ten years old. "Literally," she said, "*scordatura* means mistuning, discordance. The Italians put an *s* at the beginning of a word, my dear, and that word is shot. All the composers of the baroque period fooled around with the tuning of string instruments; they'd alter the standard tuning to facilitate the playing of unwieldy intervals, you see? But sometimes the intervals were not only unwieldy, they were uncanny."

   The minute Stella told me that, I recognized myself. "That's me. I'm the mistuned instrument." Somehow I had always known this. People kept trying to play me, fiddle with me, saw at me this way and that — they could never get what they wanted out of me. Squawks and screeches. I didn't function the way I was supposed to. When did it start? I'll think about that some other day. Maybe. *Scordare*, according to my Italian dictionary, also means to forget.

"The most unearthly, the most inhuman *scordatura* in the history of the violin," Stella told me, "was that used by Heinrich Ignaz Franz von Biber in his *Resurrection Sonata*. Here's what the violinist has to do . . . "

She demonstrated by twisting her own fat fingers into knots.

"Normally the tuning of your four strings is G, D, A, E, okay? Well, first you take the two middle strings and switch them around behind the bridge and inside the pegbox, and then you tune the A down a tone to G. The outrageous result is that the first and third strings end up side by side, tuned an octave apart (both D's), while the second and fourth strings are also side by side and tuned an octave apart (both G's)!"

My mother Elisa never talked to me about music. The pleasure she took in music was as private and sacred to her as her belief in God; in a sense the two were the same thing. She talked to her best friend, and her best friend talked to me.

"So," Stella went on, "the piece being notated as if the violin were normally tuned, the sound that comes out of the instrument bears no resemblance to what is written on the page. For instance, your eyes can be following a series of ascending notes on the stave while your ear hears them descending. Or you can read a major chord and produce a minor one . . ."

According to Stella, the Philadelphia performance of Biber's *Sonatas on the Mysteries of the Rosary* was for Elisa a moment of sheer ecstasy — it was as if this weird discrepancy between the visual and the audible had given her a glimpse into the very essence of the divine.

So here I am listening obsessively, hour after hour as I work, to the composers of that era, Biber in particular. I'm not quite sure why I need to go back three hundred years in time in order to deal with this subject. I light candles, burn incense . . . How absurd. It's as if I were intent on recreating the stifling atmosphere of Sunday Mass. But the music is so lovely. Heart-breaking. Yes. Elisa used to play it. With Stella. Trying to remember . . . When she was young. Before we killed her. All of us, singly and collectively — Jimbo, Joanna, Sammy, Stevie and yours truly. Especially yours truly.

Mother, mother (but if both body and soul have been so drastically transformed, how can she be the same person, have the same name?). Nowadays "Mother" putters around her bedroom in an expensive home not too far from here and I visit her two or three times a year — a nondescript, dithering, blathering, platitude-spouting . . .

Oh stop it Nada.

I don't know how to write about this. It's only now that it has started swelling like floodwater inside of me, threatening my defences.

Being the eldest child, and being, to boot so to speak, a female, it was I who was privy to the regular bedroom carnage, miscarriage after miscarriage as my father continued to knock her catholically up and she in obedience to the pope, Pius XII at the time, refrained from taking measures to prevent it and the sheets filled with blood and trembly velvety black clots of something like human flesh more than once a year, yes, more often than once a year though seven mouths gaped around the dining-room table already.

(Ah! My beetles are so much cleaner, so much drier, and more discreet! At least their murder makes no mess.)

The time she almost died, the blood was literally flooding out of her, she was being emptied of her substance, I was in the room beside her and I heard her screams turn gradually into sighs — almost like sighs of pleasure — these scared me far more than the screams. Afterwards, she told me she had felt herself floating away, her soul wafting above her — like an angel? — and it had been ineffably beautiful because the pain had stopped, it was all over at last, I think of this every time I listen to the love songs of Purcell or Monteverdi, Vivaldi or d'India or Lambert, the soft poignant vibrato with which the soprano or countertenor sings

Lasciateme morire . . .
Mi sfaccio, mi moro, cor mio! . . .
Makes me, makes me, want to — die — die — die . . .
Let me, living, die . . .
Au moins ne m'ostez pas le plaisir de mourir . . .
Hélas! Que voulez-vous? Je meurs . . .

It is over now, over, over, finished, there is
nothing more to fear. I am a fearless woman now.

The Resurrection Sonata

II - Childhoods

Durand is a day-labourer, a young man whose skin is already thick and cracked, a man of few words because he is all body, all brute force, for as long as it will last, after which he will be nothing. Soon he will have forgotten this whole thing — his first marriage, his life with Marthe, their long wait for a son who'd be able to help them later on . . . These events will be rapidly engulfed by the fog of his exhausting, monotonous days.

He has signed with a cross the declaration of the twins' birth in the parish register, and now he is lining up small white stones on the ground, also in the form of a cross, to mark the burial place of the little singing shepherdess. No one expects Durand to keep and raise the babies who killed his wife. He himself was orphaned in childhood and his mother-in-law, Marthe's mother, perished a few months ago in a fire. The twins will have to get along as best they can, relying on the grace of God or the generosity of human beings — both of which, admittedly, are unpredictable . . .

Father Thomas, the Torchay parish priest, gives the boy in oblation to Notre-Dame d'Orsan, a nearby priory of which he also happens to be the confessor.

As he grows older, Barnabé learns the story of the place by bits and scraps — an unusually colourful story for this rather crude and dull part of the land.

Orsan, Father Thomas tells him, belongs to the Fontevrist order, founded at the end of the eleventh century by the ever-adulated but never-beatified Robert d'Arbrissel. This hirsute, charismatic, barefoot and eloquent Breton, deeply suspicious in the eyes of the ecclesiastic powers-that-be, had preached a return to the teachings of Christ, in particular the values of humility, poverty and love. He had founded the Abbey of Fontevraud for the thousands of misfits who made up his following — beggars, lepers, ragamuffins, whores, frustrated and flouted wives . . . A handful of noble-blooded virgins and widows were also allowed to join, principally to ensure the solvency and royal sanction of the enterprise.

The Fontevrist order was unique in the late Middle Ages, not because it included both men and women (other "double orders" did exist), but because it stipulated that in all matters the men be subjected to the women. The monks were required to ask the mother superior's permission for every initiative they wished to take, submit uncomplainingly to whatever corporeal punishments she might deem necessary, and work in the outside world to support the nuns, who themselves were contemplatives. D'Arbrissel had organized things in this manner as to humiliate the male sex, which he judged excessively proud and domineering. For a while, Fontevrist brothers desirous of proving their capacity for renunciation had carried the emulation of Good Robert to the point of sleeping, as had been the founder's wont, in the same rooms as the women — but these latter, having ascertained the weakness of imperfectly mortified flesh, had ordered the construction of new dormitories by and for the men.

All the Fontevrist priories in France conform to the rules of conduct laid down by Robert d'Arbrissel, but Notre-Dame d'Orsan is especially finical about them, for it was here (O marvel!) that in the year 1116 the good founder breathed his last breath, and here (O outstanding honour!) that the relic of his merciful heart has been most preciously preserved. Every time Father Thomas tells Barnabé the story of d'Arbrissel's death at Orsan, the boy divines some sort of drama or mystery surrounding the event, but he never manages to learn what it is.

Raised in this highly singular monastery from birth, like other orphaned male babies of the province, Barnabé soon displays signs of an obliging character and becomes the monks' little favourite. As they have neither the moral inclination nor the material means of spoiling the child (the prioress ordaining even the manner in which they must dispose of their leftover food), they vie with one other at instructing him in the arts of music and gardening. By the age of twelve, Barnabé is already passionately knowledgeable about the pruning and grafting of apple trees, and during his hours of freedom he loves to stroll about in the orchard, humming the lovely melodies of vespers and matins.

He sees the nuns from afar — enigmatic black and white shapes that go floating across the courtyard, into the chapel and out of it again — but, as they have embraced the Benedictine rule of silence, he never hears the sound of their voices. Another woman, though, is often at his side, and it is she who reveals to him the exquisite beauty of the female voice — his mother.

Yes — Marthe often appears to him, without warning, now in the orchard and now in the dormitory. She watches over him, talks to him and sings him pastorales; shares his worries over the havoc wreaked in the garden by moles or hailstones; listens with him to the cuckoo's stupid call, the blackbird's intricate trill (which he has been trying, long but unsuccessfully, to imitate), the dove's soft coo — and also, when he is stretched out on his palliasse late at night, the eerie ululation of the owl. Barnabé has never feared this bird of darkness, the prophet of death that peasants nail to their barn doors to stave off ill fortune. No . . . for he happened to be listening to the owl's repetitive plaint when his mother first appeared to him. He was only four at the time, and since then she has never left him alone for long.

Marthe speaks to him in her soothing, melodious voice; a tender smile plays on her lips as she watches him fall asleep; like the Virgin Mary she is surrounded by a diffuse light, but — to bespeak the fact that she is human — her nimbus is blue rather than gold. Marthe adores her little Barnabé.

As for Barbe, though born coiffed with the caul, she is not quite so fortunate. Few people care to take on the burden of a little orphan-girl, especially in these times, these hard years of famine when so many in the province have found themselves with neither a mattress nor a shirt, not a stitch of linen or a stick of furniture to their name, and when it is not uncommon, walking across a pasture, to stumble over the dead bodies of women and children, their mouths filled with grass . . .

At first, Marthe's best friend Raymonde, whose youngest child is still at the breast, takes the little girl into her home and nurses her as best she can — but Barbe is always fed after the other baby, a great gluttonous boy, so that by the time her turn comes round there is just enough milk left in Raymonde's breasts to whet her appetite. Barbe grows weakly, puny and bitter, she wails ceaselessly with rage, and in Raymonde's heart the already lukewarm desire to feed her turns stone cold. Ultimately the problem is resolved in another way — the usual, divine way — Raymonde catches typhoid fever, writhes in pain for a few days and gives up the ghost without complaining overmuch, and little Barbe moves on to the house of a neighbour, but soon the woman cannot bear to have her around because at two and a half she talks better than her own daughter who is four, so the neighbour palms her off on a cousin who lives in the next hamlet, and so on and so forth, from hamlet to hamlet, circling the town of Torchay.

Because of these continual changes of environment, because of being immersed every six or eight months in a new stench, a new cacophony, a new family and a new poultry-yard, because of being forever shunted and shoved around, stroked or spanked by different hands, Barbe turns into a shrewd and mistrustful little girl. The word for children like her in these parts is *ch'tite*. Skinny as a doornail, hard as a doornail, too, eyes always on the watch — she is quicksilver.

She grows, and the bad years slide by one after the other. Smallpox and cholera take turns decimating the population, discharged soldiers wander through the area, plundering and smashing whatever they can lay their hands on, violent hail and rain lay waste to the crops. The poor peasants feel crushed, punished, cursed by unfathomable powers for unfathomable sins, they do what they can to protect themselves from the scourges being rained down upon them, and they punish in turn — the powerless. Barbe Durand is no one's daughter, and therefore everyone's scapegoat. By the age of six, she knows how to run fast and obey faster, draw water from the well without spilling a single drop, clean straw-bottomed chairs by whipping them with nettles, furiously knead bread dough, shell peas, chop up pears, apples, turnip-cabbages. Her quick skilful little fingers squeeze the she-goat's nipples, the milk squirts out and foams in the pail; she does not have the right to taste it. On the least pretext and often without pretext, the drunken husband or the harassed wife will yell at her, slap her across the face, beat her over the head with a stick. At regular intervals, whenever there is a food shortage, they threaten to hand her over to the *taker*. The latter's wagon passes through town thrice yearly with its sinister load of several dozen newborn babes from the provincial towns, ostensibly driving them either to their wet-nurse in the country or to Paris to be exposed, though clearly most are already at death's doorstep. Tense and silent, Barbe stares at the tiny bodies limp with hunger and exhaustion, the quivering, whimpering, whining mass of pink skin and filthy rags.

She becomes wiry and alert, capable of vanishing into thin air at the approach of danger, like a lizard disturbed in its sunbath on the stone wall.

The year she is seven is the worst of all. That year, both the summer and fall are chilly and wet, and the following winter is catastrophically cold; the seeds freeze in the furrow, which means the peasants will harvest neither wheat, barley nor oats, which means they will have neither porridge nor bread to eat, not even the usual vile mixture of wheat and rye, which means they will die. From far and wide they flock to the priory of Notre-Dame d'Orsan, whose good sisters have been handing out bread to the poor for centuries, but the Church's lands have not been miraculously spared and even the monks and nuns are starving, the peasants protest and fulminate, attempt to set fire to the buildings — and then, overcome with weakness, they give up and go home, eat grass and acorn flour, die of hunger. Die. Wolves skulk in ever larger numbers on village outskirts.

The scrawny girlchild turns out to have a confounding vitality. It seems she scarcely needs to consume food at all — she gobbles down all she sees and hears, and this is what keeps her alive. During the great famine, she acquires the habit of scrutinizing the corpses at the edge of the road, bending over to study them close up, stroking the livid, bristly cheeks of the old men, the tangled hair of the young women with babes still at the breast, the blue lips of the little boys.

And then the worst is over. The survivors drag the dead to the churchyard and bury them just below the surface (to make it easier for them to resuscitate); then they burn their palliasses and life starts up again.

Barbe moves yet again, as the famine claimed all the grownups at the farm on which she was living and their children have been dispersed. For the first time, she is taken in by a moderately well-to-do peasant family, but they insist she sleep in the stable — indeed, more warmth emanates from the animals than from the humans in this household.

One day the son of the house, who is just Barbe's age but a good head taller than she, tells her they are going to play fish. She does not know what he means, but she soon will. He drags her up to the attic where the fishing rods are stored, tells her to lie down on the floor which is gritty with mouse droppings and spiderwebs, and announces, "I'm the fisherman, you're the fish. You've gotta try to get free."

He wants to see her squirm and wriggle in the filth. She remains rigid, immobile, frozen with hatred. She thinks of her twin brother. She knows she has a twin brother, her various foster mothers have told her so, he lives somewhere in the area, perhaps not far from here, and bears a name much like her own, the lovely name of Barnabé. The boy moves the tip of the fishing rod closer to her face. There's no hook on it, there's no danger. Barnabé, Barnabé.

"Look out," he says, "or I'm gonna catch you!"

Barbe does not budge. Suddenly the fishing rod plunges deeply down her left nostril, all the way to her throat. Jolted by the pain, she screams, the boy yanks the instrument back out and blood spurts forth.

"Sshh!" says the boy. "Stop yelling, will ya? I didn't do it on purpose."

She can see from the fear in his eyes that there is a lot of blood. He walks over to a corner of the attic, picks up a dirty rag and hands it to her.

"Ya won't tell, will ya? I didn't do it on purpose."

She shakes her head, no, she won't tell, it goes without saying, he is the son of the house. He vanishes, leaving her alone and bloody in the attic.

None of this matters.

She awaits her brother.

She dreams of him. She dreams they find each other and decide to live together, babes in the woods, as in the tale of Hansel and Gretel she has heard so many times, at so many evening meetings, cracking walnuts or shelling beans by so many firesides — the two of them will travel far, far away from all the farms and hamlets, they'll build themselves a little cabin in the middle of the woods . . . Her dream never gets past this point, for she knows the woods are also peopled with wolves and witches, and until Barnabé is at her side she dares not imagine how they will deal with these creatures of darkness . . .

Time goes by as best it can, Barbe reaches adolescence, begins to menstruate and is confronted, at just the same time, with the question of her first Communion. The family decides to send her to catechism lessons with their son, thus creating several inextricable confusions in her mind. Because she is taught the notion of sin in the company of her attic torturer, the words *pêcheur* (fisherman) and *pécheur* (sinner) will forever be superimposed, and she will find it baffling that Jesus should have chosen His disciples among sinners, declaring, "I am the sinner of men." Moreover, Barbe is told that she is to blame for Jesus's death, that His blood flowed because she was evil — but that she can redeem herself by eating His Body and drinking His Blood . . . Is what trickles between her own thighs the good blood or the bad — the blood she should never have caused to flow, or the blood she must consume? The Christian doctrine contains many mysteries indeed . . . Be this as it may, before she can take Communion, before she acquires the right to don a dress for the first time in her life (though the dress, belonging as it does to the family's eldest daughter, is naturally too big for Barbe — really much too big for the stunted, emaciated body of our Barbe), she must go to confession.

The very idea makes her quake with fear. She knows Father Thomas only by sight, and is intimidated by his mottled bald head and his bulging eyes, to say nothing of the huge belly that juts forth beneath his long black cassock. She is unaware that it was he who, twelve years earlier, reluctantly abandoned a sensuous dream to come and sprinkle holy water over her little head. She fears that when the time comes to tell him of her sins, she will lose her voice completely and he will accuse her of being prideful.

On the contrary, Barbe emerges overjoyed from church after her first confession — for, the minute she pronounced her name and place of birth in a timid whisper, Father Thomas cried out in surprise and told her he was glad to make her acquaintance at long last — her brother Barnabé, he added, was his favourite novice at the Orsan priory — a boy graced by God with the most unusual gifts of ear and voice, capable of imitating everything from toads to angels — and he, Father Thomas, had spent long years searching for Barnabé's sister — and now, praise be to God, his prayers had finally been answered, and so on and so forth, so that in the end, quite forgetting the principal reason for the young girl's presence in his confessional, the good Father had asked her not for the list of her misdeeds, but only for the name of the house in which she now lived, so that he might pass it on with the utmost celerity to her twin.

On the spot, Barbe started believing in God. She wept.

All remained the same, and yet her existence was transfigured. It was as if, in the great shadowy room of her soul, someone had thrown open a heavy set of velvet curtains. Happiness flooded in like sunlight.

Barbe's heart is beating rapidly. This is her brother walking towards her. He is here. The two children grasp each other's hands and stare into each other's eyes, their curiosity rapidly overcoming their embarrassment. They are of identical height and build, they have the same glittering dark eyes, the same pointy chin and upturned nose.

Barnabé. Boy me.

Staring at him is like staring at herself in the surface of the pond — herself, but so much more serene! So much more solid! Barnabé clasps to his chest the nail-body, the lizard-body of his twin sister.

"Barnabé . . . " she murmurs, scarcely daring to allow this name, which she has chanted inwardly a thousand times, to cross her lips.

They cannot remain long in each other's company this first time — indeed, they will never be able to remain long in each other's company, their lives are not such that they can carve out large spaces in them for conversations and promenades, they are not courtly lives made up of lazy mornings and scintillating soirées; always it will be hard for them to tear shreds of time for each other out of their long days stiffened by necessity . . . Nonetheless, happiness floods in.

Barnabé says, "Let us pray." And, hearing him thank God for their reunion, Barbe trembles with joy.

Later, still holding hands, they sit down on the small stone bench at the entrance to the poultry-yard and try to sum up their meagre lives for one another — scouring their minds for memories, speaking shyly, clumsily at first, but with increasing verve and vigour as they gain confidence. Barbe has an uncannily accurate memory for facts; she runs down the list of the houses and hamlets in which she has lived, the lucky years and the unlucky ones, the people she knows — living, dying and dead — but breathes not a word of the violence of which she herself has been the brunt. As for Barnabé, he describes to his sister the odd little universe of the Orsan priory, where women give orders and men obey, where women think, pray and meditate while men work to support them, where women are silent and men speak.

"You mean you'd never heard a woman's voice until you came to see me?" says Barbe incredulously.

"Sure I had!" laughs Barnabé. "Anne du Château, the prioress, talks to me regularly — in fact she's just accepted me as a novice. And also . . . well, and also, my dear sister . . . " (Yes, he tells her this — as of their first meeting he tells her; the trust between them is carnal, instantaneous . . .) "I hear our mother's voice."

Barbe starts as if he had struck her — surely this is blasphemy, it must be. She signs herself hastily, eyes round with fear.

"But Barnabé," she says, "you know quite well our mother is dead. She died giving birth to us, we never knew her . . . "

"Yes, I know, but I see her, I swear it — it's been going on for years, since I was four. If Jesus can rise from the dead, why not our mother?"

"Sssshh!"

Barbe's little eyebrows tie themselves into a knot of worry on her brow.

"Are you telling the truth?" she whispers.

Barnabé nods solemnly.

"Well then . . . what's she like? What does she look like?" asks the little girl excitedly. It is suddenly urgent that she know.

"Oh, she's beautiful . . . so beautiful . . . and . . . it's as if she were transparent. When she stands by my bedside, I can see the roof beams through her body. And when she comes to visit me in the orchard, I can still make out the pear trees behind her."

"But then, she must be a . . . a spectre!" says Barbe in a tiny voice, squeaky with fright.

Her brother's gaze clouds over suddenly.

"Don't ever say that, Barbe. I forbid you."

Barbe blushes and lowers her eyes.

"She's beautiful," repeats Barnabé, after a brief silence. "And often in the evening, she sings to me. Her voice is enchanting. Something like this . . . "

Closing his eyes, Barnabé takes a deep breath and sounds of pure honey begin to flow from his throat — warm, liquid, golden notes; never have Barbe's eardrums been thus caressed. A shiver goes through her and she stares at her brother, transfixed with love. But he breaks off, adding casually, "She's taught me to imitate all sorts of noises, too. We started out with birds . . . "

And as his sister gapes at him, more astounded by the second, Barnabé twists his lips, sucks in and puffs out his cheeks, flares his nostrils, blows and whistles, turning himself into woodpecker, owl and wagtail — and then, changing registers, hornet, dormouse, boar. When the performance is over, Barbe yelps delightedly with laughter and throws her arms around her brother's neck.

A moment later, though, she cannot help asking again, "So . . . why does Mamma come to see you and not me? I've never set eyes on her! She's as much my mother as yours, isn't she?"

Barnabé reflects on this. What, indeed, could explain this apparent injustice on their mother's part?

"Perhaps," he says tentatively, "it's because you had the caul on your head at birth, so she thinks you probably need her help less than I do . . . "

"Born under a lucky star . . . " says Barbe with a bitter shake of her head. "Oh, Barnabé! I don't want to complain, I've found you again at long last and this is the happiest day of my life, but — tell me one more thing . . . Do you think I might be allowed to see her . . . you know, once in a while?"

"Well . . . "

He shrugs, at a loss for words. The two children sit there in silence, absorbed and happy. Then, seeing the erratic arcs of the first bats out of the corner of their eyes, they realize that night has almost fallen.

Barnabé starts to ring, tipping his head from side to side in a startling imitation of the Orsan chapel bell — and again Barbe laughs aloud in delight. Then, rising, brother and sister embrace one last time — and separate.

The *Scordatura* Notebook

September 16th, train to Long Island

Nothing.

It is always reduced to nothing.

Everything I undertake, commence to believe in —

Stop it, Nada. I'm warning you.

— as soon as my back is turned: dust.

"Poor clay!" as Byron's Lucifer keeps mocking Abel.

This morning — waking again, again, with the sense of loss. In my dreams, whole passages of the *Resurrection Sonata* appear to me, sparkling, flowing, beautiful — but then evaporate before I can capture them in words. When I sit down at my desk the work advances with such turgid slowness, such clumsiness, it feels like pushing around bags of cement, whereas as I sleep, all the themes go swirling into place like ballerinas on the stage . . .

What exasperates me about writing is its successiveness. I don't mean chronological order (of course I am free to use flashbacks if I want), simply the fact of having to write the story a sentence at a time. One yearns to create as God does, everything all at once in a burst of sheer wondrous energy —

the big bang, the tiny fetus, the thing that is suddenly, instantly *there* and then gradually diversi-
fies, specializes, extending itself simultaneously in
all directions . . . Novels are so bloody linear. Can
you imagine God making Adam in the clumsy way
of children playing Hangman — first the head,
then the neck and shoulders, then one arm, then
the other — or making a galaxy star by star? Even
the *Genesis* version of the Creation is absurdly labo-
rious, absurdly human: the first day He did this,
the second day He did that . . . grotesque!

*Just so, my dear: if you wanted everlasting life or instan-
taneous creation you should have knocked at the other
door. When you chose me as your master, you knew
quite well that Time and I were inseparable. Stories
depend on the passage of days and years, in other words,
on death. My kingdom.*

Yes but there are moments when I can't bear
it. Waking this morning I heard little Sonya, Mike
and Leonora's baby, running across the floor
upstairs, she's not a baby anymore, she's already
running, there's something —

*What a cliché, the pitter-patter of little feet, for Christ's
sake . . .*

— I know but there's something so unique
about the way tiny children run — it reminded me
of Stevie and Sammy when they were little, the
way they used to trip and tear all over the house, I

loved those two so much, I was their big omniscient sister, they worshipped me . . . I can still see, almost touch, press to my cheek, the dark blue leather of the tiny slippers Sammy used to wear when he was three, when I think of the huge cleated clodhoppers he jogs in now — and the way we *are* together, the three of us, the forced conversations, each of us pretending to be interested in what the other is doing, Sammy off on some new computer jag in Duluth and Stevie studying his poisonous spiders and me with my lugubrious books — and not caring, just not caring, my brothers and I really do not care about each other anymore, shit, who are we, what is this life?

I thought not caring was the very cornerstone of your philosophy.

Yes but it was dreadful lying there in bed this morning and listening to Sonya run, her pure desire and energy uninfected by thought, history, knowledge, death, it made me want to weep and retch

had to get out of the city immediately —

leaped at my phone, called Stella — dear Stella, wonderful enormous irreplaceable Stella, my fat sweet *yiddische mama* — and she said, "But of course, dear heart. Come immediately, we'll have lunch," and in half an hour I was at Penn Station.

And just now, standing on the platform as I boarded the train, a young man was holding a very small child up to its grandmother to say good-bye, it must have been eight or nine months old, you could see its weight in its father's arms was *nothing*, and again . . . oh . . . this moment is already over, it is dead, the weightless child has already become a gum-chewing teenager, a computer-punching yuppy, a cancer-wracked mother, a putrefying corpse — oh!

Quoth the Raven: Nevermore . . .

I know, I know — all this has already been said, and better said, by your beloved poet Poe, among others. You're terribly sarcastic this morning. I hate it when you're like this.

I can shut up if you want me to.

Yes, do. Shut up for a while. I'll call you when I need you.

(He laughs, sardonically of course. A preposterous idea, that *I* should order *him* around. But we know each other well, and now I am certain I can count on his coming back. I used to panic and think he wouldn't.)

But *why* is it that everything is always fading, withering, dying, falling away from me, away from me — *why* all this loss, this perpetual, relentless, incontrovertible-despite-all-evidence-to-the-contrary loss?

Train back

Stella never disappoints me. Never in all the years I have known her, since I was born, has she given me a single moment of boredom or irritation. She's so funny! When she laughs her whole body shakes, breasts bouncing, stomach and hips trembling like jelly, feet, hands and head wagging, every cubic inch of her taking part in the laugh, just as everything used to take part in her playing of the cello, people would have to close their eyes so as not to be distracted by the unbelievable sight of her jiggling bosoms (she says "bosoms" plural, just as Mother used to — once Stella took a bad fall in her bathtub and when she told me about it later over the phone, she said, "You should see my bosoms, they look like the Rainbow Coalition!") . . . Despite her bosoms and the rest of her, the billowing jiggling overflowing plush of her, jowls and upper arm-flesh jumping rhythmically but half a second after the music's beat, Stella never missed a note on stage. Her bow would keep sawing back and forth, she'd sweat quarts and lose pounds during a concert and need a seven-course meal to make up for it afterwards — but what a musician! What a woman! I attended at least fifty of the Ensemble's performances before she finally retired to Long Island — "to read the Greek dramas and spoil my grandchildren silly," as she puts it.

(How had *she* managed to coordinate kids and career? I asked her once. "We had money," she said flatly, with a little shrug. "Jack earned plenty and he was not a stingy man. Lots of help around the house. Cleaning ladies, babysitters, cooks that pitched in when I was out of town. It makes a difference. But it doesn't mean my kids turned out any better than Elisa's, you know. And they still hold it against me, they're still convinced all their neuroses are my fault. There is no perfect formula." Wise Stella.)

It was so healing to be next to her, strolling amidst the driftwood and the rocks. Her mind is still all there, memory better than mine whereas she's a good ten years older than Mother, must be eightyish now although, coyly, she has always refused to reveal her age to me — "Oh come on Nadia, what do you want to know that for, it would just make you think I'm an old lady and that wouldn't be nice of you, now would it?"

Her heart has weakened, though. Our pace on the beach wasn't as brisk as it used to be, and she started panting after about ten minutes. She was popping her nitroglycerine tablets more often, too. "Don't pay any attention," she told me, winking. "I've always been a druggie. I take whatever my doctor tells me, I don't even ask what's in it, I don't give a damn, hormones, cortisone, rat poison, give it to me! There are about seventeen particoloured little pills a day by now."

I remember once she came over to Perry Street for dinner, she was staying with her sister in Brooklyn, by the time she left it was past midnight but she insisted on taking the subway. "Don't worry, darling," she said, "no one wants to rape *me* anymore!" "It's not that," I protested, "but you *know* all those stairs are hard on your heart, and you've had a long day already — please take a cab, do it for my sake . . . " "Nadia," she retorted, interrupting me, "I run a far greater risk of having a heart attack when I see the amount on the taxi meter than when I climb the stairs."

Why am I writing all this down? So precious. Never want to lose her. Only living witness of my mother's glory? No it isn't that. It's just — Stella.

I gave her an update on Elisa's wandering brain.

"It reminds me of Hölderlin's piano," she said. "Do you know about Hölderlin's piano?"

I didn't. Apparently the Princess of Homburg once gave Hölderlin a grand piano, and he took a pair of shears and cut the cords — but not all of them. Then he sat down and started improvising, never knowing which notes would sound and which would remain silent.

"That piano," said Stella, "was the image of his own soul."

When we got back to the house, I told her about my Witness obsession. We were sitting in her kitchen full of blue glass, blue china, blue collected things that somehow are not knick-knacks. She let me talk, munching brownies and sipping tea and licking her fingers, listening intently.

"You see," I said, "I keep thinking (there is a whole lobe of my brain set apart for sentences that begin with 'I keep thinking') — I keep thinking *there has to be a Witness*. It's probably my Catholic upbringing . . . "

"Oh, don't worry," said Stella, chewing delicately. "Us tough old ex-communist atheist Jews have exactly the same problem."

"It's hard to shake the idea that SOMEONE must have this incalculable mess figured," I went on. "Sometimes I sit up in bed in the middle of the night and say to myself, You mean nobody's watching, nobody's keeping track, we're not going to get our due? Ever? Stella, we can't be flailing around *ad vitam æternam* amidst cosmic indifference, can we? Seriously. The crimes of Enver Pasha, Hitler, Stalin and Pol Pot can't sit there in the middle of the universe, arrogant and answerless, eternally unpunished, can they? Yes I know they can but *can they?* You mean every single one of those little black kids dying of hunger and AIDS and diphtheria is an entire rich human soul filled with dreams and memories and songs — and they can just be flatly bluntly permanently wiped off the slate? *By the thousand?* Come off it. I know it's true, but it *can't* be true."

I'd rather think of them as beetles.

Stella laughed sadly, nodding, wiping her mouth on a paper napkin. I think she had a couple of abortions herself, as a young woman. Before, after, in between the three children who made it as far as birth? I don't know. Her only son ended up getting shot to bloody smithereens over Korea.

I continued my spiel.

"I keep thinking life is some sort of school year, you know, and that at the end we'll all get a report card summing the whole thing up, full of amazing revelations. The Witness will take in our entire existence at a glance and tell us Yes, hm, well, you listened to Schubert's *Quintet* sixty-three times, ate seven hundred and forty-one sesame bagels . . . No, huh? Oh, Stella — how come to terms with the fact that there will be no Day of Reckoning whatsoever!"

"'Fraid not, deah," said Stella, finishing off her last milky drop of tea and setting her cup down with a clink. "Nope — ain't nobody up der dat's lookin' down at us and gohn' do our reckonin' for us. We all jes' gotta reckon wif what we got as bes' we cain."

Her imitation of the Southern Black accent was superb.

Perry Street, later (2 a.m.)

The dæmon *is* a demon. He is, yes, also, a torturer. The banishment from paradise is called: self-awareness. I know when I first felt its sharp cold blade slide between myself and my skin. Yes — I know exactly when I stopped being like little Sonya upstairs, carefree, running towards something with nothing in mind but my wish for it, and then reaching it and having it and being utterly absorbed in it, utterly content . . .

This is one of my "formaldehyde images," as I call them. Memories that don't change, don't move, don't disappear, but sit there lined up on a shelf in my head, mute and horrible, like the nineteenth-century human and animal organs kept in glass jars at the Paris Museum of Natural History.

I was four, just as Barnabé was four when his mother first appeared to him. (Perhaps, come to think of it, it was on this day that Elisa first appeared to *me* — as she was, as she would be — different from myself, hostile to my self . . .)

Eric, her replacement as first violin in the Ensemble, had dropped by (he's dead now, all of this is long dead, all except the nada nada napalm damage it has done) — for tea and to meet the new baby, Jimbo it would have been that time, probably mewling and pewling away in a corner through-out the scene, tearing Elisa's nerves to shreds . . .

I liked Eric. He was tall, straw-haired and big-boned — he didn't look like a musician at all, more like a Swedish farmer, I was sitting on his lap that day at the table, and when tea was over he took out his instrument and handed me the bow. I started shoving it back and forth across the strings as he moved his fingers on the bridge and, stupid-ly of course (*now* I say "stupidly of course"), I was amazed, proud, delighted at the beauty of the sounds that came out. *It actually felt as if I were play-ing an instrument!* But when I boasted about it to Father later that evening, Elisa said drily, "Don't be ridiculous, Nadia. Eric was doing the playing."

That's all.

Nothing, isn't it?

Nada.

Never again would I touch a musical instru-ment. And never again would I be carefree. The blade was under my skin. There it was: I had thought I'd been happy, whereas in fact I'd only been ridiculous. *Scordatura*. You play one note, another note comes out. Strings, pen, smile, heart — everything twisted. Try as I might, Mother, I never managed to produce the music you wanted to hear. There was no way to bring a smile to your lips.

When I started writing poetry and showed you my first poem — a sad one, in all likelihood a soupily smarchily sad one, but still — you said, "Well, if the next pregnancy kills me that will sound just lovely at my funeral, dear."

I know, you'd just had another miscarriage, tearing up the stairs to the bathroom screaming your head off in fear, blood pouring out of you, *great gouts of blood* dear Macbeth on every step of the staircase, puddles of blood in the hall and on the bathroom tiles — later I would have to help you wipe it all up, quickly, quickly, get rid of the evidence before Father returned, that was the only time I actually caught a glimpse of the thing, the fetus, that had spewed from your innards as the screams kept spewing from your throat — you picked it up and wrapped it in tissue paper and threw it in the garbage pail, yes, God had decided to take this soul, too, back into His keeping before it got born and baptized and hungry — but was it my fault? *Was it my fault, Mother?*

(How does it happen Ronald was never around when this was going on? Another time, I remember, Elisa's mother happened to be visiting when the horror happened, I was excused from cleaning-up duty that time and Grandma came down at the end of the afternoon, her face blanched and pinched, her lips pressed tightly together, shaking her head and muttering in her clipped Hungarian accent, "He could be careful, your father, he could try being careful" — and I hadn't the faintest idea what she meant, I spent weeks trying to figure it out — how could my father be careful? What did he have to do with it?)

I have never told Stella these things.

I have stored them away in formaldehyde, they are my *stigmata diaboli*, the numb spots of my soul, where the devil first touched it.

Pinch me, burn me, stick needles into me there, and I feel nothing. "My heart belongs to Daddy" . . . my soul belongs to the Father of lies.

Oh come now, stop feeling sorry for yourself. Just think of all I have given you in exchange.

Yes I know . . . Ubiquity, immortality, resuscitation, divination — seven-league boots are nothing compared to the gifts you've showered on me! Oh, little Tom Thumb clinging to the ogre's wife as she strides through forest and field — look! How not believe in miracles? All of us can do it! Take giant steps, ogre steps backwards and forwards in time, sideways in space . . . and *be*, authentically, in ancient Israel or Greece, *be* in twentieth-century Communist China, *be* a Trinidadian dishwasher in a greasy spoon restaurant in the city of Spokane, Washington . . . quicken the dead and murder the quick . . .

(I have never understood why Gœthe's Faust only aspired to hang out with the Superstars of the past. Helen of Troy, for Christ's sake! Why not have chosen a tiny, wizened old *fisherman* of Troy? Surely Mephistopheles was capable of taking him to anonymous cottages, and not only the roiling clouds of Olympus?!)

Yes, the pact was worth it . . . I don't want to be here on Perry Street. I want to know all there is to know about Barbe and Barnabé. They are nobodies. Utter nobodies. And I love them already.

The Resurrection Sonata

III - The Awakening

"Mother . . . "

"Yes, my son . . . There's something on your mind this evening."

"Tell me, Mother . . . why is it you never appear to my twin sister Barbe?"

"I chose you, Barnabé, because I knew you were in jeopardy."

"In jeopardy? Me? But Mother, I have the most peaceful life in the world, I divide my time between orchard and cloister, walking and meditating, I love everything I see, hear and touch, I take pleasure in the conversation of the monks and in the silent enigmatic presence of the nuns. When I sing God's praises, people tell me I have the voice of an angel — but I know it's thanks to you, Mamma, it's *your* voice that fills my heart, swells up my breast, quickens in my throat . . . How could I possibly be in jeopardy, dearest one?"

"It is not in my power to see the future, Barnabé. And even did I know your fate, I would not have the right to impart this knowledge unto you. One thing is certain, though — Barbe will pull through. There is no need for you to worry about her."

Barnabé remains pensive.

"We loved each other instantly, Barbe and I," he says. "It was as if we'd always known each other. And our physical resemblance is uncanny, feature by feature . . . It gave me the oddest feeling."

As Marthe gazes at him, her blue aura seems to pulsate faintly with sadness.

"Soon you will start growing whiskers, my son. You will become a man and your sister a woman; the resemblance between you will fade. But I know your love for her will grow ever stronger and stronger, until the day you die."

Strangely enough, whereas Marthe's second prediction would come true, the first was inaccurate. Upon reaching puberty, Barnabé would remain glabrous and slim, his features would not harden nor his body grow strong and virile, and his voice, instead of breaking, would evolve into a natural countertenor, startlingly clear and precise, thus enabling him to go on singing the soprano part in psalms and canticles. Barbe, for her part, would remain a bony, flat-chested little thing — so that the twins, while forever living apart, would continue to look alike to a truly exceptional degree.

It is at this time, shortly after her reunion with her brother, that Barbe's life undergoes a major change — she leaves the farm and is taken on as a maid-servant at the Torchay inn. Hélène Denis, the obese and jovial innkeeper, widely known and vaguely feared throughout the land, had noticed the young girl one market-day and been struck by her air of alertness, the astonishing alacrity with which her fingers picked up eggs and slipped them into villagewomen's baskets, never cracking a single one. And so Hélène — famous for knowing what she wants and saying what she thinks — had offered Barbe room, board and employment on the spot.

"You'd sleep in a real bed and eat two meals a day. I have a daughter about your age — how old are you, my skinny one?"

"They say I'm thirteen, Madam. I've already made my first Communion, I'm clean and I don't steal," says Barbe in a single breath, for the offer tempts her.

"Well then, come along with me! My daughter Jeanne is fourteen, you can help us with the cleaning and keep her company, she's tired of listening to strangers jabber their heads off from morning to night. Her daddy, God rest his soul, was gutted by a bull when she was but a year old so she's never had brothers or sisters — do you think you might be a sister to her, my girl? And what is it they call you?"

Barbe takes an instant liking to Hélène. Made shy by the very force of her feeling, she blushes violently and lowers her eyes as she pronounces her full name.

"Ah! You must be Marthe's little girl! Poor Marthe! True enough, I heard she . . . You see, I used to know your Mamma, long ago. We'd lost sight of each other but I thought the world of her, she was such a sweet slip of a thing — and my heavens, what a singing voice she had! She didn't even need a dog — her sheep would follow her around for the pleasure of hearing her sing! I remember the two of us prepared our catechism together . . . Ha! ha! What a catechism! Oh, yes, we certainly learned our Gospel lessons, Marthe and I! That we did! Oh, it's all coming back to me!"

Hélène laughs uproariously, setting off such a seism in her massive body that Barbe's mouth falls open and her eyes widen; but never will she find out what was so hilarious about the religious instruction of her mother and this woman.

Jeanne Denis, the innkeeper's daughter, though but a year older than Barbe, is already a young woman, blond and buxom, with a mischievous gleam in her eye. At first, she is taken aback and slightly repelled by the wild thing her mother has brought into the house — this wiry ugly girlchild with stick legs and a face made of sharp points and angles. But she rapidly discovers Barbe's intelligence; the two young girls become friends and start sharing secrets.

Barbe cannot stop thanking God for all the favours He has bestowed on her in so short a time. She no longer suffers from the cold, as every room in the inn has its own fireplace; her chores are less exhausting than on the farm and she performs them with gusto — rubbing the brick floor-tiles with linseed oil to bring out their lovely redbrown colour, emptying the chamberpots each morning, using night soil and pigeon droppings to fertilize the garden that flourishes the length of the building's west wall, washing and folding the thick linen sheets, and, when all her other tasks are done, helping Hélène serve up meals in the great dining room, wiping down tables and washing glasses while listening to her conversations with the guests.

Hélène knows everything. Sitting in state in an armchair of solid oak which her body overflows in all directions, hands and lips constantly in movement, she expresses herself with a sonorous voice and enormous, irresistible bursts of laughter. Barbe notices that the men listen to her with respect and she, too, begins to pay attention. The frontiers of her universe recede a little every day. Hélène discusses past and present dramas, small and large events alike. The terrible fire of 1693, which razed 103 houses in the city of Bourges (Barbe loves the precision of the figure), to say nothing of the palace and royal holy chapel. The horrifying tale of a relapsed Protestant in nearby Issoudun, who thrice refused the holy sacraments on her death bed, and whose corpse was therefore attached to a wagon and dragged face-down through the city, then hurled onto the refuse-dump. Taxes, all sorts of taxes, forever on the rise. Was it not a scandal to impose the large salt-tax on this province, one of the most miserable in the kingdom, with its labourers already unable to pay their tallage?

"The tax-collectors saw it with their own eyes when they did an inquest here two years ago," says

Hélène, warming up to her subject. "Just to make sure we weren't partying it up from one Midsummer's Eve to the next. They had a meal right here in this very room, I saw them just as I see you and I can tell you, they looked pretty pale, it almost spoiled their appetite, up there in Paris they're not used to seeing people eat dirt and tree bark . . . At Saint-Vic around that time, there were those poor men who ate their own hands and arms, you remember? To say nothing of the woman over in Ronzay who turned her own baby into a stew . . . Of course, that's only hearsay, it may not actually have happened. But you know why Mister Sun King has to bleed the peasants white? To pay for his pure gold piss-pots, that's why! Yes, they say that when he sits down on his throne there's always a piss-pot underneath — no really, I swear it's true — there's a hole in the seat and he's got his fat bottom all ready-set under his robes, just in case he gets an urge in the middle of a ceremony . . . "

The guests laugh, eat, drink and pay — life is wonderful.

Barbe shares not only Jeanne's bedroom but even her large poster bed — it is the first time she has ever slept on a real box mattress.

Also for the first time, she discovers the delights of gibble-gabble. Jeanne is considerably more informed than she on certain matters.

"Did your masters ever fiddle with you?" she asks Barbe one evening.

"Fiddle?"

"You know . . . Did they ever put their hands up your dress to diddle your breasts or your bottom?"

"Oh, no! I guess it's because I haven't any breasts or bottom to speak of."

They shriek with laughter.

"Once, though," Barbe goes on, "the son of the family — you know, when I was on the farm — well, he shoved a fishing rod down my nose. I don't know if you'd call that fiddling or diddling, but I spouted blood all afternoon."

"Ugh! That's disgusting."

"What about you? Do they touch you?"

"Ha! All the time. You see, they're all men, the guests here, they're travelling alone, just passing through, so they have nothing to lose, you see what I mean? I must have been about seven the first time it happened."

"What does it feel like?"

"Well, it feels funny. It's like a shiver — like a draft of air going through you all of a sudden. It's not too bad. You'll see. It won't be long."

"And you just let them . . .?"

"Ha! They take you by surprise. But you must be careful not to let them get you into a corner and rub themselves against you, especially if they've been drinking. That's the beginning of the big danger."

Barbe, who has witnessed the coupling and birthing of farm animals since earliest childhood, nods pensively. She has been aroused at the sight of he-goats, donkeys, horses in rut. She thinks she knows what her friend means by *shiver*.

"So," Jeanne goes on, "you should just push them away — but gently, you know, with a smile. Mamma says it's not their fault, they can't help it if their thingamajig leads them around by the nose."

More shrieks of laughter.

"Do you know any healings?"

"No."

"Oh, I'm sorry. I forgot."

The magic formulas can only be handed down from mother to daughter or from grandmother to granddaughter. Barbe, having no family, is excluded from the healing chain.

"What about you?"

"Yes, Mamma's teaching me. I'm lucky because she's got a real gift. People come from far and wide to see her . . . "

"So which ones do you know?"

"So far the only one I'm sure of is healing asp bites. But it's important because asps are really witches in disguise, so if they bite you you're in bad trouble."

"Well, I'll stick close to you next Sunday when we go looking for hyacinths in the woods. Just in case . . . "

"Oh, no!" says Jeanne, laughing. "As long as Mamma is alive, I don't have the right to use it. All I can do is keep it in my heart and make sure I don't forget it."

"Could you teach it to me?"

"No . . . I'm sorry, Barbe. It's not that I don't want to, I'd do anything for you, but it can't be between friends, you know. It's not allowed."

Icy cold. Loneliness. Barbe feels her soul retracting like a slug teased with a twig.

"But you know," says Jeanne, changing the subject, "they say Richelieu himself believed in healings."

"You mean the cardinal?"

Barbe has only vaguely heard of him, but she knows the two words *cardinal* and *Richelieu* go together.

"Yes! When he was at death's doorstep, and the king's doctors and the relics and everything else had proved useless, he sent for an old peasant-woman from around here to be brought to his palace."

"No!"

"Yes! I swear it! And this old lady just *despised* the cardinal, so she decided to sweeten his final moments here on earth as best she could. And you know what she did? She made him drink a pint of white wine where a horse-flop had been soaking for weeks."

"Yecccchh! That's revolting!"

The two girls roll around on the bed, holding their noses, grimacing, pretending to throw up.

"So you know, when you get pregnant, they say the soul doesn't enter the baby right away when the man plants it, only a while later. It takes forty days for a boy, and eighty for a girl. So if you get rid of the baby before the soul comes in, it's not so serious."

"But how do you get rid of it?"

"Oh, there's lots of ways. Mamma knows a million recipes, it'd take me all night to recite them to you!"

"And when the baby's born, it's the same thing — the mother is impure for forty days if it's a boy, eighty days if it's a girl. That's why Candlemas, on February Second, is called the purification feast — because it's forty days after Christmas, and that's when the Virgin gets pure again."

"But that's impossible! The Virgin Mary can't be impure! If you're a virgin and you give birth to a baby who's the son of God in person, how can you be impure?"

"Because that's the way it is. Because you're a woman, and if you have a baby you're impure, even if you're the Virgin Mary in person!"

"And you know, there's this convent called Loudun not too far from here, where all the nuns got possessed by devils. My grandparents went there on their honeymoon, and grandmamma said there were crowds pouring in from all over the country just to see the good sisters thrash about on the floor."

"How did the devils get inside them?"

"Well, they go in through here — just like men! And then afterwards you have to drag them out the same way, it's called exercising. Sometimes there'd be twenty or thirty different devils in the body of one single woman, and the priest would have to exercise them for hours on end, and when they finally started coming out, the woman would roll around on the ground saying blasphemies and dirty words — no, I'm not making it up! In the middle of church and everything! Grandmamma said she never heard such horrors in her life! And once, when they were exercising the Mother Superior — she was called Jeanne, like me — you know what happened? She puked up a pact."

"What's a pact?"

"A pact with the devil, don't you know that? A little tiny packet with all sorts of things in it. This one had a piece of a baby's heart that was sacrificed in a witches' sabbath, plus the ashes of a holy wafer, plus some blood, plus a drop of seed from her priest, Father Grandin — because you know, all the sisters at Loudun said he'd forced them to do it with him."

"But that's impossible . . . " says Barbe.

"What's the matter with you? Every time I tell you something you say it's impossible. It's true! Father Grandin even ended up getting burned at the stake, so it must have been true! . . . And you know what else? This same Jeanne, the prioress, once she thought she was pregnant!"

"Pregnant!!"

"Yes, she hadn't had her curse for months, you see, and her stomach kept swelling and swelling . . . So first she thought of using remedies to kill the baby, but then she figured no, that would be sending an innocent soul to hell, so she decided to cut her own stomach open, take the baby out and baptize it, then smother it — after which she'd die herself. So she went to the kitchen and stole the biggest butcher's knife she could find, plus a basin of water for the baptism, and then she climbed upstairs into a little cell-room with a crucifix . . . "

"Stop it!" says Barbe firmly.

"No, don't worry, everything turns out all right in the end, because you know what? Before she could cut her stomach open, she started coughing up big clots of blood and it turned out she wasn't pregnant after all — it was just the blood of her moons that had collected inside her until finally it rose up into her throat . . . "

"Stop it!" says Barbe, covering Jeanne's mouth with both hands.

It is not really the macabre details of her friend's story that bother Barbe — her own murderous birth has been described to her on many occasions, and she is beyond being shocked by such images. No, what bothers Barbe is jealousy — while she cares deeply for both Jeanne and Hélène, she also feels a slight pinch of resentment that she herself had neither mother nor grandmother to initiate her into the mysteries of being female.

"And you know — a customer told us this the other night, he saw it with his own eyes — over in Gargilesse, there's a lying-down statue called Saint Greluchon because you can see his *guerliche*, well, you won't believe it but you know what the women around there do when they can't have a baby? They pay a visit to the saint and scrape off a little piece of his *guerliche*. Then they put the powdered stone in milk and drink it for nine days in a row! I don't know if it works, but the man said there was almost nothing left of the poor statue's *guerliche!*"

"Did you ever see a real one?"

They gibble and they gabble, sometimes late into the night. They are so excited about their friendship that they seem never to suffer from fatigue during the day — even as they go about their domestic chores, they are mulling over last night's conversation in their minds, and looking forward to tonight's.

The *Scordatura* Notebook

Perry Street, November 17th

The material world conspires to defeat me. I am by no means as smooth, sleek and straightforward-sailing-like-a-figurehead-siren as I like people to believe. *Au contraire*. Each morning I stride out into the world head high, arms swinging, the very picture of haughty elegance and grace . . . Gradually, however, innocuous factors converge to bring me to my knees, and by the end of the day I am alone in the arena, exposed to crowds of malevolent onlookers that point and guffaw at me as I writhe in shame and mix my tears in the dust.

For example. This morning, as it was chilly, I put on my long rust-coloured suede coat: a lady of seemingly unruffleable loveliness came out into the Manhattan fall day, descended my front steps, took the subway at Sheridan Square and emerged twenty minutes later at the Forty-Second Street Library. Even when my nose began to run and I checked my pocket for a kleenex only to discover that the pocket lining was badly torn, I scarcely batted an eyelash. Anyone can have a torn pocket. It is not a crime. It is scarcely even my fault. It is reparable. It is virtually negligible.

At lunchtime I left the library and bought a slice of pizza to eat while walking. There is nothing wrong with eating while walking. Millions of people do it without giving it a second thought. It is a perfectly normal and ordinary thing to do, in this frantic age and on this harried continent. Well, and then I went to the post office to mail a package to Laura in France, but the line-up wasn't as long as I'd expected and before I'd finished devouring my hot sticky mushroom-and-melted-cheese pizza my turn had come. I hurriedly wrapped the napkin around the pizza and shoved it into my pocket, where its weight caused it to slip through the hole in the lining and plummet to the bottom of my coat. There it was, grotesquely stuck between coat and lining, where I could not get at it unless I chose, in front of gaping giggling onlookers, to remove my coat and plunge my entire arm into the hole in my pocket. As I blithely pretended nothing had happened and proceeded to pay for my stamps, the spicy oil I had poured liberally on my pizza began to drip onto my shoes and the post office floor . . .

How can you do this to me, dæmon?

O. I try to laugh.

These days at the library I'm reading everything I can get my hands on about what came out of the various orifices of the nuns. Where else would devils take up residence but in women's innards? Infernal chaos, at once dark and burning — just like home to them! The priests, too, had fairly chaotic ideas about female anatomy — at Loudun they performed miraculous enemas, forcibly irrigating the good sisters' colons with giant syringes — and, almost invariably, the demons gave up and left.

The situation of the possessed sisters at Auxonne was even more startling. "They claim, as do the priests, that the latter cured them of their hernias by means of exorcism, forcing the bowels that had come dangling out of their wombs back inside, and instantly healing the wounds the wizards had inflicted on their wombs by ripping them. Sticks covered with wizards' foreskins came tumbling out of their wombs, as well as pieces of candles, sticks covered with tongues and other instruments of infamy such as guts and other things used by the wizards and magicians to perform impure acts upon them." — Dr Samuel Garnier, *La Barbe Buvée et la prétendue possession des Ursulines d'Auxonne*, p. 14-15.

Admittedly, this is a bit too much for my Barbe to hear about from Jeanne. But one cannot help wondering what in heaven's name was going on — had the good sisters used these various sticks and candles for masturbation and then just sort of *lost them* inside themselves? And just how did the holy priests go about extracting them from their wombs? Perhaps the whole phenomenon is merely a variant on the old folktale: the kind, generous little girl is rewarded by having a gold coin drop from her mouth at every word she utters, whereas her nasty and selfish stepsister's every word turns into a toad. From the wombs of good women issue forth babies, but from the wombs of evil women —

nothing but sticks covered with tongues and fore-skins!

(It turns out, moreover, that for centuries the toad was a symbol of the uterus. It was quite usual, for instance, to thank the Virgin Mary for a successful delivery by offering her a votive toad! Hmm, the witches are not so far away . . .)

What is possession? The good sisters were possessed by Beelzebub, Asmodeus, Lucifer, Leviathan, Dagon — it was *they* who swore and blasphemed through the nuns' innocent lips . . . Men who rape and murder little children say exactly the same thing: a "demon" or "monster" lives inside them, gives them orders, forces them to commit these heinous crimes as they themselves look on — horrified, helpless witnesses of their own acts.

In just the same way, the Evangelists protested, "*I* didn't write that, it was dictated to me word for word by the Holy Ghost!" Every prophet, every poet has had his hand guided by someone: deity, angel, muse, envoy from Above or from Below.

L'Autre inhabits us. We swarm with disembodied voices and invisible presences.

What about myself? Am I not possessed — voluntarily, passionately — by *you*, dear dæmon? I could not live without you.

And . . . what about my father when he is drunk?

Go ahead, get it off your chest. If you don't, we won't be able to move on to more serious matters.

Dinner with Father last night. A disaster. How much longer I will be able to stand this I don't know.

When I let myself in with the key, he didn't even get up from his chair to say hello. I saw him from behind. I'm still not used to seeing him as an old man — his head quite bald now, a few unkempt tufts of grey sprouting here and there, his body heavy and lumpy — he who was once so elegant, so debonair. He was at the kitchen table, more or less slumped over the newspaper, there was a bottle of gin next to him but he had not passed out, no, he was sobbing.

When he heard me set the flowers on the counter he wheeled around dramatically and cried out, "Nadia, this is the most terrible thing I've ever read about in my entire life, I can hardly *believe* it."

Sobbing so hard he had to stop and get hold of himself before he could go on. I stood there feeling hard, fleshless and heartless as usual. Waiting, knowing I had no choice but to wait, and that he would not wish to be comforted afterwards, but would wallow the entire evening in this newfound pain, as gleefully as a pig in mud.

"Look," he said at last, snuffling back what snot he could and wiping the rest on his sleeve. "Just look . . . "

The story was something I had heard about vaguely on the radio, Robert Peary's having brought five or six Inuits back to New York with him from the North Pole, and medical experiments having been performed on them to determine whether and why their bodies were more resistant to the cold than ours. The experiments had resulted in the Inuits' deaths, and now, a century later, after endless litigation, their bones were about to be repatriated to the Great North. Of course what Ronald was crying about was not the repatriation but the deaths, the incredible callousness of human beings uprooting and deporting other human beings for the sole purpose of medical experimentation, the calm scientific sadism of white men dealing with non-whites . . . Yes, of course, Father, all of this is true . . .

"Have you anything in the fridge?"

He let me start fixing an omelette, but before I got as far as grating the cheese he was at it again.

"I can't *believe* it, Nadia, I just can't *believe* it." He moaned, he groaned, he gulped down another half glass of gin and tonic. "There's this little Moroccan girl? Nine years old? On some beach in the Netherlands? I didn't even know they *had* beaches in the Netherlands, for Christ's sake, I thought all they had were dikes. Dykes and fags and junkies. Don't laugh so hard, you'll burst an artery. My artery fartery daughter. Sorry about that. Anyway, so she's wading and splashing around in the water and suddenly she goes under — she doesn't know how to swim — and you know what happens? Two hundred fucking Dutch people get up from their beach towels and stand there and *watch her drown*. And she *drowns*, Nadia! She's *dead*! That little girl is fucking *dead*! And you know what the nice Dutch people said when the journalists arrived on the scene? 'That makes one less of 'em'."

"'One fewer' would have been more correct."

"Are you crazy or what? Who gives a shit if they said one fewer or one less, they were talking Dutch anyway, the gist of what they said was, 'Fortunately, there is now one dirty Arab, or Arabs, fewer on our nice clean beaches', that's what they said!"

"Father."

"What?"

"Can't we just have a pleasant meal together, the two of us? I only see you about once every six months, and I do read the newspapers every day myself."

"Yeah, you read 'em, but it all slides off you like water off a duck's back. Sometimes I wonder how you managed to attend church and Sunday school all those years without learning a thing about Christian charity. You don't give a damn about other human beings. All you care about is your stupid characters who don't even exist."

I chopped lettuce and tomatoes methodically, waiting for him to reverse gear; I could have timed it virtually to the second.

"No, I don't mean that, Nadia. That's not what I meant to say, all I meant to say was, WHO SAYS I shouldn't cry for that little Moroccan girl, or for Robert Peary's mutilated Eskimos? WHO will cry for them, if I don't? Did you ever cry about any-body or anything in your entire fucking life?"

"Father? Can I serve the omelette?"

I'm so patient with him. Never raise my voice. Chilly and impassive as a block of ice.

Perhaps Ronald is right. Perhaps *in vino veritas*. Perhaps sobriety is the brick wall that protects the rest of us from our emotions. Without it we would not, or at least should not, be able to read the daily newspaper. Drunks weep and rage and shout, perorate, stumble and insist, make themselves ridiculous — we all know this, we all recognize "men in their cups" — but perhaps they are at once cowardly and brave. Yes, brave.

By the end of the evening Father had gotten all friendly and cushy and mushy with me but he was still weeping. Despite my attempts at diversion, there was no way I could stop him from going to the bedroom and dragging out his box of love-letters from Mother. Letters written fifty years ago, some during their courtship and the rest during the one and only European tour she managed to go on after their marriage.

Hub, she called him, in one of the letters he showed me, spattering it with his tears. "Dear hub hubby luvey-dove mine. I keep thinking about the way you made love to me last week and it gives me wings. I've never played so well in all my life. Who would have thought that little thing between your legs could set off standing ovations in Vienna and Stockholm? Well it sure can, Ronny honey-bun."

I felt soiled. I felt as if he were brandishing his dirty underwear under my nose, as if these micklesicklesweet words had nothing to do with me — whereas they did, in fact they had everything in the world to do with me, for even as Elisa pasted a stamp on the envelope addressed to Fordham Road, the result of their love-making was budding in her tummy, and that result

oh I feel sick, sick, my hand weighs a ton

There were two of us in there. I lived nine months with my brother; he was the one that got strangled in the horrendous confusion of our birth and I got off scot-free.

What would you have called him, dear parents? They have always turned away, angrily refusing to answer that question.

I cleared the table, washed the dishes, tried yet again to change the subject. But Ronald could not resist repeating, for the six hundredth time at least — weeping still, weeping always, eyes glittering, cheeks bathed in tears — the tale of how they met. This time I shall write it down and have done with it. Kill it, stab it to death on the page.

Ronald in those days was a charmer, a smiler, with slick black hair combed sideways on his head, a Scottish-Italian kid from Avenue B who'd taken some bad knocks in his youth, spent fourteen years in factories before he finally managed to pull himself up — "by his own bootstraps," as he invariably put it (oh how he fatigued us all with his boasting and his clichés, in fact his social ascendancy owed nothing to his bootstraps and everything to his lips, his gift for smooth-talking fast-talking sweet-talking) — to the status of storeowner in the Bronx. Not-too-fancy leather goods.

The story tells how Elisa and Stella and the other members of the Ensemble, fresh off the plane from Chicago, were walking down Fordham Road of a Saturday morning carrying their instruments and suitcases, bumpity-bump, thumpity-thump . . . (What in heaven's name were they doing in the Bronx? Cheap hotel rooms? A game at Yankee Stadium? Fond memories of the *viole de gambiste's* childhood? The story doesn't say.) There they were, Elisa by far the youngest, "ten years younger and ten times as gifted as the rest of them," my father now says proudly and I clench my teeth . . . The story goes on to tell how Elisa's suitcase — a bad one, a cheap one, a rotten flimsy one her impoverished Hungarian parents must have picked out for her at the local five-and-dime — suddenly fell apart, spilling forth its contents, delicate female things, nightgowns, blouses, lacy lingerie, onto the dirty New York sidewalk . . . A bunch of kids immediately dived to pick them up for her, laughing and jostling the bizarre-looking group of musicians, so that he, my father, Ronald, pricking up his ears at the scuffle, had glanced out his shop window to see what was going on . . .

"And believe it or not, Nadia, that was *it*."

"Yes, Father."

"I saw this *angel*. There must have been something like fifty people milling around on that sidewalk, but all I could see was this *angel*, standing there laughing helplessly with her suitcase in two pieces in her hands, and no one knew what to do with the stuff they were picking up off the street, and so I didn't even *think*, you know? I was thunderstruck, hypnotized, whatever you want to call it, it was as if my whole body was suddenly lit up from inside, my hands and feet were tingling, and I just ran to the back of the shop and picked out the nicest leather suitcase I had in stock and took it outside to her and said, 'Madam, would you do me the honour of accepting this small gift as a token of my admiration?' Smooth as you please. It was like somebody else talking through my mouth, I felt so happy and sure of myself, and when Elisa looked up at me she had this surprised look on her face at first, like she was going to say you can't be serious, and then right away she saw how serious I was so she got serious too and we just stood there in the middle of the sidewalk looking at each other very seriously while everybody filled up the new suitcase with her stuff and snapped it shut and handed it to her, and suddenly this huge blush came over her face and she turned around to her musician friends and said, 'See you guys half an hour before curtain!' I'll always remember that, it was the first time I heard her voice, 'See you guys half an hour before curtain!' — some gumption, huh? — and then she slipped her arm through mine and we just walked off together. I don't even remember what coffee shop I took her to, I was floating on air."

He took a very long gulp from his glass of gin and tonic.

"Floating on air," he repeated, with a noise that combined the functions of a sigh and a belch.

"Father. I have to be going now."

That woke him up.

"*Why* do you have to be going, may I know? Would you be so kind as to tell me *what* is so urgent in your life that it is impossible for you to listen to your own father's memories of your own mother? As far as I know, you're not obliged to punch in tomorrow at any goddamn factory the way I did for fourteen years, you don't have five kids to wash and dress and get off to school the way your mother did, you don't even have a husband anymore so what's the rush? Why are you always in such a fucking hurry, Nadia? Can you tell me that?"

I was outwardly stiff and inwardly trembling, cold, cold with rage.

"Do you think it is irresistably pleasant to stand here and be sworn at?" I managed to say, almost in a whisper.

"Oh, get out of here," he said, slamming down his glass in disgust and turning away from me. "Just get the hell out. Go on, that's what you've wanted to do since you first got here, so go!"

I put on my coat, picked up my bag and walked out. Somehow I mustered enough maturity not to slam the door. But as I went down the front steps he came staggering after me . . .

"Wait — Nadia — please. Don't be angry. Don't go away mad. Don't go away hating me. I'm sorry. I know I get carried away . . . Wait a minute. Please, wait just one minute. Can you wait *just one minute* while I go and get my coat? I'll walk you to the subway."

And so I wait for him, and I forgive him, and he looks so frighteningly elderly and pathetic as he comes back outside, struggling with his overcoat, and by the time I finally get to Perry Street I am defeated, annihilated, dead.

The Resurrection Sonata

IV - The Storm

The inn at Torchay being located just across the square from the church, one of the most endearing of all the small Romanesque churches in the area, Barbe acquires the habit of going there early in the morning, before the guests get up and start ordering bread for themselves and oats for their horses.

It is springtime, the sky is just barely growing light as she inches out of bed, careful not to disturb the sleep of lovely Jeanne, grabs a shawl and picks up her wooden clogs, slipping her bare feet into them once she is out of doors.

Bird sounds — the raucous insistent cries of roosters, gradually replaced by the amorous chattering of sparrows and turtledoves . . . the morning air so delicious and no one around to taste it but me, Barbe, tiny breasts now beginning to bud, and the sky blushing pink at the horizon . . .

She enters the church, where it is still dark and very chilly, moves up to the altar and kneels down on the flagstones — always at the same spot, facing the beautiful dark orange fresco above the altar, a Christ Ascending. She waits until she can clearly distinguish the contours of His body in the shadows, then closes her eyes and waits to feel His presence — ah here He comes, yes, He is approaching, she feels Him lay His hand upon her shoulder, sometimes even on her head, He is a youthful man, warm and gentle, Who listens to everything she has to say, more attentive and more tender still than Father Thomas — He is pure Light, pure Love, pure Forgiveness. When He touches the eyes of the blind they cry out in astonishment, for suddenly they can see again; and ever since He touched her own ardu-ous and desolate existence, streams of felicity have been flowing in all directions.

One Sunday when the two young girls come home hand-in-hand from Mass, Hélène (who never goes to church herself, on pretext that she would need to use every tablecloth in the house to sew herself a presentable dress) holds two baskets out to them.

"Go pick me some wild strawberries, my pret-ty ones. I'm told there are masses of them down at the bottom of the hill, in the thicket to the right. I'll serve them up at noon with cream and honey — oh, the guests will lick their lips, mark my words. Off with you, now! Yes of course, you'll get some, too — if there are any left over!"

Barbe and Jeanne dash away. Cavorting like a couple of young goats, they reach the crest of the hill and fly downwards, Barbe in the lead — for she is the lighter and more sinewy of the two, her breasts do not bounce and jounce like Jeanne's at every step. At the bottom of the hill, she sees the thicket Hélène mentioned, takes a running leap and bounds across the ditch . . .

The pain is so extreme she nearly faints.

Catching up with her, Jeanne realizes at once what has happened. Barbe's ankle is sprained — she must have landed on a stone that slipped — but what is to be done? Jeanne does not know that particular healing, and it is unthinkable for Barbe to walk back up the hill with her ankle so evilly swollen; as for Hélène, her weight does not allow her to travel — it has been five years since she ventured any farther away than the marketplace, which is directly in front of the inn.

Meanwhile Barbe is writhing on the ground, moaning pitifully . . .

Jeanne runs back up to the village, reascending the slope more swiftly than she came down it. As soon as Hélène finds out what the problem is, she makes a decision — and, as usual with Hélène, as soon as she makes a decision it becomes reality.

Four hefty guests carry the innkeeper's oaken armchair, already heavy in itself, out to the street, and Hélène settles into it. They are instantly surrounded by a small crowd of bantering housewives and curious kids. Then — with difficulty, with pride, with great grunts of effort and satisfaction — the men lift the armchair off the ground and, swaying and stumbling, carry fat Hélène down the hill. The crowd of onlookers straggles after them, growing larger by the minute, turning into a procession, everyone laughing and prattling, thinking how this will make a good story for months, perhaps for years to come.

Hélène's hands do not so much as graze Barbe's ankle. They move above it, tracing precise designs in the air, but Barbe is in too much pain to even attempt to see what they are doing. As for the innkeeper's muttered words, they are wiped out like a sigh by the hubbub of the crowd.

The whole thing lasts no longer than ten seconds, after which Barbe gets to her feet and picks up her berry basket. She knows better than to express her thanks.

"We'll be back with the strawberries in a jiffy, Madam Hélène," she says instead. "Are you coming, Jeanne?"

As the two young girls move off into the thicket, the men crouch at the edge of the brook, splashing their faces with water in preparation for the redoubtable return trip.

The month of June arrives, and Hélène suggests that Barbe invite her brother over to celebrate Midsummer's Eve with them. Though a devotee, the boy has not yet taken his vows (he will not be able to do so until next year, when he turns fourteen); for the time being he can still move about quite freely and eat whatever he pleases.

Midsummer's Eve, in these parts, is considered to be a pagan, not to say Satanic festival — it is on this night, claim the priests, that the devil's followers are summoned to the greatest orgy of the year — so the peasants tend to avoid celebrating it. Instead they have Brand Sunday — the first Sunday in Lent, when all the young men go tearing across the fields in the middle of the night, waving long, flaming firebrands to stimulate the earth's fertility. But

Hélène was born into a family of potters, and potters are an exception to the rule — they celebrate Midsummer's Eve. Indeed, potters are thought to be shady characters, almost tantamount to alchemists or wizards — they live apart, on the outskirts of villages, their dealings are dubious and their craft dangerous: they handle fire, the elements . . . Hélène herself has always been regarded with distrust, especially since she married the son of the notary public's widow — it was not a proper marriage, Sylvain Denis was far too good for her — and then, scarcely a week after signing the purchase of Torchay inn (under the lord of L...'s nose, it might be pointed out), Sylvain had been disembowelled by a bull in an adjacent field — very suspicious indeed — and it was then that Hélène started gaining weight, spouting opinions on everything under the sun and receiving patients from other villages . . . Healers are a fishy lot — one never knows whether their powers derive from God or from the Other.

Be this as it may, Hélène has always remained attached to Midsummer's Eve, a happy reminder of her childhood — and, turning a deaf ear to the buzz of the busybodies, she celebrates it each year without fail. For weeks now, the girls have been gathering deadwood and stacking it behind the inn; there will be one marvellous bonfire tonight . . .

The three of them laugh as they knead bread dough, pluck guinea hens, slide long rectangular pear pies into the oven, chop up cabbage and onions. Hélène is in an excellent mood — she is telling them about a piper whom she knew as a little girl; he lived at the edge of the forest and he was a leader of wolves. Drawn by the sound of his bagpipes, she explained, the wolves would swarm into his yard by the dozen and dance circles around him — he knew how to cast spells on them, subdue them, compel them to do his bidding — and if a local reveller got into the bad habit of coming home drunk in the middle of the night, the piper would send out two wolves to accompany him. The beasts would follow the drunkard down the road, always at the same distance, walking when he walked, stopping when he stopped and running when he ran, until the poor man was fairly mad with fear — but upon arriving home, he still had to repay his unwanted guides by feeding them a loaf of bread . . .

Barbe listens wide-eyed, a floury finger in her mouth — is everything Hélène says to be believed?

"And when a wolf died," adds the innkeeper, "the piper used to cut out its liver, dry it and crush it into a fine powder, then put it in his pipe and smoke it."

"Oh, Mother, please!" says Jeanne. "You'll spoil our appetite."

The guests have already had their evening meal. It is late, but the red ball of the sun is still suspended above the horizon, the solstice weather is lovely this year, the evening air so fragrant, Barbe and Barnabé have set up a table and chairs out of doors, behind the inn, on the flowered terrace which looks out over the entire plain, with its pleasing, irregular alternations of garden and hedgerow, wood and pond, pointed steeple and pointed poplar, as far as the eye can see.

The meal is served.

Everyone I love in the world is seated around this table, Barbe says to herself as the food is blessed. When she reopens her eyes, her gaze meets that of her brother and their faces break into mirror smiles.

"So I hear you're planning to become a little Orsan monk?" Hélène asks Barnabé, plunging her fork into the mountain of cabbage on her plate.

"Yes, Madam."

"And you're prepared to take orders from women for the rest of your life?"

"Of course, since the founder decided it should be so, nigh on six hundred years ago."

"You do know some priests of the order kicked up a fuss about it, don't you? Not that long ago, either. My mother remembered it well — she's the one who told me the story. They were fed up with not being allowed to decide anything for themselves, they found it humiliating to be whipped by women, or tossed into prison for the least bagatelle. So they started complaining, they got the priests of all the other priories to complain, too, and things started looking pretty bad for a while. But it so happened that the abbess of Fontevraud at the time was Sister Jeanne-Baptiste — you know, Henry II's little bastard. Well, she told her half-brother Louis XIII that if he dared change so much as a comma in the statutes of the order, all the Bourbon dames would stop giving him their support. Louis wasn't stupid, he got the picture right away, and ordained that the sisters retain their privileges.

"Well," says Barnabé with a faintly ironic smile, "so long as the king was in agreement with the founder . . . "

"Ah — your sister is right, you're adorable. Speaking of Good Robert, has anyone at Orsan ever told you the true story of Mister Holy-Heart?"

"I know that it's kept in the chapel," says Barnabé, "and every year at Whitsuntide thousands of pilgrims flock to the priory to pay it hommage."

"Well, let me tell you, that poor little piece of the founder has had a hard time of it," says Hélène, laughing and digging into her second plateful of guinea hen and cabbage. "I have the tale from Father Thomas himself, and believe, me he knows Fontevrist history like his *Ave Maria*."

She loves talking with her mouth full, and manages to do so without the slightest indelicacy.

"The problem, you see, was that d'Arbrissel, in that icy winter of 1116, made the mistake of dying *here*, in a tiny little priory in the middle of nowhere — whereas he wanted at all costs to be buried at the mother abbey of Fontevraud. Even before he gave up the ghost, he could see the prioress Agnès gloating over him as a potential relic, the object of pilgrimages and therefore a major source of wealth for Orsan. Well, he was right! As soon as he entered his death throes, the priory was invaded by a bunch of nuns from Fontevraud — including the abbess, of course, who went by the improbable name of Pétronille de Chemillé — and no sooner had the founder breathed his last breath than they grabbed the body, rushed to the cloister and locked themselves up with it. But then the archbishop of Bourges, who was a personal friend of Agnès's, brought in a pack of local lords and warriors who promptly stove in the cloister doors and kidnapped poor Robert, sequestering him in the chapel. At that point, the Fontevrist girls simply stripped off their coats and shoes — it was the month of February, mind you — and started marching barefoot around the chapel, refusing to eat or drink until they got their founder back. Crowds began to pour in to Orsan from far and wide . . . Finally, the abbess threatened to appeal directly to Rome, and the local lords got the jitters — they figured perhaps it was not such a good idea to fool around with someone named Pétronille de Chemillé. The archbishop eventually threw up the sponge, too, and Agnès was forced to hand over Good Robert. But, refusing to be totally outdone, she took care to rip out his heart first! Then she sent the corpse back to the abbey just as it was, chest agape, without even taking the trouble to embalm it. Frankly, d'Arbrissel must have been a bit gamy by the time he got home — a good thing it was wintertime."

"Mother, for heaven's sake!" says Jeanne, with a grimace of disgust. "We're eating!"

"So now Agnès had her precious relic," Hélène goes on irrepressibly. "She locked it up in some sort of pyramid, and for the next few centuries everything went along fine — Mister Holy-Heart contented himself with performing a little miracle every now and then, just to keep his hand in. But then came the terrible year of 1569, when the Huguenots rode up and laid waste to the convent. One of these great German brutes strode into the chapel and started thumping on the pyramid to see what was inside. Suddenly everything went dark — he lost his sight, and his guilty arm was para-lyzed."

"No!" says Barbe, impressed.

"But afterwards," says Jeanne, interrupting her mother to speed the story up, "he was smitten with remorse. He did an entire novena in the church, and the good founder finally restored his sight."

"You call that remorse?" mocks Hélène. "When you're blinded and it bothers you? Hmph! Some remorse! Anyway," she goes on, pushing her chair back so that her stomach can breathe more freely, "some years later, a man from Fontevraud comes over to clean the pyramid and — oops! bad luck! — the coffer slips out of his hands and smashes to the floor, reducing the relic to a little heap of dust. Well, they sweep up the ashes as best they can and this time they put them in a tabernacle. But a while later another man comes over from the abbey, supposedly to work on the priory archives, but all of a sudden he starts feeling sick — ooooohhhh he feels soooooooooo siiiiiiiiiiiick — so, just to make sure of a swift recov-ery, he decides to take the heart with him when he leaves. Of course the prioress bristles up, there's another tug-of-war, and finally they agree to divvy up the ashes — three-fourths for Fontevraud and one-fourth for Orsan. In other words, what you've got now is about one half teaspoonful of Mister Holy-Heart! It's hardly surprising there's been a dearth of miracles in the last few decades!"

Barnabé cannot help laughing. He is now utterly at ease, so that when Barbe begs him to do some imitations he consents, wondrously mimicking the screeching voice of the Orsan portress, the mellifluous platitudes of good Father Thomas, two young monks singing together in weird harmony . . . and then, as his audience laughs harder and harder, Hélène's oaken armchair creaking as she sits down in it, Jeanne yelping as a wasp buzzes madly about her head, the frightened snorts of a horse in the throes of a bad dream.

Later, when they have laughed to their hearts' content, when their stomachs are gratified and stars have begun to appear in the sky, the four of them light the bonfire and, holding hands, sing and dance around the flames. Fat Hélène can do little more than bob rhythmically on the spot, but the three young people jump and spin, take running leaps over the fire, laugh and leap and laugh until their breath is spent.

They separate at dawn, and in her two hours of scant sleep Barbe has a disturbing dream. In her dream, she sees a wizard filling up his pipe — not with tobacco, nor with the dessicated liver of a wolf, but with the fine pink-powdered heart of Robert d'Arbrissel.

Summer swells and ripens. Barbe feels she has never in her life seen summer before — as if her first thirteen years had been spent staring at the ground, into the mire and muck, or her own inner gloom — whereas now Hélène and Jeanne teach her all manner of things — the names of flowers — nasturtiums, poppies — and when is the best time to pick the tiny syrup-plums — and also the names of special roots and plants, used to induce this or that effect . . . Yes, Barbe senses that she is being initiated — unobtrusively, almost imperceptibly — into certain mysteries. Here is what happens when you feed men horse-chestnuts, leeks, or carrots — do you understand? Yes, and when a woman wants a baby boy, what you must give her is thistle juice. Now, take a good look at this plant here — what does it remind you of? Exactly! That's why it's called satirion — its double ballock-shaped roots will turn any man into a satyr!

Other remedies, however, for other ills, are concealed from her. Barbe asks questions, bothers and begs Hélène to explain to her the uses of ox gall, white violets, colocynth pulp — but the innkeeper merely winks at her. "Later, sweet one, later," she says. "A time for everything and everything in its time." Similarly, in addition to the familiar plantations in the garden that runs the length of the inn's west wall, there are certain unknown herbs that Barbe does not have the right to touch — it is Jeanne who looks after these, fertilizing them not with the usual night soil but with bat droppings, which she collects on special twice-weekly visits to the church.

One Sunday in August, a day of unbearable heat and humidity, the innkeeper sends the girls in search of wild cucumber. She knows exactly where they can find some — on the far side of La Prade Pond, a fair distance away but they have no choice, they must go now, yes, immediately, before evening. No, she will not tell them why, all she will tell them is that it is urgent, a woman's life is at stake.

"Is it someone from Torchay?" asks Jeanne — who, unlike Barbe, knows what wild cucumber is used for.

"None of your business, you nosy thing! Now go do your mother's bidding, or I shall turn you into a may-bug — in the twinkling of an eye!"

The two girls set off — but at a far less eager pace than on the day of the wild strawberries. The air is leaden, the sky an abnormal grey-yellow, breathing is like inhaling warm water, they wish they could walk fast to get it over with, but as soon as they hasten their step, sweat pours down their backs and foreheads and their clothes stick to their skin. They walk without speaking, the thick air imposes silence on the entire landscape, the sheep lie motionless and prostrate in the fields, even the flies and bumblebees have renounced buzzing.

No one should be out of doors right now, it is obvious, they would give anything to take shelter behind the cool stone walls of the inn or the church. Barbe tries to think of Jesus but her head aches and pounds, they keep walking, keep walking, in defer-ence to Hélène and to save some unknown woman's life — but it is awful, it is unfair, no one should be forced to walk through this molten lead . . .

Flash-*crack*! There is virtually no lapse of time whatever between light and sound.

They glance at one other. They are now walking along the pond's edge but the cucumber patch is on the far side — Hélène told them to take their bearings from a dilapidated fisherman's shack — another half-league at the least.

Above the pond, the lightning literally sunders the sky, leaving the giant brilliant engraving of its forks on their dazzled eyelids. And at once — *crack*! — the thunder pierces their eardrums. It is not the usual rumble or drum-roll, but a dry, deafening report . . .

Suddenly the sky goes dark, breaks apart and floods them with its contents, gushes and sheets of water, they are soaked within a matter of seconds — it is a fabulous relief, a joy, they begin to run, oh, at last they can run again, they find it thrilling, exhilarating to be running in this incredible downpour, they laugh as they run — then, hearing the Torchay church bells clang, they exchange a look of surprise, Father Thomas will be angry, it is against the law to set the church bells ringing because of a thunderstorm . . .

Flash-*crack!* Barbe senses . . . Either what she senses is a non-sensation, or it is no longer she who senses it. Something, Barbe or the world, is no longer there. In far less than the twinkling of an eye. In no time at all. Outside of time. It is like the annihilation of orgasm — if Barbe knew what orgasm was, and if

she was capable of thought. Or like a wild horse, gal-
loping backwards through the cosmos. And it is cold
— it has turned your body and soul to ice before it
can even begin to do so. Barbe senses all of this, if one
may use words at all to describe so wordless a phenomenon — and scarcely has she begun to sense it
than she has already sensed it and she is back again,
the world is back, nothing has happened. Everything
is as before, except for the powerful stench of thunder in the air . . . She sees that she has run too fast
again — faster than Jeanne; she will have to wait for
her, and tell her . . .

She stops. Turns in her tracks. Stops. Oh,
Jeanne fell down . . .

Her friend is lying on her back beneath an oak
tree. Whatever is she doing under an oak tree? She
was right behind me on the path . . . Barbe stands
waiting for her friend in the downpour, which is
already lessening, turning into a reasonable rain, a
sweet, innocent summer shower — and look, the
sky is calmer now, a diffuse, unearthly light sifts
through the thinning clouds and the whole scene is
transfigured. A faint, iridescent mist rises from the
pond, scintillating like gold dust in the oblique
rays of the sun, and through it one can make out, as
in a dream, the rushes and water lilies. The earlier,
ominous silence has melted into a divine peace —
and look, Jeanne, look at the way the water is glittering over there, you'd think a million gold coins
were dancing at its surface . . . Come, my Jeanne . . .

Barbe walks slowly over to her friend. The
strange thing, the really inexplicable thing, is that

Jeanne is totally naked. Her dress and apron are scattered in pieces on the grass around her, she is wearing nothing but a sandal on one foot and a tatter of blue cloth on her left thigh. How did you manage to do that so quickly, Jeanne, how can you possibly have gotten undressed and torn your clothes to shreds and lain down on the ground while my back was turned? What kind of a game is this, sweet friend — some sort of thunderstorm ritual you never told me about? Ah . . . how lovely you look, your legs so shapely, your stomach so round and white, and your breasts — oh, I'm jealous, you never wanted to show me your breasts and now you're baring them to all the world!

But seriously, Jeanne, you must get up now — someone might come past and see you here like this, it wouldn't be right — come on, get up, please, come see the way the water is glittering, I've never seen anything like it, it's pure heaven . . .

Turning back towards the pond to look again upon the trembling, scintillating scene, Barbe's gaze is drawn by a bizarre, whitish heap — just ten paces away, on the far side of the path, next to the first rushes.

She takes the ten paces, bends, and freezes, freezes, forever and forever, oh God, please make it, make it not, God, God, God . . .

It is Jeanne's brain.

The *Scordatura* Notebook

January 8th

Each of us carries around within himself the centre of the universe.

This seems to me of capital importance. Just as in the cosmos there is no objective up or down, whatever we are thinking about is where the centre of the universe is. So we must be very careful what we think about, mustn't we?

Jonas came over last night. He called and came. What always happens happened again. We are so stupid. We can never believe it's going to happen again. I cannot get angry with this man though perhaps I should, perhaps it would be better for both of us if I did, he's married to Moira, for twenty years he has been in love with Moira who is frigid and crazy, she's a sculptor, a gifted cyclothymic artist, in and out of mental hospitals, countless electroshocks, two suicide attempts (one by wrist-slashing, the other by Valium and vodka), two children also (I don't know how *that* happened, but I suppose if the Virgin Mary can do it there's no reason Moira can't) . . .

Jonas loves her, desires her, desires only her, desires her so badly he thinks he will die if he cannot make love to her, only she never never wants to, her body whenever he approaches it is always passive and stone cold, and so he comes to me, because I am not a prostitute, because I'm an old friend, a kind understanding friend, he comes to me filled with his desire for his wife, and I know this and accept it because Jonas is a poet and I have always admired his poems, and also because the sensation of his hardness through his clothes and mine, when he first takes me in his arms, is so warm and fine, and then, and then, it happens every time, the more we are naked the less he is erect, and by the time the bedclothes have been flung open and our skins exposed there is nothing left to do together, no slightest hope of coaxing him back to arousal, and it's defeat again, shame again, his apologies, my demurrals, clumsy kisses that try to say it's all right whereas it's not all right, either for him or for me, and then we have some whisky and some talk by the fireplace.

Last night as usual he talked about Moira, it's the only subject that interests him, her recent work is frightening he says, women with gaping holes in their stomachs, women covering their heads with their arms, women tearing off their own hands and feet, he is afraid she may be about to lose it again. The last time it happened was during a ceremony in her honour, she was supposed to walk to the podium to receive a medal and instead of walking she went down the aisle on all fours, howling and slavering like a mad dog. I cannot bear to hear Jonas tell this story anymore. The first time he told it I was moved to tears at having been taken so fully into his confidence, shown such deeply private horrors — but then I heard him tell it to other people, casually, over a glass of beer, and realized with a shudder that he was actually boasting, that in fact he was proud of Moira, proud of her craziness and her frigidity and his own patience with these problems . . . And then, in a recent collection of his poems, I came across the same images yet again, wife as mad dog, wife as stone statue, and now I don't want to hear about it anymore. I know, I know, what can one write about if not the things one is haunted by, but somehow, no, it bothers me.

Also, I have no desire to compete with Moira for madness. How could my pokey little neurosis ever measure up to her gorgeous full-fledged deliriums?

Unusually vivid dream after Jonas's departure: I was pregnant, and the child I was carrying had rudiments of arms and legs, even a head . . . *but it had no heart*.

Obviously connected to what I had just written about d'Arbrissel's heart being torn from his chest. But I know the true meaning.

Myself: the heartless child.

Father just called to wish me a happy New Year and to apologize for what happened in November — I hadn't heard from him since. Whenever he calls, I try to ascertain the degree of his inebriety from the way he talks. He knows this, can feel me listening for slurred words, and is able to do a passable imitation of a sober person. There are only two infallible criteria: repetitions and superlatives. When thoroughly soused, he repeats every sentence at least six times, with minor variations from one to the other, and the word "most" recurs obsessively. (The most beautiful, the most horrible, the most astonishing thing he has ever seen or heard or done in his entire life . . .) Just now I would say he was only on his second or third drink of the evening, which is not bad for six-thirty p.m. He told me he had never felt so ashamed of himself as on the way back from the subway station that night. I hung up as soon as I could without being hurtful.

Now that the old hatred is gone, what he stirs in me is nearly intolerable. Pity, of course — but also, if I look more closely, aching nostalgia. The wish for him to be again the man that he once was. My handsome daddy — I thought he was handsomer than all the other daddies put together; when he dropped me off at school I wanted to be sure the other girls would see him kissing me good-bye. He was a strong young man with white teeth and muscled biceps, he used to catch me up in his arms and toss me into the air . . . A gruffly tender man, embarrassed by tenderness, who once stroked my thick unruly hair and told me I should be proud of it, it was just the colour of chestnuts . . . A funny man who, when he dressed for church of a Sunday morning, struggled to straighten the knot in his tie with grimaces of strangulation . . .

Why doesn't he telephone the other kids? I'm not the only one left within free calling distance, there

are still Jimbo in Brooklyn and Joanna in the Bronx —
but they, of course, have "family responsibilities"; he
hesitates to barge in on them, whereas I am perfectly
free and permanantly available, all I do is write.

*You wanted, I believe, to tell the story of the double con-
cert. Tartini. The* Devil's Trill Sonata . . .

Yes. The double concert. Yes.

So she wrote all those "hubby" letters as the
Baroque Ensemble toured Europe, and I remember
her telling me more than once — it was as close as
she ever got to joking about this — "When I came
home that time, your father grabbed me in his arms
and swung me off my feet and said, 'I'll never let
you get away from me again.' I had no idea he
actually meant it."

That was her joke.

Here is what happened the first time Elisa gave
a concert in Manhattan after the European tour.

By now she was four months pregnant with
my brother and myself. (My brother Nothingness,
dead twin of living Nada. Would you have called
him Nathan? Norman? Nasturtium? *Why did you
tell me it was a boy?*)

It was a free Sunday afternoon concert at the
Riverside Church. A program of violin sonatas by
Giuseppe Tartini, with Elisa as soloist. The church
was nearly full — much fuller, probably, than it had
been that same morning for the religious service.
(Stella always says she derives a certain amount of
comfort from the fact that, even in our age of canned

perfection, people continue to feel the need for live music.)

I've always had the impression I witnessed this scene myself but obviously not; my eyes were still glued together with amniotic fluid — the movements of Mother's body must have rocked me rhythmically as she played and the music itself may have reached me faintly, at four months a fetus's ears are already formed . . . Anyway, no, it was Stella who told me the story. She was not playing that day — it was the other cellist's turn — so she was in the audience. And, shortly before intermission, in the middle of the final *Adagio* of Giuseppe Tartini's *G-Minor Sonata*, she heard the sound of footsteps coming down the aisle towards the stage. Noisy, uneven footsteps. Not someone walking carefully on tiptoe. Someone staggering with ostentatious carelessness.

She turned around to look — and, with horror, recognized Ronald. Drunk as hell and mad as hell. She considered sticking her foot out into the aisle to trip him, lay him sprawling, prevent him at all costs from reaching the space in front of the altar where his wife was making heavenly music. But she was afraid — she now admits wryly — he would bite her leg.

When Elisa realized who was making the disturbance, she blushed purple. (She had never seen Ronald like this before — happy drunk yes, talkative loveable tipsy drunk yes, but totally purposefully pissed and furious no.) She continued to play, Stella says, setting her chin into the instrument and bowing away without missing a note — a true professional.

Ronald wove his way up to the transept, where, contrary to Stella's forebodings, he did not jump on Elisa and wrench her violin from her hands. No. He ambled over to the opposite side of the stage, where the grand piano had been pushed to make room for the harpsichord, and — after numerous parodical flourishes of hand and head — sat down at the keyboard and launched into a raunchy rendition of "Ramblin' Rose". Not only playing it, singing it. Terribly. Loudly. Even as his wife continued to perform Tartini's *Adagio*.

Why you ramble, no one knows . . .

Several people in the front rows leaped to remove Ronald's hands from the keys, but he shoved them away with a grunt and went back to banging out his chords.

My Ramblin' Rose . . .

The concert ground to a halt.
My mother's career was over.

He needed to feel he could support a wife and family.

Yeah, right. You keep out of this. You men always stick together.

Shortly after they were married, Sigmund Freud wrote a letter to his wife Martha asking her to forgive his occasional explosions of ill humour. "Since

I am violent and passionate with all sorts of devils pent up that cannot emerge," he explained, "they rumble about inside or else are released against you, dear one" (letter dated Nov. 10, 1883, quoted in Ernest Jones, *Sigmund Freud: Life and Work*, vol. I, p. 214). I have always wondered what Martha Freud felt upon reading this letter. Did she understand what her husband meant? Here is the alternative: either they rumble about inside, or else they are released against you. Dear one.

My mother never understood my father's devils — of that I'm certain. She was in love with him, she wanted nothing more than to look up to him and found a family with him under the benevolent gaze of God, I'm convinced that in her mind the family was construed in advance quite simply as the extension of the Baroque Ensemble. There would be various combinations of instruments but Ronald would forever be playing the *basso continuo* and she the first violin, helping the others tune, then conducting with her bow (there was no such thing as a conductor in the baroque period — the other players simply kept the first violin's bow within their field of vision as they played) . . .

No. He had married the bird to throttle it.

More clichés.

Go to hell, will you? I need to think this through.

I don't know how Elisa reacted to the interrupted concert, or when exactly she agreed to leave the Ensemble, these are questions I have never asked her. One never asks the essential questions.

She stashed her instrument away in a closet somewhere. At first she probably thought of the break in her playing as a temporary one — during the final weeks of her pregnancy, then nursing me. It would have been uncomfortable and inconvenient to try to do complicated bowing movements over breasts that bulged with milk. And then somehow the moment never returned — that special moment when one's head is free and one can unhurriedly open up one's music stand, set the pages on it and take off for heaven . . .

The first surprise, the first false note in their marriage concert, was the sudden, incommensurable importance of food. Elisa had been an aerial creature, a slender, virtually weightless thing in love with sound and movement, accustomed to travelling light, flitting in and out of cafés or pastry-shops, indifferent to what she ate. But once married, and soon pregnant, heavy with child, then children, in her arms, in her stomach, at her breast, on her back, three then four then five of us, tugging at her skirts, her hand, her brain with our demands, she was forever having to make shopping lists, plan meals in advance, carry heavy bags home from the supermarket . . . I remember the way her thin arms strained, veins puffing up from the weight, and on her face the constant expression of effort and surprise, surprise at how hard it was and how alone she was, doing it.

She prayed to God for strength and patience, but He just kept sending her more children, some alive and some dead, all of them exhausting.

Stella would come to see her every time she was in town, they'd have coffee and angel food cake together and gossip about the music world. We kids would try to get some morsels of the cake before Stella gobbled the whole thing down single-mouthedly, but we adored her for her incredible appetite and also for her jollity, every time she came over we'd be sure to hear our mother laugh, some-times we walk into the kitchen and the two of them would be sitting there in gales of laughter, heads thrown back, tears streaming down their faces . . . Once I overheard Elisa asking Stella why it was she always seemed in such good spirits and Stella exploded with laughter, her whole body quaking and crumbs flying from her mouth as she answered, "Because I'm alive! *They didn't get me!* "

(At the time I didn't know what she meant. Now I do.)

Wherever she went, Stella lugged her cello around with her in the trunk of her station-wagon. She would ask Elisa if she felt like playing a little Telemann and Elisa would decline. There was always some excuse, she wasn't feeling well or she was pregnant again or her violin was missing a string.

Clearly she needed their conversation and laughter more than she needed music, in those days.

More and more false notes.

She started falling into trances of inattention at the breakfast, lunch or dinner table. She'd serve all of us and then just sit there chin in hand, staring off into space, eyes glazed over. Sometimes Father would reach across the table and snap his fingers loudly, half an inch from her nose; she'd come to with a start and he would scathingly reprove her for "day-dreaming".

Only once, as far as I remember, did Elisa dare to complain. Formaldehyde image — a Sunday lunch. Yes, she must have complained at having to do all the housework; that's the only way I can explain this scene, this image, unbearable, of Ronald jumping up from the table so violently that his chair fell over, striding across the room and slamming open the cupboard under the sink, grabbing the cleaning rag then hopping around the kitchen like a grasshopper, landing in a crouched position and pretending to scrub the floor, leaping again, leaping and scrubbing again and again, yelling at Elisa all the while, did she expect him to do this in addition to that, and what I remember most clearly of all is that his hair, always so sleek and smooth, was mussed, a piece of it had gotten pushed up away from his forehead and I saw — this was the first time I saw it and it scared me almost as much as his raging at my mother — that his hairline was receding.

Why are you writing all this?

I need to write this in order to be able to write that. And the other way around.

But it is bathetic, my dear. A waste of time. Follow me . . .

Follow me and I will make you fishers of men, is that it?

Don't be silly. I have nothing to do with Jesus. I am Satan the two-faced, Satan the father of lies.

I'm beginning to wonder, you know. I'm beginning to wonder if I don't love Satan in just the same way as Barbe loves Jesus, or Barnabé his mother . . . Yes, humanity needs you badly — all of you, the non-existent. And it needs all your little helpers and apprentices too, the witches and voodoo priests, the poets, painters and madmen who — ceaselessly, unflaggingly — bring non-existent things into existence, perform miracles, heal broken legs and hearts, ease pain, make bitter tears sweet, turn water into wine and saliva into nectar, transform hard solitary flesh — at the touch of a wand, the pierce of an arrow or a needle or a poem — into molten gold!

Please stop waxing eloquent, Nada. Lay off on the ideas. You know your intellectual defences put the lives of your characters in jeopardy. Calm down, now. Be still. And listen.

The Resurrection Sonata

V - The Road

"But where will you go, little sister?"

"I don't know, Barnabé. As far away as possible . . . "

The twins are speaking in low voices, casting anxious glances about them — Barnabé managed to convince Father Thomas to set up this meeting between them in the Orsan chapel, but no one must discover them here.

"You have no idea, Barnabé . . . As soon as they found out what happened, everyone in the village turned on me. The thunderstorm was my fault, I was a witch, I'd stirred up the elements on purpose. For years to come, every sick person, every barren woman in Torchay will blame their problems on me, you can count on it . . . I killed Jeanne because I was jealous of her, I was nothing but an evil orphan-girl, a filthy slut, a bitch — oh, I heard some dreadful things dear brother . . . "

"But not Hélène, surely? Tell me, Barbe — Hélène didn't talk to you that way, did she? She who loved you so dearly . . . "

"No, Hélène didn't blame me. Even as she wept, she tried to comfort me. She knows I would never have hurt a hair on Jeanne's head . . . Hélène is so strong, it's incredible — you should have seen the way she took care of all the details of the funeral, summoning first the carpenter to take measurements for the oak-wood coffin, then the organ-master to choose the music for the service . . . I saw her go off to church, there was a man supporting her on either side but she held her head high — and I didn't even have the right to go with her, Barnabé, can you believe it? I couldn't attend my own Jeannette's funeral on pain of sparking another riot — oh, dear God! . . . And afterwards . . . it was Hélène who advised me to leave. She said the villagers were stupid, narrow-minded people and they'd never forgive me, they'd fear me and hound me for the rest of my life . . . She gave me a few of Jeanne's clothes . . . and this amulet to protect me from wild beasts . . . plus enough food to last me several days of walking. She told me to go as far away as I could — someplace where no one will have heard about the fatal storm . . . "

Barnabé strokes the back of his sister's neck. Pressing her forehead against his, she clenches her jaw until it trembles, but her eyes remain dry.

"My poor, poor Barbe," he murmurs. "And yet, Mamma has always assured me that you'd lead a life of luck, as you were born with the caul. Ah, the ways of the Lord are unfathomable indeed."

Barbe draws back slightly and stares into her brother's face.

"*You'll* never abandon me, will you, Barnabé?"

"Never. I swear it," says Barnabé solemnly. "But as you know, I'll be taking my vows soon, and after that I won't have the same freedom of movement — I'll need the prioress's permission every time I wish to leave the monastery. But Mamma and I will pray for you, Barbe, every day the Lord makes. And you'll find some way of letting me know how you are? You must *promise* me you'll do so — or else I won't let you go, I'll hide you here, I'll turn you into a pear tree so that I can come and see you every day and sing in the shade of your branches."

He imitates the sad cooing of a partridge.

Barbe smiles, grateful for his clumsy attempt to make her laugh.

"I promise," she says.

The twins hug passionately, then part without another word. They sense that this conversation has marked the end of their childhood.

Lying on his palliasse that night, his eyes roaming over the familiar beams and rafters that make up the inverted boat shape of the dormitory roof, Barnabé waits and concentrates. At last he begins to perceive the blue aura.

"Are you there, Mother?"

"Yes, my son."

Her face appears to him, ever young and smiling — Barnabé suddenly realizes that his mother is now but a few years older than himself, and this awareness makes him slightly uncomfortable.

"I wanted to ask you . . . " he says. "Can you see Barbe? Can you watch over her?"

"I can see her, but her destiny is not in my hands. Nor have I the right to tell you what will become of her."

"But . . . are you sure she'll be all right, Mother? Are you sure she'll find happiness eventually?"

"Please don't worry, Barnabé. Barbe has nothing to fear. It is *your* destiny that appears to me as . . . marred by shadow."

"But whatever do you mean? What could possibly happen to me in this monastery? I'm perfectly happy here — planting things in the earth, praising God with my voice, talking to you . . . Oh, if only there were some way I could get Barbe into the convent!"

"That is out of the question," says Marthe, interrupting him with surprising vigour. "Barbe must follow her own path, and you must do nothing to stop her."

"Yes, Mother," says Barnabé, shaking his head sadly. "And now . . . would you sing me that pastorale again . . . the one I love so much?"

And Barnabé's dead mother, the young shepherdess to whom he owes his pure, melodious voice, begins singing in the monks' dormitory, for his ears alone:

"Thy lambs, little shepherdess, are straying far and wide,
They're down there in the meadow, almost out of sight.
Thy lambs, little shepherdess, are straying far and wide,
They're down there in the meadow, almost out of sight."
"My lambs they are a-gamboling down by the brook,
My shepherd-boy will bring them in when crieth the rook."

Barbe's path is dry and dusty, exhausting in the rays of the late August sun. She had all but forgotten the taste of fear during her months of light-heartedness at Torchay, but now she rediscovers it and is perpetually tense and on guard, as sensitive as a wounded animal. Despite her will to be brave, and despite the amulet she wears around her neck, she finds it difficult to avoid thinking about wolves, especially the ones who follow night-travellers, always at the same distance — the mere idea of this intimate pursuit, the animal's footfalls sarcastically echoing one's own, is enough to turn her blood to ice. She is careful to find a place to sleep early in the evening, so as never to be on the road after nightfall. One morning, waking up nose to nose with an enormous slavering black beast, she fairly faints away in fright — but no, it is not a wolf, nor the horrible greyhound the legends describe, it is only a farm-dog, from the farm near which she had fallen asleep, sniffing anxiously at this warm yet motionless body it has come across in the ditch. Feeling her stir at last, it licks her cheek — she bursts out laughing and the two of them, equally relieved, go rolling about together in the grass.

In the daytime, whenever she sees or hears other people coming down the road, she slides into ditches, darts behind hedgerows, slips amongst the tall grasses next to ponds. Little does it matter whether they are pedlars, beggars or migrant workers — everyone frightens her. She learns to turn herself into a reed, a sapling, a stone; she learns to blot out her own gaze so as not to attract the gaze of others. People walk right past her, all but touching her, and do not see her.

She prays. She thanks God for having arranged things so that this trip could take place in the summer rather than the wintertime . . . But then it occurs to her that God also sends thunder and lightning in the summer — and had He not sent that storm, she would never have been forced to flee.

"Tell me what to do, my Lord. I'm listening with all my soul."

But the presence of Jesus, so powerful in the cool and quiet of Torchay's little church, is somehow dissolved out here in the open countryside by the overwhelming vitality of nature — miniature trajectories and pursuits, all sorts of things croaking and buzzing, bellowing and bleating, swinging and falling . . . The longer she lives out of doors, the more fearful Barbe becomes. She fears not only snakes, nettles, insects, but even wind and birds' nests . . . She no longer knows where nature stops and where she begins, she feels transparent, permeable, as though sounds and objects could pass through her, she has somehow lost faith in her own existence, her own separateness from the rest of the world. At dawn and dusk, when the sun's rays are oblique, she feels somewhat better — but the days are still long, and often, in mid-afternoon, she suffers attacks of nausea and vertigo.

Between clenched teeth she repeats her brother's name, a thousand times, ten thousand times.

After five long days of walking, she begins to ask for work as a maidservant in every town she comes to. Her eyes are two burning embers — and she knows it; she must lower them or people will immediately grow suspicious. They grow suspicious anyway — she is too skinny, too dusty, too burnished by the sun, this is not a good sign, she might very well be a vagrant wretch, a gypsy, and such as those are not wanted around here . . .

September arrives. In the ditches that serve as her bed, the morning dew suddenly becomes cold and penetrating. Barbe ceases thinking; she even ceases praying; she eats blackberries and grass; she walks because Hélène told her to walk, no longer knowing what she hopes for — and, were she to drop dead of hunger, cold or exhaustion, she would not care.

But such is not her destiny. No, her destiny is not, like that of her brother Barnabé, a straight line. It is a weirdly winding path, full of knots and arabesques.

One day, after a great many days, she arrives in Sainte-Solange. In a pale square of autumn sunlight just in front of the church, she sits huddled for warmth on a stone bench. She knows neither where she is nor how long she has been walking; she scarcely remembers her own name. As she is sitting there, legs splayed apart, hands dangling between her thighs, eyes empty as the knapsack that once held her food, a young woman comes up to her.

"Are you ill? Miss? Are you all right?"

Barbe has not even the strength to lift her head.

The young woman looks about her. Does anyone know this poor girl? No. No one has ever seen her before.

"Listen, we must help her. She's very weak. Look at her . . . "

"Hmph!" say the townspeople. "As if we didn't have a hard enough time helping ourselves, nowadays! We can't be expected to come to the assistance of every wench and beggar . . . "

"She's not a beggar, I'm sure of it. Come, just help me carry her to my place, I'll take care of the rest."

"Your Donat won't be thrilled to find her there when he gets back."

"Oh, I'll take care of him, too!" retorts the young woman gaily. "Come on, please give me a hand — it won't take long."

Towards mid-afternoon, Barbe wakes to find herself in a large, curtained bed — her first bed in weeks. The young woman is sitting in an armchair by the window, spinning hemp. She greets her with a broad smile, revealing a gap where her two front teeth should be. Barbe does not ask where she is, she has not yet recovered the use of language, she is still a beast of the woods . . . Sinking back, she sleeps deeply until evening.

She is awakened by loud voices coming from the kitchen at the far end of the house. Two voices — a man's and a woman's. Barbe cannot make out the words, but she gathers that the subject of the quarrel is herself. Hastily, she gets out of bed . . . and collapses in a faint on the floor.

That evening, for once, Marguerite Guersant wins out over her husband Simon, whom everyone but she calls Donat because he was a "donated" child — abandoned as a baby on the church steps at La Chaume.

"Just wait long enough to see — it'll only take a few days," Marguerite insists. "We'll nurse her back to health and then decide if she's strong or not — she looks strong to me, and we need *someone*, I've had no help around the house since Madeleine went off to be married, I do all the work myself, even the dirtiest chores! It's not right, for the wife of a good labourer like you! Folks will think we haven't enough money to pay the wages of even one servant — how do you expect me to look them in the eye?"

"What about me? Do you think folks respect a man whose wife takes in beggars off the street?"

"At least come and have a look at her, Simon!"

They find her on the floor, bones jutting every whichway, looking like a pile of kindling. As they pick her up and lay her gently back on the bed, Barbe's eyelids flutter open.

"Bejesus, she's as ugly as a weasel!" grumbles Donat discontentedly.

"Shhh! She can hear you . . . You'll see, all she needs is a good meal and a good bath and she'll be quite decent, leave it to me."

Deep down, Marguerite knows she has chosen this girl just because she is not beautiful.

The next day, Barbe is given a palliasse to sleep on — the curtained bed, of course, is the couple's own — but anything is more comfortable than a ditch. As the partition between their room and hers is nothing but a blanket suspended from the ceiling, Barbe is soon brought up to date on the Guersants' marital difficulties. They have been married seven years, and in that time Simon has gotten no fewer than four of their maidservants pregnant; Marguerite dismissed all of them out of hand, as soon as she learned of their predicament. Simon bitterly reproaches his wife for not giving him a child — in the evening, especially if he has stopped off at the tavern on his way home from the fields, he rants and rails at her. "People will think someone must've tied the aiglet when we got married and I can't do my job as a man!" This, he claims, is why he needs to make sure of his virility elsewhere. "And look — you'd think it was a joke — everyone gets pregnant but you! It's your fault if I still haven't got a son after seven years of marriage! I'm sick and tired of listening to your excuses . . . *Do something*, Goddammit! I can't go on like this!"

Donat weeps. At first this surprises Barbe, but everyone else in Sainte-Solange seems to be used to it. Every time he drinks, it is the same thing — his smile gradually fades away and he begins to shed tears of self-pity; if he goes on drinking his sadness will give way to rage and when that happens things

can get very bad indeed; he can become unrecognizable — an energumen, a mad bull. If the fit comes
over him in the tavern, a brawl inevitably breaks
out; if it happens at home he batters his Marguerite
— a sock in the jaw was what cost her her front teeth
— then throws her down on the bed or even right on
the floor, spits in her face and shouts horrors at her,
then tears off her clothes and goes ploughing into
her, banging her head on the flagstones, his face distorted, sweating, red. In such moments he resembles
the devil himself, and Marguerite has no choice but
to squeeze her eyes shut and beg God not to let her
conceive this time, either — for the offspring of such
an embrace could only be a monster.

Despite his excesses and his fits of rage, Donat
is well liked and respected by the parishioners of
Sainte-Solange. His hooked nose gives him a singular, powerful profile. Moreover, he has some learning: having worked as a youth in the vineyards of a
local lord, he picked up bits and snippets of knowledge, learning to read and even to write a little.
When sober or only slightly tipsy, he has a ready
tongue in his head. People love to listen as he tells
stories — whether invented or true-to-life matters little—of salt smugglers in the city of Le Blanc, or high-
way bandits, or the time the child king and his mother laid siege to the castle in nearby Montrond . . . Of
a Sunday afternoon, especially in the wintertime, his
tales bring a splash of colour to the dull grey atmosphere of the tavern — helping the men forget their
fatigued and aching muscles, their departed youth,
their pallid children.

Thus, as soon as she is better, as soon as she has gained back a little strength and a little weight, Barbe — reassured by the comforting anonymity of Sainte-Solange, albeit she has no clear notion of where the town is, how far away or in what direction from her dear brother Barnabé — begins a new life.

The *Scordatura* Notebook

February 6th

Oh, dæmon . . . Only give me the courage, the vision, the necessary cruelty to go through with this, allow it to unfold without rushing or crushing it.

In fact, there was nothing heavenly at all about the *G-Minor Sonata* Mother was playing that day at the Riverside Church. It is more commonly known as "The Devil's Trill." People often think it is so called because of its diabolical technical difficulty. But that's not it at all (for me, if I may say so in passing, "devil's trill" is the best possible verbal equivalent of what happens when a man takes that sweet pointed morsel of me between his fingers or his lips and lets it sing, setting off a vibration in my soul, strings stretched nearly to breaking point, ribcage arched to form an echo chamber for the close sharp waves of sensation) — no, the true reason is that Giuseppe Tartini, born at just around the same time as my heroes Barbe and Barnabé, had a dream.

In this dream he had made a Faustian pact with the Devil, selling him his soul in exchange for the fulfillment of his every wish. He lent the devil his violin to see what he would do with it — and lo and behold, Mephistopheles proceeded to perform a sonata of extraordinary beauty. Tartini awoke overjoyed, rushed to his writing desk and feverishly attempted to set down what he had heard. Forever afterwards he would say regretfully that though *"The Devil's Trill"* was by far the best sonata he had ever written, it was vastly inferior to what he had heard in his dream.

This is it, exactly. To sense, to *know* that the real thing is non-existent, and existing things unreal. The divorce, oh God. The teeth-gnashing frustration, forever and ever, *amen.* Why are we vouchsafed, like Tartini in his dream, these glimpses of paradise — of what it would be like to *really* live, *really* fuck, *really* write?

The cold blade under the skin.

"Don't be ridiculous."

You are one thing and life is another.

How live without a Witness?

Not only Per my once-husband, but Sol, Jonas, Juan, every man with whom I have lived or been in love, to say nothing of all my "best friends" in school and college and young adulthood, my men and women soulmates over nearly half a century of existence — each of these people in turn has been my Witness, as I have been theirs. All the outpoured confessions, the heart-to-heart talks, the shared secrets, starting over once again, trusting once again, each time with the same naïveté, the same foolishness — listen to me, here is what happened, my father did this, my mother did that, take my life in your hands, see it, embrace it, be the one who knows and accepts me as I am, as I shall be for you . . .

But there was always some little thing. Some shortcoming, blind spot, failing in the other person that disqualified him or her for absolute Witness status. Always a *soupçon* of reserve, of witholding. Besides, my friends, however wholehearted their approval of me, never totally approved of one another and this irked me no end, as it made me — my *self* — seem inconsistent. Jonas spoke ill of Sabina's poetry, Sabina could never understand what I saw in Per, David and Laura each tried to convince me that the other was a monster . . . Equally disturbing, equally inadmissible were differences in literary taste — could I love someone who loved Paul Claudel? Could I submit to the caresses of someone who mocked Tsveta'eva? Could I take seriously someone who took Jean-Paul Sartre seriously? If Janet worshipped Sylvia Plath and Laura was allergic to her and I felt equally close to Janet and Laura . . . then who was I?

How unfathomably complex all this human interaction is, each of us flitting around with our own little norms by which to judge other people, while straining at the same time to meet *their* norms — but straining *discreetly*, pretending not to strain, pretending we're really only ourselves and need no one else's approval . . . There is no gold standard, always only this endless shifting negotiation and compromise, this ridiculous waving of one's foot in search of a piece of firm ground to stand on . . .

What one wants, really, is a second self.

Only another "I", standing at a respectful and observant distance from the first, could possibly have the benevolence and empathy required to play the Witness role . . . This is the role Barnabé plays for Barbe, the role I have dreamed of all my life for Nathan, or Nothin', the dead twin brother — "boy me," as Barbe puts it — with whom I have incestuously yearned to live, as with an invisible lover, discovering the world through his eyes, or rather *transforming* the world through his eyes, coating it with gold, minute by minute, year by year . . . Ah yes — with Nothin' as with none of my tritely human friends and lovers, I'd at last be able to truly LIVE, revel in jazz, grovel in baroque, munch on bluegrass, wash it down with whisky and never get a stomach ache or a hangover, smoke a million cigarettes and never get a sore throat let alone lung cancer . . . With him I'd never have the impulse to look at my watch because making love and making breakfast would be equally thrilling, dancing at three in the morning and taking the subway at five in the evening equally fulfilling, our most quotidian conversations would turn into works of art, instead of which . . .

Nearly all the people I once thought of as my Witnesses have disappeared. Some have moved away; others while remaining in the city have drifted away (with or without chips on their shoulders), and the rest have died — of AIDS, of accidents, by their own hand or by the hand of God or whoever that sadistic joker up there is, perpetually wreaking havoc with our loves and hopes, tearing up our plans for the future and stamping out our memories of the past like so many sparks in the grass after a bonfire . . .

Of course, nice people continue to drift in and out of my daily life, my nightly life, but I cannot start again. It is over. I'm too tired to believe in other people's stories, and too tired to tell anyone mine. It is too long a story by now. These shards of love, this jigsaw puzzle of emotion. I would rather lie, make up a new identity for myself with each new lover, as I do with each new book. Or say nothing. Couple with strangers in silence. I could be a whore.

Last night Sol and I met at the Village Vanguard. (Sol is black from Brooklyn, a painter, and — how to put this, I don't like to feed clichés, though as Jonas once told me *"a cliché is a piece of language that's just dying to climb up into a good poem"*, so why not feed them once in a while — Sol is black from Brooklyn, a painter, and he is also without question the best lover I've ever had, the things we do to each other's bodies are sublime but I don't much like his painting and he doesn't particularly care for my novels, he finds them too morbid, too violent, "philopsychotic" as he puts it, what he likes best about me is my laughter and he says it hasn't found its way into my computer yet — that's all right, I've never required that my lovers love my books . . .)

"It makes me so sad," I told Sol, "to think I've been coming to this wonderful place for thirty-three years now."

He looked askance at me, shrugged his lovely shoulders and ordered a bottle of champagne to celebrate my sadness.

Now, always, when I am "somewhere," doing "something" — for instance at the Vanguard, with the champagne *and* the cigarettes *and* this beautiful black man I know I'll be making love with in a few hours, *and* the fantastic music playing, the musicians' bodies rolling and jiving with it — there is still, stronger than ever, the yearning to *be there*.

Where is "there"?

Where is "it"?

As a child, I had no doubt but that "it" (which I also called "the real thing"), would come along later, when I grew up and escaped from my chaotic family and started making all my dreams come true. Devil bastard. Now, at forty-nine, I see that "it" will remain forever just beyond my grasp, and that I shall die without having managed to live.

"Why the word *second*, as a measure of time?" I asked Sol.

"Huh?"

"We're always in the second, the seconds ticking by. Whatever happened to the *first*? We keep running after the firsts, running late, always a *second* too late. Where did the *first* go?"

"What are you talking about, Nada?"

"Where is *the thing itself*? I mean, is there any such thing as the real thing, apart from Coca-Cola?"

He laughed and kissed me on the lips, a full wet fleshy kiss. "You're a funny girl, you know that?"

Around midnight I looked over towards the cloakroom and saw two very young women talking animatedly to one another, standing close and thin and lovely warm together, aged perhaps nineteen, both with long wavy manes of hair, one raven, one copper, heads bobbing up and down so that even their hair was filled with expressiveness, hands stroking each other's cheeks and shoulders, eyes laughing . . . O *they were there*! They were there and I was not, had never been, not even at age nineteen.

And then Sol came back with me to Perry Street and we made love and it was as full and deep and fine as love without love can be . . . But still, the soul numbness does not change, does not go away — not never no more.

O men — I only give you my cries and moans, I only give you my gasps and tears; the rest (my lies, my silences, in other words my deepest essence) remains untouched by you.

Everything, now, is a translation. My books are translations, for instance — clumsy botched attempts at transcribing what my dæmon has revealed to me. The original does not exist. The original — like paradise — is by definition lost.

As a result, my readers, like myself, will care far more about the fate of homeless Barbe, skulking and slinking down the back roads of central France three hundred years ago, than they do about the fate of the homeless woman dying on their doorstep. Barbe is vivid, breathing, fragile, frightened; what happens to her matters to us deeply. Non-fictional sufferers are mere shadows at the periphery of our vision.

Discouragement: my father is right.

Once again you are beating about the bush, my dear.

Yes. I admit it. But I don't have the courage to write the rape scenes yet, really write them, be inside the person who does that.

Yet you know . . .

Yes, I know I know. Of course. I've inherited from Father what I despise in him the most — the overreaction, the screaming, the smashing. Rape is no different. It merely implies going to the outer limits of a rage that gradually becomes a pleasure, a tingling exhilarating heart-pounding physical rush. Oh yes, dæmon, *diaballein*, it is in these moments that you *throw us across, transport* us, yes, literally plunge us into transports which we know do irreparable damage to those we love . . .

(Good thing I killed all those kids. Had they lived, they would have had to start analysis at three.)

Per could not fathom my fits of anger. Could not recover from them.

I loved him. My daily Dane. Who could have dreamed I would one day wake up and not know where this person was, what he was doing, wearing, eating . . .

In the morning I used to come in after my shower and lie down on his back, length of naked body upon length of naked body, I can still feel the shape of his buttocks in the hollow of my stomach, I'd kiss him behind the ears, my wet hair would drip all down his neck and he never complained, not at all, he grunted with contentment, he liked me to lie on his back, he loved me

. . . or something like that.

Nada.

Nada the blank space, the non-entity, finally succeeded in driving him to desperation. What would happen . . . I'd like to get some words on this. What would happen? For example that summer evening in Copenhagen. We had friends over, the windows wide open, good jazz playing, we were all drinking white wine, lots of it, and suddenly someone mentioned a review they had seen of one of my books. It happened to have been a despicable review, a catty arch tight-assed female review, and Per just said casually, between two swallows of wine, "Well, it's better to be reviewed negatively than not at all, and indeed the reviewer's hostility was so extreme, so blatantly overblown that it will probably incite readers to seek out the book just to see what could have provoked such an outpouring of bile, so in the final analysis it may even be a perverse form of publicity and help sales." I felt a bad shiver go through me. For the moment all I said was, "Per, the next time you decide to say something asinine, would you please warn me so I can go powder my nose until it's over?" Per glanced at me, surprised, hurt, and the conversation moved on to something else. For him the incident was closed. For me it had just opened. I knew I had a good hour ahead of me, until the departure of our guests, in which to fan the icy flames, think of things to say — insults, swearwords, horrible insinuations — that would wound Per to the quick, and as I made up my speech, repeating it to myself over and over, faster and faster, all the while continuing to smile and drink and chat with our friends, the cold white wine coursed through my veins and my blood turned into rushing ice, sliding glaciers, the anger mounted until my head was crashing and spinning with it — so much like the gradual wanted rise of erotic arousal, yes, keep rising, more, better, higher, don't go down, the explosion will be fantastic — and as soon as Per had gently closed the door of our apartment behind the last guest I jumped on him, a witch, a woman possessed, frenzied, frothing at the mouth, eyes rolling, tongue lashing, how could he know anything of what literature was, what it meant, where it came from, he was an artistic illiterate, he lived in the dry dead world of numbers and equations, he had no idea what it meant to draw things from one's guts, from the roiling darkness of the unconscious . . . I don't know what I said, a lot of bullshit, it doesn't matter, I was utterly given over to the bliss of my rage, the bliss of injuring him, seeing him cringe and bleed as the bladewords slashed at him again and again — seeing him worry too — Is Nada crazy? What will she do next? — Ah! The wine glasses. The wine glasses. So exquisite, their fine flower shape, cerise-tinted blown glasses from Murano we had bought together on our honeymoon — yes, that was the perfect solution, and my bony witch fingers stretched out and picked them up and hurled them to the floor, one after the other, slowly, voluptuously, all six of them, like multiple orgasm, as Per stood there paralyzed, hand on forehead,

. . . and he forgave me. He forgave me that time, too.

Oh dæmon! Is it the same you who possess me to smash glasses and to write books?

Well, both are tremendous fun! Now don't be naive, Nada. You know quite well that your books are destructive, too — of illusions, for example — and that your temper tantrums are creative — of new scenes, new sentences, new characters . . .

You are ready now . . . come with me.

The Resurrection Sonata

VI - The Weasel

Marguerite Guersant's bet has paid off — "the weasel" is of no interest to her husband. Indeed, she is of interest to no man — at age fourteen she has no curves to speak of and, even apart from her scrawniness, there is something masculine, hard and repellent about her body. But she is a good worker, her mind is quick, and within a few months, despite their age difference, she becomes something of a confidante for Marguerite, and learns a number of surprising things about the life of married folk.

"What did it mean when Mister Guersant talked about tying the aiglet?" Barbe asks her mistress one day as they are kneeling by the washing-place, scrubbing dirty clothes together.

"Oh!" says Marguerite, laughing. "He doesn't believe a word of it, the big donkey! You know, when a couple gets married, if somebody in the church ties knots in a string or a ribbon they have in their pocket, then the man won't be able to do his duty as a husband. You make three knots, all the while repeating the groom's name in a low voice, or else you say *Tibald, Nobal and Vanarbi* and make the sign of the cross between each knot — that's supposed to be really powerful."

"Ah . . . "

"More and more folks are getting married in hiding these days, just to make sure they won't find themselves knotted afterwards! They ask the priest to come and unite them in the woods in the middle of the night. But my Simon and I got married in church — he's not a man to fear that sort of nonsense!"

"And how long does it last, if you get knotted?"

"Well, until the spell is undone — anything from a day to a year or even more. The husband of one of my best friends was knotted, and she told me that instead of fondling each other in bed they used to bite and scratch at each other like a couple of wild animals! One night, they even saw the devil in person — he'd slipped in between their bodies and was making faces at them!"

"But did they get better?"

"Oh, yes — her husband went and peed through the keyhole of the church where they got married, and it worked right off — she was pregnant within a few days . . . but she died in childbirth, poor thing."

"So did my mother," says Barbe, almost in a whisper. "She died giving birth to my twin brother and me."

The confidences, however, move only in one direction — Marguerite Guersant cares little about the personal history of her maidservant.

"They even say," she goes on, "that if it lasts long enough, little bumps start popping up along the aiglet — one for each child that would have been born if the couple hadn't been knotted."

"Oh, I don't believe that!" Barbe exclaims. "Do you?"

"I don't know . . . It's not my problem . . . "

A brief silence ensues, during which the two women continue energetically scrubbing and whacking clothes on their crenellated washboards.

"You may have noticed," Marguerite adds somewhat coyly, "that Mister Simon has no difficulty in fulfilling his marital duty."

Flushing, Barbe nods slightly.

"I'm the one who can't get pregnant," her mistress confesses, heaving a great sigh. "It's been years now, and heaven knows I've tried everything you can think of — pilgrimages, ex-votos, prayers to the Virgin — I must have shed tears enough to drown the poor woman! — and when nothing worked, I started running around consulting people who know remedies — I even went as far as Ronzay! — and I followed all their advice, too. Heavens, you should have seen me — the things I stuffed into my mouth, up my nose, everywhere you can stuff things! Laudanum suppositories, fumigations with darnel and vetch, God knows what all . . . but to no avail. It seems the Lord has decided once and for all not to give me a son for my Simon . . . "

She heaves another sigh, shrugs her shoulders and starts whistling through the gap between her teeth.

Another day, she warns her young maidservant about Father Jean, the priest of Sainte-Solange.

"He's a real rascal, you've got to watch out for him. They say he likes to maul young girls when they come to confession, threatening afterwards to reveal their secrets to the whole town if they denounce him."

"Did he ever touch *you*, Madam?"

"You bet he did! Once as I was leaving the confessional, he grabbed my rear end just like that, and started squeezing and pugging me without an if-you-please — you would have thought he was kneading bread dough!"

"And what did you do?"

"Well, I just told him, you've picked the wrong woman, Father Jean, because it so happens I have nothing on my conscience. You try that one more time and you'll have the whole parish on your back."

Thus, Barbe is careful to say as little as possible when she goes to confession. She speaks in a low voice, her eyes on the ground, and Father Jean is so bored that he sometimes taps his foot with impatience.

Months pass, and Barbe's new existence takes shape. Her daily routine is so monotonous that there is something soothing, almost pleasant about it. She is a good maidservant, silent and obedient, virtually invisible. She eats alone, after her masters, and sleeps without dreaming. Her nights are punctuated by the grunts and cries of Simon Guersant, on the other side of the blanket between their bedrooms.

Her daily chores revolve mainly around the farm animals and vegetable garden — it is the mistress of the house who sees to the actual cooking. With her usual alacrity but in something of a daze, Barbe goes about breaking necks, chopping off heads, peeling carrots and skinning rabbits, collecting blood for sauces, washing guts, removing brains, detaching hearts and livers from their wreaths of fat, ripping out feathers, eyes, weeds, and learning to wield the clippers when shearing-time rolls around.

She passes through the town square but once a week, to take the bread dough to the banal bakery. It does not take her long to spot the local gossips, and she strives to enter their good graces by virtue of her cleanliness, modesty and self-effacement. Never again must she be talked about; never again must she need to endure anything like that abominable day in Torchay, when those she had thought of as her good neighbours had turned into ferocious demons, bent on tearing her limb from limb. Never again must she find herself on the road, wandering and transparent, at the mercy of the elements and the beasts.

She asks nothing of her life — not even that it go on. Ever since that August day when she saw her best friend's brain lying on the ground next to the pond — a whitish, motionless heap containing all the dead girl's laughter, her memories, her thoughts — she has felt inwardly obliterated.

Had Jeanne gone to heaven with or without her brain? Had they buried her brain along with the rest of her, or had someone picked it up and tossed it onto the refuse-heap? Barbe does not even know. And if Jeanne's brain was missing, did that mean her soul was missing too? *Where was her soul now?* Was it wandering around in limbo, searching for her body?

Disturbed, obsessed by these questions, Barbe allows time to flow over her, indifferent to the procession of the seasons.

She still thinks, often, of her brother Barnabé, who must be a monk by now — but how can she possibly keep her promise and send him news?

She takes only one initiative, from the depths of her near-somnambulant state: little by little, as the months go by, she scours the nearby woods looking for the simples Hélène taught her to use, and transplants them into a corner of the vegetable garden. She lavishes great care upon these herbs, slipping them surreptitiously into the morning soup when her masters complain of headache or diarrhoea.

Her clandestine, groping experiments are sometimes successful, sometimes not.

She has a brief moment of wakefulness each morning and evening when Robert Raffinat, whom everyone in the town calls Little Robert, goes past the house. Little Robert is neither very young nor particularly puny — it is his mind that is small; he is a simpleton. (It is said that a travelling circus

passed through town during Mrs. Raffinat's pregnancy; she accidentally glimpsed a monkey, and
the beast's grimacing face perverted her husband's
seed in the womb.) A huge grin on his face, eyes
permanently widened in amazement, body askew,
legs swinging in a weird hopping-step, Little
Robert takes out his mother's two pigs every morning, wanders far and wide with them in search of
herbage, and returns with them at night — this is
the only job he can handle. When he catches sight
of Barbe at the bedroom window, Little Robert
always waves to her enthusiastically, as though
they were long-lost friends. Barbe responds with a
smile and a nod — she knows Jesus loves this big
brainless booby as much as He loves her, perhaps
even as much as He loves Barnabé.

If the truth be told, ever since Barbe came
Sainte-Solange, Jesus has ceased to answer when
she speaks to Him. Often, for fear of disturbing
Him, she dares not even call upon Him anymore,
and her prayers have gradually been drained of
their fervour. Eating His flesh and drinking His
blood at Sunday Mass has become a mechanical,
meaningless gesture. The host, dry and brittle,
sticks to the roof of her mouth; it no longer brings
her life. The mystery does not occur — but she can
confide this to no one, least of all the priest.

The months slip past, stretch into years, and
Marguerite Guersant is still not pregnant. Even the
remedies Barbe gives her on the sly — birthwort
and mandrake — remain without effect. It now

seems certain she will remain childless. All the more certain since, as she weepingly confesses to Barbe one day, her Simon no longer approaches her, no longer even looks at her — he has found someone else. Barbe is already aware of this — as, indeed, is the entire parish: Donat has fallen for Marie Bourdeaux, the miller's pretty wife.

Marguerite is convinced that Marie slipped something into the glass of water she gave Simon one day, when he brought his grain to be ground at the mill. She herself, Marguerite, leaves no stone unturned in her effort to get him back. Incredulously, Barbe watches her mistress's final desperate attempt to prevent her husband from doubling on her. She takes the house cat — a great, scabby old tom — and hides it under the washtub for two whole days with nothing to eat or drink; then, with Barbe's help, she ties its four paws together, covers them with butter, and feeds it some bread soaked in her own urine; the poor cat has no choice but to nibble at the repulsive mixture — "Now," says Marguerite triumphantly, "everything should be fine."

But she is wrong. The love affair goes on.

Marie, too, is married — but she has no compunction about decorating her husband André's forehead with two full-fledged horns. The cronies jabber, poor Marguerite weeps, the priest sputters and admonishes, but still the affair goes on. The lovers get together early in the morning or late at night; they blaspheme together, laughing — saying that after all, the other Mary, the Virgin, cuckolded her old Joseph, too, when she let God lead her down the garden-path, though their antics could scarcely have been much fun, seeing that God had no body! They scream with laughter, and when the miller's wife gets pregnant they say well, the Virgin got knocked up by somone other than her Joseph, too. Three years in succession, Marie presents her husband with babies sporting Donat's hooked nose; the fourth year starts out in the same way but in the third month of the pregnancy, shortly after Midsummer, an asthma attack carries off both mother and child.

Early the next morning, a group of friends come to the vineyard where Donat is working, to break the news to him — the miller's pretty wife gave up the ghost during the night. All day long in the glancing sunlight, Donat trims the vines and reminisces about plump Marie's white skin, the way she used to giggle, and the way her little fists used to pound into his back when he clasped her to him — he had really been in love with that little woman — his body aches, his soul aches, his whole being aches, he does not want the other labourers to see his pain but it is all he can do to hold out until the end of the day. Then, having no idea how to face up to Marguerite with this real suffering in his veins, he feels the urge to drink.

The regular customers fall silent when he walks through the tavern door — Donat is in mourning, they all know about it and respect his grief; it is nothing to laugh at. He won't be telling us any good stories today — no, words deserted him several hours ago; the man who loves to palaver has not unclenched his teeth since he heard the bad news.

Donat motions to the tavern-keeper, who immediately serves him up a glass of the local rosé. Without greeting or so much as glancing at the other customers, Donat takes a seat on his usual bench. His movements are hesitant; he has never felt this way before — oddly friable, as if parts of his body might break off and go smashing into pieces on the ground. . . .

Just then, a stranger bursts into the tavern.

Foreign body. Instinctively, the regular customers bristle up. What man is this? Discharged soldier? Brigand? Hard to say. But big, brawny, already clearly drunk. They don't like it. Especially just now, in this unaccustomed atmosphere of compassion for Donat. The stranger lurches forward with an ugly look on his face. Oh, no, not this, not today . . . He sits down at the same table as Donat and bangs on it with his fist.

The tavern-keeper lifts his chin to ask for the stranger's order. The man mutters something and receives, in return, a large glass of red wine.

The others go on staring at him in silence. The air is heavy.

"Thought I was comin' into a tavern, not a church," he grumbles, raising his glass to his lips. "Haven't you folks out here in the sticks learned to talk yet?"

So saying, he downs his wine in a gulp, breaks the glass between his teeth and spits the fragments disgustedly onto the table. One of the shards of glass slides along the polished wood and grazes Donat's bare arm. The arm goes up by itself, hitting the unprepared stranger in the face.

And suddenly sheer pandemonium breaks loose — unleashed black rage, the rage of tired, exasperated men — Donat's friends coming to his defence, the stranger flexing his muscles, picking up chairs and stools and hurling them across the room, bruising shoulders and crushing feet — the rage mounts in all of their heads, growing sharper and sharper, like the sound of a furious wasp, or like a violin reaching up to the highest piercing squeaks and rubbing away at them, Donat is now standing to one side of the room, at a remove from the uproar, his gaze plunged into the void — he is too weary, too preoccupied to take an interest in this fight — it doesn't really concern him — he listens absently as the other men grunt and pant and swear, as fists and feet go thudding into temples and stomachs — dull, heavy sounds of impact — muffled cries, hoarse groans . . .

And then, as suddenly as it had started, the whole thing stops.

Donat glances up. Someone has just bashed in the stranger's head with a poker. His back to the wall, the man crumples slowly to the floor, uttering a long wheeze of surprise which drowns in a gurgle of blood.

Silence returns. A long moment elapses as the men struggle to recover their breath, their composure, their command of language.

"You go on home," they tell Donat, as soon as they can speak. "Go on, get out of here. We'll look after this. We'll tell the priest and doctor what happened. You've got nothing to do with it — you weren't even *here* tonight, Donat — do you hear? Don't even think about it. Just go!"

Donat walks home feeling giddy. The summer dusk stretches out endlessly, the air is calm and fragrant with the smell of wheat, the little ponds by the roadside are puddles of gold, the croaking of frogs scratches pleasantly at his ears and he feels as if he is floating rather than walking. He knows he is not drunk, he only had one glass of wine, and yet his body no longer aches, in fact he no longer feels anything at all. I must be dreaming, he thinks. How can it still be daytime, still the same day as this morning? He cannot get over it. And when he reaches the house the dream continues; everything appears to be glazed with gold; the weasel is there but Marguerite is still out milking; they are running late today because it was a big washday . . . The weasel yelps in surprise and pain when Donat grabs her arm, skinny and hard as the branch of a walnut tree, and drags her over to the bed, the wedding-bed, the barren bed, the large curtained bed on which no child has ever been conceived, so many deaths today, his little Marie, and their baby smothered alive in her stomach, and now the stranger, too, some other mother's son, his skull stoven in, his eye dangling from its orbit as if in extreme astonishment, his head reduced to mush, jaw crushed, cheekbone smashed, neck inundated with blood, and, still in the same silence, a silence of stone and terror, Donat wades more and more deeply into the blood, immersing himself in the weasel's viscera, and as her piercing little yelps annoy him, distracting him from his dreamlike gilded intoxication, he grabs one of Marguerite's kerchiefs that is lying on the dresser and stuffs it into her mouth, gagging her, and keeps at it, keeps at it, quite oblivious to the way her hard skinny little body wriggles and twists beneath him, so great is the confusion of this day, so dark are the shadows into which he needs to plunge, needs to keep on plunging, further and further, eyes closed, jaws clenched. Then, sensing from deep within the warning twinges of the implosion, he slides into it, falling, losing himself utterly, as if his very being were distintegrating, scattering like stars across the firmament . . . after which, still dizzy, his head still spinning with the godawful joy of broken bones and stifled screams, he lays his cheek on the weasel's flat chest and weeps.

There is blood. At twenty, Barbe was still a virgin. No one had ever wanted her, no one had ever invited her to the balls, evening meetings and seasonal hiring fairs at which young men and women strike up an acquaintance, always she had remained apart, and the thrilling dangers of which Jeanne had warned her, all those years ago in their bedroom at the Torchay inn, had never materialized . . . Now, her face and neck reddened by Donat's whiskers, she fetches a wet rag and energetically rubs the bloodstains on the coverlet, praying God that Mrs. Guersant will not notice the dampness later this evening, when she goes to bed.

She returns to her own room, on the far side of the blanket. A moment later, she hears Marguerite come home, heat up Donat's meal and serve it to him, chattering like a magpie all the while. Always so gay. Always so sweet to her husband.

Even sweeter than usual, because the town mourner stopped by this afternoon to inform her of little Marie's death, and she is hugely relieved.

The *Scordatura* Notebook

March 1st

An excerpt from the doctor's autopsy report:

"We found a very-murderous contusion next to his left eye; after having opened said Deluteau's head, we found that the arch of the cheekbone had been fractured, and once said dilatation had been carried out, giving us the opportunity for further research, we concluded that the contusions and fracture had been inflicted by a terrible contusive instrument, and that this blow had provoked a counterblow to the opposite side of the head which had brought about a bursting of the entire opposite side of the head."

That's not the half of it, though.

"After further research, we found a fracture in the temporal of a roundness of approximately two inches in diameter, and a crack in the parietal on the same side, opposite to said blow, which had brought about a rupture of the blood vessels in the head, so that the blood had overflowed from one to the other of said fractured parts, in such a way that the brain found itself so bloodied by the abundance of blood that the violence of the blow and concussion brought about an effusion of the whole organ, which, having not much elasticity, was unable to recover from this state and, consequently, the distribution of spirits necessary to movement throughout the rest of the body ceased in the instant, causing death." – Doctors Michel Texier and Léonard de Bize, quoted in André Alabergère, *Au Temps des laboureurs en Berry*, p. 179.

Well at least that's clear.

If the occipital cortex of a person's brain is electrically stimulated at the secondary level, the person will "see" complex images, sometimes even objects — people, trees, animals . . . Our memories are quite literally *stored* in a specific section of that grey cauliflower, and can be jolted back to life. If condemned persons on the way to the gallows "see their whole lives pass before their eyes," it is likely because the secondary level of their occipital cortexes is being stimulated like mad.

When Deluteau's brain was bloodied by the contusive instrument, did he catch a glimpse of his mother's face, or perhaps his favourite oak tree? When Jeanne's brain jumped out of her head — when my friend Sabina's brain was caved in by the steering-wheel of her car — were they teeming and flashing with memories of childhood? And when the white-coated soul doctors zap Moira's brain with high voltage, are they tossing the images of her life into the air like a deck of cards — in hopes that they might fall in a playable order next time round?

It's all a matter of electricity.

The bolt out of the blue.

Coup de foudre — love at first sight — Ronald describing how he was "thunderstruck", "lit up from inside", "tingling" when he first set eyes on Elisa. Oh the mysteries that roil and boil in there. Life. Love. Deep, dark, unfathomable.

How apt that Benjamin Franklin, inventor of the lightning rod, should also have been a fervent advocate of the Enlightenment. And that, a century later, Sigmund Freud should have written his revolutionary treatise on the unconscious at just the same time as the homes of Europe's intellectual elite were being equipped with light bulbs. In order to promote Reason and Rationality among the masses, it was indispensable to overcome darkness, fill up the houses of those superstitious peasants with electric brilliance, show them there was *nothing* under the bed, *nothing* up in the attic, *nothing* prowling out there in the awful shuddering ink-blackness of the garden, the forest, the marsh . . . Come now, all ye enlightened modern citizens! Let us banish obscurantism! Socialism is the power of the Soviets, plus electricity! Let us dispel gloom, and the monsters crawling and coupling there! Long live transparency!

But our brains yearn to astound us, and know how delectable is fear. They crave the murk of non-reason, dream, spell. They thrive on shadows, for shadows enable them to travel to distant times and places. What further proof do we require of the transmigration of souls? All we need do is close our eyes, take a deep breath, and uuuuuuuuuup the chimney we go — like witches — or — dooooooooown the rab-

bit hole we slide — like Alice — or — acrooooooo-
oosss the sky we sail — like Peter Pan, Santa Claus,
Sindbad the Sailor! Our brains are our broomsticks,
sleighs, wings, burning bushes, magic carpets, oint-
ments, Aladdin's lamps . . . Just rub them and poof!
— reality vanishes, to be replaced by astonishingly
lifelike images.

Avoidance.

No, no. I'm getting there.

Elisa must have felt God had abandoned her; she
must have wondered why He had deprived her of
music, her most ardent form of worship, and hum-
bled her with menial repetitious tasks and an iras-
cible mate. Even while submitting to the divine
will, she did her best to be brave.

At first she thought she'd be able to stand up to
Ronald. Hold her own. Preserve her pride. She was
struck dumb, numb, the day he threw one of his
shirts in her face because it was badly ironed. She
who was familiar with the aching dissonances of
Heinrich Ignaz Franz von Biber's *Mystery Sonatas*
could quite simply not believe that this was to be her
reality from now on, and that the man she had fallen
in love with, and who continued to be so witty and
charming in the presence of strangers, could turn
upon her in petty rage and throw a shirt in her face.

Her face. My mother's face. Her delicate fine-drawn
twenty-two-year-old face with its sparkling shy

eyes and its pointed nose and chin. Elisa, her name was, before it became Mother.

I know, I know, Ronald's own milieu, the poverty, the absent father, the violence too, the chain of violence, the ubiquitous violence he blubbers over now when he comes across it in the newspaper, the Russian soldiers stacked naked on bunkbeds in the morgue, young dead men lying on their backs with their genitals visible and their feet splayed, their dear dirty big bunioned feet parted in V's, row after row of V's, and to think that every single one of these young men had a mother who brought him up, purchased pair after pair of shoes for him as his feet grew, washed his ears and genitals and then respectfully refrained from washing them because he was a big boy now, big enough to wash his own genitals and ears, then big enough for military service, just a spot of tedium to put up with and then everything will be all right, you'll be able to pick up where you left off, your girlfriend, your career plans, your walks in the woods, oh dear it seems there's this little uprising over in Chechenya that needs taking care of . . . and now all of them are dead.

"Okay, so there have been ten times as many victims among the Chechens, I know that, Nadia, I just happened to see this photo of the Russian morgue, *can you imagine being the mother of one of those boys?*"

"No, Father, I cannot."

(I can, of course, because of Stella's Andrew. I can imagine. But I try not to. It's essential that I limit my liability.)

All lives deserve weeping over. No wonder we invented a God who could take on the monumental task of caring about each and every one of us!

Ronald himself is to be pitied rather than blamed, of course. Naturally. His own Scottish mother, jilted at nineteen by his Italian father, telling him that try as she might she had not been able to pierce his goddamn fontanelle with the knitting-needle, repeating it until the day she died . . . What can you do with an image like that in your brain but drink and drink and drink to drown it, kill it, kill yourself . . . Yes yes, I also understand his fear of being a father, of the terrible responsibility that entailed, so many people depending on him, and how he must have dreaded yet been tempted by his own father's spectacular gesture of abandonment, giving it all up, throwing up the sponge at the first little difficulty . . .

Oh I'm so tired of it all, so tired of understanding.

I *cannot* care, there is no logical reasonable way to care, I have to say nothing matters because if I allow one tiny speck of human reality to matter it drags with it the endless litany of suffering, bodies tortured, blasted, raped, stabbed, electrocuted, gnawed to the bone by illness, minds devouring themselves alive, newborn babies with AIDS left lying naked on their backs in the icy void of the outside world, birds shot to death in the air, sheep used as substitute humans in experimental nuclear explosions in Kazakhstan in 1964, and the camps, the thundering Huns, the thundering guns, and my mother's face as she stared in disbelief at my father's rage . . .

I'm trying to get back to the other face — the one she had when I first knew her. Why so few images? Everything slides together and all I see are the soft swishing materials of her summer dresses I so loved to bury my face in . . . But she was always getting up and moving away, never tranquil, never at rest, there was always another child squalling, demanding her attention, it was impossible to lie there on her lap and feel her stroke my hair and hear her sing to me for more than five minutes in a row.

She used to sing around the house, though, when I was little. I do remember . . . Elisa singing to some *lied* on the radio as she chopped potatoes, onions or walnuts . . . singing lullabyes in Hungarian as she tucked us in at night . . . humming hymns as she packed a basket for a picnic at the Bronx Zoo . . .

She was determined to remain graceful and gay, to make a lovely home (*homemakers*, women like her were called back in those days) for her husband to return to after work. All the clichés of the Fifties twinkled in her eyes as she removed her apron and rushed to open the door when she heard his step on the stairs . . . All the clichés without exception ran rampant in our household, including Elisa's discovery that Ronald was cheating on her. Lipstick on his collar, as she stuffed one of his shirts into the washing machine? Maybe even that. I don't know.

(Sometimes I wonder if Juan's wife ever found out about me. It's painful to think of oneself as "the other woman" when one likes women as much as I do.)

To make matters worse, I can also see the whole thing from the point of view of Mother's rival and — damn it all to hell — I'll bet she was a nice person, too.

Ronald was delightful in company, so attentive and funny, he knew how to look at women and how to talk to them, spinning one tale after the other, acting out the roles of politicians or baseball players or society ladies he had seen on TV, all the while smoking cigarettes, crossing and uncrossing his legs, tossing his hair back, slipping in an off-colour joke now and then, he knew how women love to listen and to laugh, nothing pleased him more than to make a woman laugh, her gales of giggles were like a balm on his festering sore of a soul, a healing, a resurrection, and her shy glances and first tentative touches were like strong shots of pure ego — proof that he was charming still, loveable still, a remarkable human being despite his father's defection and his mother's rejection, he deserved to live, he had the right to walk upon this earth . . .

But when Elisa found out about the other woman, it was not merely another false note in the concert her baroque-ensemble family was playing. No. It was a cataclysm.

She screamed. Screamed, intransitive. For hours, it seemed. Sitting in the kitchen, arms jabbed straight between her knees, hands locked together, she rocked back and forth and screamed. Elisa, so beautiful. Our mother, unrecognizable. Of course we had no idea what was wrong, what could possibly be so very very wrong. I was the oldest, I kept Jimbo and Joanna occupied with games in the bedroom, trying to take their minds off the unholy sounds coming from the kitchen. Every time Ronald came near her she would grab something and throw it at him. Pots, pans, sugar tins, a bottle of milk, the kitchen was a mess.

"*How could you?* You take Communion every week, how dare you go to church, how dare you accept the body and the blood of Jesus Christ when you're so deeply immersed in sin, how dare you go to confession, you must lie to the priest, another sin?"

Words like these were probably pronounced, though I didn't actually hear them. Adult drama, awful, sickening, confusing. It eventually blew over. We children understood neither what had caused the rent in our mother's soul, nor what eventually brought a smile back to her ruby lips.

The cold blade . . .

Yes. Sorry. Got a bit carried away there.

At that time, the cold blade, the distance between my self and the world, was named God. I prayed desperately for my parents to stay together, to love each other and be happy again. Their discord seemed a message addressed to me, it was somehow my fault and I was the one who had to atone for it.

God watched me. His eyes were glued to me every second of the day. He knew everything about me, down to the nittiest grittiest details of my problems with clothes. The way the elastics under my turned-down knee socks were either too loose and kept falling down around my ankles or too tight and cut off my circulation. The holes in the toes, knees or crotch of every pair of leotards I owned. The pants' zippers that pinched the skin at the side of my stomach if I pulled them all the way up, or revealed a triangle of white panties if I didn't. The scratchy lace collar that left my neck aflame. The hook-and-eye fasteners in my Scottish plaid dress (a birthday gift from Father's mother) that kept coming undone so the kids at school made fun of me by sticking their pencil crayons into the aperture. Scuffed shoes. Broken belt buckles. Lost buttons. Botched repair jobs with safety pins. Clothes were a torture to me (they still are, cf. the other day's Torn Coat-pocket Tragedy) — no doubt a God-given trial, and I had to prove I could endure it with serenity.

I strove to earn God's approval, love, forgiveness. Each morning I resolved anew to get through the day — just this once, one single day — without sinning in thought, word or deed. A day of perfection. Smooth. I knew that perfection had to be

smooth, weightless, sightless — yes, if I could just
manage to float through the entire day in a sort of
dreamdance, it would be immaculate. No rude noises, no dirty jokes or gestures, no slapping of Jimbo or
Joanna, no raising of the voice in anger or impatience
. . . Nothing but kindness, gentleness and melted
honey, like Our Lord Jesus Christ . . . He was the
model on Whom I kept my inner eyes unswerving-
ly trained. I talked to Him under my breath from
morning to night so as not to forget. Let me be
good, I pleaded. But it never worked. I wonder
why?

Boy, you're a lot better off with me, aren't you?

Yes, but when push comes to shove, the two
of you are in cahoots. Given that I never managed
to be good no matter how hard I tried, I can only
conclude that God enjoys evil. Deep down, He likes
you, dear dæmon.

I never asked Him for His affection.

No, but you asked Him for just about everything else. All the great theologians agree that the
devil needs God's permission to intervene in
human affairs — otherwise there would be something in the universe that escapes His control. And
considering the amount of evil in the world, one
can only conclude that God must have granted
each and every one of your requests, from poor old
Job up to the present.

There's always some good reason to make people suffer, isn't there? Especially in the area of sex, because that's the original sin area. "Hey, God. Can I make Ronald commit adultery with that luscious brunette who waits tables in the doughnut place over on the corner of Jerome Avenue?" "Sure, that sounds like a good idea. That way I'll be able to test the strength of Elisa's faith in Me. Go right ahead, you old devil." Is that the way the dialogue between you went?

My whole existence has been a struggle against the illusion that niceness brings about good and meanness evil. Already as a child, I noticed that if I came to the dinner table full of goodwill and grinny Pollyannishness, my parents would be liable to sour and disgruntle me, whereas if I made it clear from the start that I was in a bitchy mood, they would invariably respond with tender-loving attention.

By the same token, when people tell me that my books make them cry, I am happy. Intensely so.

Yes. Crime pays, doesn't it?

It certainly does . . .

Shall we go commit a few more, then?

The Resurrection Sonata

VII - Wounds

Barnabé is now a young man, slight without being undergrown, radiating kindness and good humour. Each morning, like the other monks of the order, he dons a black gown, a leather belt, and the odd-looking hat with two flaps known as "Roberts" in memory of the founder. Since he pronounced his vows, Father Thomas has taught him to read and write and now he is never so happy as when he can spend the afternoon in the scriptorium, deciphering and recopying sacred texts. He also leaves the monastery, however, as often as the prioress allows him to, carrying the message of Christ's love to the most miserable hovels of the land, where ill health and ill luck run rampant. Whenever possible, he also brings laughter.

Just now, as the summer sunlight wanes, he is paying his final visit of the day — to a solitary man, old at thirty and wizened with misery. These past few months, not only have his wife and two sons been carried off by dysentery, but his goats have stopped giving milk and he has become destitute almost overnight. He shakes his grizzled head, wrings his hands, mumbles in his beard.

"Sure thing it's the fault of Simonnat, who lives over at the Forges of Ronzay. He always had it in for me, that one, no doubt about it, I must have looked at him sideways one day last spring and now he won't be satisfied until I'm dead and under the ground, oh dear God, what is to become of me!"

Taking his head in his hands, the man begins to sob.

"Do not accuse your neighbour, my friend," says Barnabé softly. "He has nothing to do with the illness of your goats, I assure you. These things happen."

Barnabé emits a few plaintive bleats and the peasant starts, glancing at him apprehensively.

"I get around quite a lot," the young monk goes on with a smile, "and in the past year I've seen at least a dozen men who have the same problem as you — Simonnat can't be *that* powerful, can he? And why would he have it in for every goat in the land?"

He imitates the amphigory of a wizard over his conjuring-book, then airily dispels this image with a wave of his arm.

"No," he says, laying both his hands on the man's shoulders, "please don't grow bitter. You must simply pray to God to make your animals well again. You know, my good man, we musn't find fault with God's better judgment. He had His reasons for calling your wife and sons back to His side. I know it's hard — but come, let us pray together, and you'll see, the Lord will comfort you . . . "

Falling to his knees, Barnabé closes his eyes and prays in silence. Then, in his startlingly clear soprano voice, he sings the *Magnificat* from the

Vespers . . . *Deposuit potentes de sede, et exaltavit humiles; Esurientes implevit bonis: et divites dimist inanes* . . . By now the labourer is rigid with stupefaction.

As Barnabé is on the point of leaving, he clasps the poor man's calloused hands in his. "You heard that, didn't you? It means the humble will win out in the end. So — be humble, my friend. And don't forget to love yourself a little, otherwise you won't be able to love your neighbour. Above all, never despair. If your soul is at peace, God may well allow your wife and sons to visit you from time to time."

Slipping the bewildered peasant some bread and a few walnuts, Barnabé kisses his hands and withdraws.

Orsan is several leagues distant, and Barnabé's heart rejoices at the prospect of this long walk home at nightfall — he loves nothing better than to meditate, while walking, on the marvels of the Book. These days, his mind is absorbed by the enigmatic passage from the tenth chapter of the *Apocalypse*, in which a Voice from on high orders Saint John to "seal up those things which the seven thunders uttered and write them not." What, exactly, had the seven thunders utter-ed? Humanity will never know, since John obediently refrained from writing it. But then why did he write that he had not written it, if not to torment and titillate us, inciting us to speculate about what this message might have been? Perhaps the most sublime message of all is one we can wonder about indefinitely, thanks to the fact that it was silenced?

The sky's blue deepens, drifting towards indigo, and Barnabé's heart thrills higher at every step. His pace, while firm and vigorous, is unhurried; his body moves freely and easily beneath his black gown; he praises God for the beauty of the sunset, and for the swallows, joyfully tracing their calligraphy on the clouds above . . .

These are to be the final images of his life.

When he comes to his senses, all is dark. Even in the first instant, he cannot mistake this darkness for nighttime — not only because the summer sky, a moment ago, had been filling up with stars, but because the blackness is also excruciating, unspeakable pain.

He is lying on his side, in the ditch. He lies there all night long, losing and regaining consciousness; every time he comes to his senses, the waves of pain that flush through him are so overwhelming that he knows nothing, neither who nor where he is, and he falls back into a faint.

He is found the next morning by Suzette, the little milkmaid from the neighbouring farm, as she is carrying her two milkcans into town at dawn. At first she thinks the young man in the ditch must be a sleeping vagrant, but then, noticing his religious habit, she stops up short in surprise. Approaching, she sees blood on his neck. She shudders, sets down her milkcans, moves a little closer . . . She would hate to touch him if he was dead — if you touch a dead person whose soul has gone to hell, the devil can slip inside you and never leave you in peace again — but no, the little monk is breathing. Gently, very gently, Suzette shakes him by the shoulder. He remains inert. Pulling at his shoulder, she turns him over. Barnabé's head falls to one side and his face is revealed to her — cheeks bathed in blood, gaping holes where his eyes should be. She leaps backward with a shriek, knocking over one of the milkcans in her panic, then races back to the farm, teeth chattering, body aquiver. Her mother takes one look at her, decides she must be possessed, panics in turn, slaps her across the face, wakens the father — "Come quickly, our Suzette is talking every whichway, I can't understand a word she says — an eyeless man — God help us if she's seen the devil in person and he's climbed up into her head, soon she'll be foaming at the mouth, come quickly, get up, we must act at once!"

Suzette's parents go out to the stable, pick up the heavy wooden pail and fill it with water from the pump. It takes their combined strength to heave it into the air and empty it over their daughter's head. The girl is flattened into the mud, spitting and hiccuping, but the treatment works — within a few seconds she has recovered her spirits.

"There's an eyeless monk," she gasps. "Over there. In the ditch. He's still alive."

It will never be known who did this to Barnabé. A band of roving criminals, highwaymen, discharged soldiers, returned convicts — there are so many people on the roads, it is impossible to make an inquiry, no one even bothers to try. In all likelihood, his attackers leaped on him from behind with the intention of robbing him — and then, seeing that he was a man of the cloth, and therefore a man of no means, tore his eyes out for a lark, so as not to go away empty-handed.

Also so that he would be unable to describe and denounce them.

Barnabé remembers nothing. His final image before blindness is that of the swallows' arabesques, their swift loops and swirls, the upstrokes and downstrokes he had been comparing in his mind with calligraphy. He strives to recover the sensation of rough hands seizing him, the sound of a scuffle, his own fall, perhaps his own scream . . . but all he can come up with are the swallows. The whole event has been abolished, sucked down into the blackness of oblivion. Had he put up a fight? He wishes he knew, for it would give him a clue to his true nature. Had his body arched up, resisted, struggled, allowing the survival instinct to take over, or had his soul been wise enough to place itself in the hands of God? He must resign himself to never knowing. Eventually, he thanks God for this as well — that every trace of the trauma has been erased from the slate of his memory. Is this not yet another proof of divine mercy?

Apart from his eyes, he is unharmed. There are no broken limbs, no cuts or bruises anywhere. Simply, his eyes are gone. He wonders what became of them. Did his aggressors decide to keep them as a sort of trophy, or did they toss them into a pond down the road a ways? Barnabé does not know which of these ideas disturbs him the most.

Father Thomas, overcome with pity for the young man who has always occupied a special place in his heart, carries the bad news to the parish of Torchay. As soon as she hears it, Hélène Denis squares her shoulders, goes to the kitchen and puts together a little bundle; then she insists on being driven immediately to the priory by wagon. There is no going against the wishes of Hélène. One of her guests grudgingly agrees to give up his day.

Thus it is that the monk's wounds are attended to by the fat innkeeper.

"Have you any news of your sister?"

"No. It's been more than six years now. What about you?"

"Same thing. Not the least sign."

"Yet I know she is alive."

"You know it?"

"Yes. I'm sure of it."

"Well, I'm glad to hear that. Barnabé . . . I can't help remembering the story I told you when you came over for dinner on Midsummer's Eve — do you remember? The blinded German?"

"I remember, Hélène."

"It is odd, isn't it?"

They go on to discuss the recent death of Fontevraud's brilliant young abbess Gabrielle de Rochechouart, known as "the Pearl of Abbesses."

"She was called back on the Feast of the Assumption," says Barnabé. "As if to be carried aloft in the very arms of the Queen of Heaven."

Hélène's train of thought is more down-to-earth. "They say her sister Madame de Montespan will be attending the funeral ceremonies at Fontevraud?" she asks .

"Yes, so I've heard. The prioress will be making the trip as well, of course, but we brothers and sisters aren't allowed to go. All we can do is say a few extra Masses in the chapel."

"Ah, if only I could meet Madame de Montespan! If only she'd let me take care of that lascivious old Sun King of hers! My remedies are more effective than La Voisin's — the attempt would not fail a second time, I promise you!"

"You're joking, of course," says Barnabé, with a smile whose nervousness he does not quite manage to conceal. A shiver runs down his spine as the healer's hands flick back and forth across his face.

Hélène spends but an hour or two at Orsan, dabbing the young man's wounded eye sockets with leaves and compresses she has dipped in various liquids. Though the active ingredients are known to her alone, their effect is swift and sure — the young monk suffers no pain following her visit, and his sores do not putrefy.

A few days later, for the first time since his accident, Barnabé senses his mother's presence beneath the dormitory roof.

"Is that you, Mother?" he murmurs.

"Yes, my angel. Yes, my child."

"I can't see you anymore."

"Of course you can, Barnabé. Try differently. Try from the inside."

"Ah yes . . . now I begin to discern the outline of your face, your body . . . But Mother, tell me — is this the shadow you once warned me about? The one you said would cover a part of my destiny?"

"No, Barnabé. This is not your shadow."

"But Mother! . . . I can no longer read, write or draw, to say nothing of paying visits to the poor . . . I don't want to complain, you understand, but . . . if this darkness in which I'm compelled to live until I die is not my shadow, then *what will be?*"

"This is not darkness, Barnabé. It is merely a new kind of light. No doubt this is why God endowed you with so fine an ear — because He knew you would one day be deprived of your eyes. Don't be sad, my son. You'll learn to see everything from the inside, just as you see me tonight. Believe me, you still have so many things to discover!"

Meanwhile, Barbe's life in Sainte-Solange has resumed its monotonous course. She has decided to say nothing to Marguerite about what happened between her and Donat — her mistress seems so cheerful these days, so very much in love with her husband . . .

Besides, Barbe knows that what happened that day had nothing to do with her, but rather with the death by suffocation of the little miller's wife and the dreadful tavern brawl that had broken out afterwards . . . Yes, she has understood this much; and so she nearly forgets.

She is even less inclined to discuss it with the priest, given the depraved behaviour in which the latter, according to increasingly specific rumours, has been indulging with certain female parishioners. Indeed, Father Jean outraged everyone by leaving town just after Marie Bourdeaux's death, thus obliging her poor widower André to keep the corpse at home for nearly a week, wrapped merely in a shroud, in the dog-days of late June. When the priest finally showed up, André Bourdeaux refused to attend his wife's inhumation.

And yet, impalpably, something has changed in Barbe. *She feels herself* — her skin, her living body. And, being more aware of her own existence, she also becomes aware of others; when Donat enters the room where she is working, she starts involuntarily — and it is not a movement of fear, rather the reflex response of one animal to the presence of another. On sunny days, she scrutinizes her reflection in the surface of well or pond, studying her pointed features, her nascent wrinkles, her weather-beaten skin — what does she look like? What sort of person is she? Who is this woman that Donat took, as a male takes his female?

From beyond the blanket, the familiar sounds start up again — and, for the first time, they bother her.

She has trouble sleeping.

She feels as if she were emerging from an endless torpor, a slumber of many years. She begins to think about her life. At night, she mulls over the images of her childhood, a chaos of bodies and blows, and then the brief span of happiness at the Torchay inn. Memories of Hélène and Barnabé resuscitate in her mind — these people are her only family — what has become of them?

At last she resolves to ask Marguerite exactly where Sainte-Solange is located with respect to Torchay. To her surprise, Marguerite says she knows Torchay well — she used to drive that way as a child with her father the weaver, as that was where the best hemp grew. "It's just over yonder, on the far side of the hill, something under two leagues away!"

Barbe's head spins. As usual, the mistress is indifferent to her servant's state of mind; she does not even inquire as to the reason for Barbe's question. Adrift in happy memories from her own childhood, she whistles softly through the hole in her dentition.

Shortly after this conversation, Barbe is in the goatshed milking the goats and it happens again. The thing. With Donat. She does not hear him come in, he approaches so stealthily that the straw beneath his feet does not even rustle, but all at once he is there, right up against her, so silent there can be no doubt as to what he wants. Barbe does not look up but her fingers freeze on the she-goat's dugs. The man puts a hand on her shoulder and suddenly she finds herself on the ground, lying in the straw next to the goat, uncertain whether he pushed her or whether she slipped off the stool by herself, but what is happening now is something she half wants, yes, something that a part of her wants, because it is what brought her to her senses, made her realize she was Barbe instead of nothing at all, and that Barbe was something, Barbe *had* something someone else wanted, and now that want is back again, pressed up against her, swollen, hard as wood, the piece of flesh she has never seen thus raised on a man, only on he-goats, bulls, boars, but now it wants her, yes, it knows where it must go and that is towards her, inside of her. Even as he pants and rears up high above her, Donat takes care to clamp his hand firmly over the weasel's mouth to prevent her from yelping as she did the first time, but in fact she would probably not have cried out at all this time — indeed she puts up scarcely any struggle for she feels wondrously weak, yes, for Barbe who has been tense and rigid all her life, it is a wondrous weakness that goes running through her body like sap, carrying relaxation and relief to the tips of her fingers and toes, she twists her head to one side but does not close her eyes, so that what she sees instead of the man is the she-goat, munching away indifferently at her straw, and what she feels is an unbelievable movement within her body, her own heart beating as if to burst, her loins flooding with something totally unprecedented, what on earth is happening, oh may it never ever stop, oh Jesus, Jesus, Jesus, I am alive.

The *Scordatura* Notebook

Lake House, April 14th, 4 a.m.

An abominable dream. Walking with Elisa in the Bronx Zoo — all of a sudden we see a picnic basket on the grass and, very matter-of-factly, Elisa tells me to open it. Inside there is a cat — not dead, I see, but wounded, its head bashed in . . . I am horrified, but Elisa tells me to take the cat out of the basket and turn it over. Then she says, "Oh, we really must put it out of its misery — look!" I look and see that where the brain should be is a small translucent sac filled with liquid, like a womb. Inside are two eggs, two fetuses. I understand; the cat's brain is pregnant and Elisa wants me to crush it so that nothing can be born from the corpse. "Come, now," she says — calmly, authoritatively — and I, shivering with revulsion, staring at the cat that is neither dead nor alive — "But . . . are you *sure?*"

Atrocious, horrendous images. Why would Elisa want me to kill my twins? This novel still so inchoate, so utterly vulnerable, hovering between life and death . . . Head splitting, hands shaking, I grab this *Scordatura Notebook* as if it were a rock and I a person drowning in a storm at sea. Help me, help . . .

Later (10 a.m.)

I'd gone to visit her yesterday.

I wanted to know about the countertenor. I wanted her to tell me simply, frankly, woman-to-woman, because there should be no more secrets between us, because it is too late for secrets, because all the roles have shifted and slid and switched and we are no longer mother and daughter . . . So selfish of me.

I must not ask her to help me with this. There is nothing left in her to give me.

"Mother," I kept saying. "Try to remember. Please, make an effort, concentrate, listen to me, I need to understand. There was a countertenor in the Baroque Ensemble, Edmund Something, do you remember?"

She smiled benevolently, nodded, glanced out the window, muttered something about last night's snowfall, then started telling me the story of the time her friends in primary school had buried her in snow and gone away and left her, drifted off, smiled, tapped her fingers on the windowsill . . .

"And what about you, Nadia? What are you up to these days?"

At least she knew who I was; sometimes she calls me Joanna or Charlotte (her favourite cousin back in Chicago, long dead).

At least she was speaking to me in English; sometimes she can only express herself in the Hungarian of her earliest childhood.

"Edmund," I insisted, unkindly. "A countertenor. Can't you hear me, Mother? Don't those
words mean anything to you at all?"

"Oh darling," she sighed. "I've known so many,
many people in my lifetime . . . " And then after a
pause, brightly — "Well, that's all right. It takes all
kinds to make a world, doesn't it?"

So I shall never know. How comb the earth for
a countertenor of four decades ago by the name of
Edmund? He is likely in a similar state of merciful
amnesia, if not pushing up daisies.

What I do know is that he was more than just a
faithful friend like Eric. He kept in touch with her long
after she had left the group, long after marriage and
motherhood had silenced her violin. He was in love
with her. I could feel it in the music, in the fullness of
his lips and the ardour of his eyes as he sang. How
many times did I come upon them singing together in
the living room? Perhaps only once or twice (one never
knows with memory), but I had the sense of something permanent and vital, feeding Elisa's soul. They
would stand side by side in front of the music stand,
sight-reading duets, Elisa singing the soprano part in a
slightly wavering yet lovely voice, the voice I knew so
well from lullabyes and hymns and *lieder*, Edmund
singing the alto with great gusto and accuracy . . .
Perhaps they even sang that lovely bantering pastorale, perhaps this was where I first came across it —

"Thy lambs, little shepherdess, are straying far and wide,
They're down there in the meadow, almost out of sight.
Thy lambs, little shepherdess, are straying far and wide,

They're down there in the meadow, almost out of sight."
"My lambs they are a-gamboling down by the brook,
My shepherd-boy will bring them in when crieth the rook."

Did their thighs sometimes touch, just barely accidentally graze each other as they stood there singing? I doubt it; I doubt there was even that much overt eroticism between them . . . At the end of each song Elisa would burst out laughing to make fun of herself for even trying, and Edmund would smile and murmuringly protest that she was wonderful, his colour would deepen and, turning the pages, he would suggest another title.

This happiness of his wife's drove Ronald crazy. It was not career, it was not social prestige, it was not sex or money, it was pure happiness, and he saw it was something with which he could not compete. It hurt him terribly.

Thus, whereas it was he who had broken their wedding vows, he behaved as if Elisa were the guilty one. One Saturday morning, I remember, he launched into a cackling falsetto mockery of Edmund's countertenor, prancing about the apartment wagging his rear end and cocking his wrist at an angle, while Mother, her eyes glazed over, unseeing, unhearing, went woodenly through the motions of doing the laundry, changing sheets and folding diapers and ironing handkerchiefs.

Of course Edmund stopped coming.

And Mother stopped singing, even around the house.

I must have been nine or ten when she decided it was time I was initiated into the sacred mysteries of Housework.

Ironing. I found it odd to sprinkle water over the things that had just come out of the dryer, but that was how it was, a mystery, one did not challenge this sort of revealed truth. After dampening them, one rolled the clothes into long sausages and stacked them neatly near the ironing-board, then, after testing the iron with a wet finger (sizzle), one commenced. Elisa had me begin with cotton handkerchiefs, then gradually progress through ever more esoteric realms — dishtowels, pillowcases, T-shirts, blouses, skirts — and at last, at the summit of this relentless ascension towards divine wisdom, I acquired the right to lay my hands on those most holy of vestments: Ronald's White Shirts. "Take your time," Elisa admonished me, perhaps recalling the one that had been thrown in her face a number of years before. "It takes even *me* at least ten minutes to iron a white shirt properly." First one did the collar, then the cuffs (unbuttoned, opened flat), then the sleeves, and finally, the right side of the shirt, the middle, the left side, doing one's best not to crush the sleeves one had already gotten smooth.

Sewing and darning. It always made me feel strange to slip the wooden egg into the sock my father's big toenail had eaten its way through like a termite, but I enjoyed drawing the yarn gently back and forth across the hole, then "over and under, over and under like basket-weaving", until I had the mesh as dense as it could be.

Then cooking. Ah! The arcana of lumpless Béchamel sauce, at last revealed!

All this precious female knowledge, elaborated and handed down over the centuries from mother to daughter, like the magic healing formulas Hélène Denis passed on to Jeanne, ended abruptly with my generation. I can throw a meal together, but I have not ironed a white shirt or darned a sock in the thirty-odd years since I left home.

(yawn)

Yeah, right. I know, you're a pure spirit, all these petty details of the human body bore you stiff but they have everything to do with my story. So be patient, I'm getting there. *You're* not the one who's mortal.

What I wanted to say was this . . . Perhaps Elisa would have survived, surmounted her pain, maintained with God's assistance some measure of integrity and pride, had Ronald been the only one to betray her. But another, worse traitor was gradually driving her to distraction and despair — and ultimately, I think, into the fuzzy bliss she has been basking in for years — *her own body*.

That was what defeated her, again and again. That was what made her grovel and quake, weep and vomit, shuddering at the sight of "human souls slithering, flailing, drowning in blood" (her words) . . .

Her body was what broke her reason.

Formaldehyde image: I remember every single word of this exchange. I was perhaps thirteen, just beginning to get my head and shoulders up out of the family muck, having my first adolescent inklings of philosophy — oh, not readings, just inklings, just thinklings — and one day after school I began talking to Mother, or rather talking out loud to myself in front of Mother, about *everyday enigmas*.

"There is only one everyday enigma," she said flatly, interrupting me, "and that is the enigma of the Odd Sock."

"What?"

"Yes, Nadia." She looked at me; both her gaze and her words were laden with solemnity. "The Odd Sock. *Where does the other one go?* Can you answer that?"

I thought she must be joking so I laughed.

"It's not funny, Nadia. Not funny at all. You know, had I saved them over the years, I should by now have a bushel basket full of Odd Socks. Proof enough, if proof were needed, that Reason Explaineth Not All."

And as Reason began to explain less and less, she lapsed into another world, sank away from us, arranged her features in a permanent vague smile, the very one I could not get past yesterday afternoon . . .

Who is my mother's Witness?
And who, if not my mother, can be mine?

Surely you're not going to start up with that *again.*

At one point, I remember, I was convinced my readers were my Witness. Taken not individually but as a group. They formed a single collective entity whom I thought of as endowed with eyes, ears, heart and brain — a breathing, feeling creature, now expanding now contracting, but always benevolent, attentive and sensitive, forgiving and loving me. In the all-encompassing, all-condoning presence of this abstract being, even my defects were part of my qualities.

I was absolutely certain of this for a number of years.

It is wrong.

It happens quite often, that one is absolutely certain of a thing, and that it is wrong.

11:30 p.m.

That one cannot live without such-and-such a person is almost always wrong, for instance. Juan and I were convinced we couldn't live without one another — I remember how my soul would growl with hunger if I had to go more than a day or two without at least hearing the sound of his voice over the phone — and look: it's been nearly ten years now since I heard from him, and both of us continue to pursue our brilliant careers.

(I cannot bear this. How do people bear this?)

When we met at the conference in Oslo, both invited for prize-winning novels, what happened was an unprecedented fusion of body and mind. These divisions simply didn't matter anymore, didn't make sense. Do you love me just for my body? Well that's wonderful. Do you love me just for my mind? Well that's fantastic. You mean you're willing to make love to me just because you read my book? You mean you think my beauty bespeaks enough intelligence to warrant your spiritual interest? All miraculously mixed. Our being together was *right*; it was as simple as that.

We talked about it with our bodies joined, we talked about it over oysters and Chablis, we talked about it reading each other's work out loud and laughing and frowning and making suggestions; life was sheer music, oh yes — when you fall in love, reality becomes ineffably beautiful, the surface of the earth shimmers as if you were seeing it through tears of happiness and you have no doubt that love can conquer all . . . Juan and I walked arm in arm through the ugliest industrial sections of Oslo and they were sheened with gold because our hearts were so huge, our writers' hearts, our shared attentiveness to human suffering, the bond between us that seemed almost a blood bond, yes surely it was Juan who, of all the men I have known, came closest to embodying my lost twin brother . . .

After our separation at the airport he was with me all the time. He inhabited me, invisible but omnipresent; I looked at the world through his eyes and I loved my life, myself, even my husband better; the fact that Juan was breathing somewhere on this earth gave enhanced meaning to everything I did. I'd walk down the street pointing things out to him, laughing at the witty remarks he made, sharing my worst fears and doubts with him . . . I was much braver in the dentist's chair, capable of putting up with the pain thanks to the aura of this man that hovered in the room, loving me. My writing, too, improved because I read it aloud for his absent ear, and because his absent lips had kissed the hand that held my pen. The idea of Juan *truly* transformed my existence, just as the idea of Barnabé *truly* protected Barbe from the sadistic fishing rod, and as the idea of Satan spared seventeeth-century witches agonies of pain when inquisitors inserted long needles into their bodies.

I was convinced it was a perfect setup and that my life was finally on the rails, nothing could possibly burst or collapse; I'd be able to reconcile husband and lover until the day I died.

Per and I were still living in Copenhagen at the time, and Juan was in Mexico City. Every time I went back to New York to visit friends or teach a workshop, he'd come up and meet me. I even grew uncharacteristically solicitous of my brothers and sisters and made trips to Colorado or Illinois every couple of months or so to check up on how they were doing. I'm not sure how Juan explained these odd jaunts to his wife, he never told me, he wasn't like Jonas, he rarely spoke to me about his wife and kids, he was too busy licking my toes and stroking my breasts and brushing my hair and reciting García Lorca to me over breakfast . . .

But once he had a reading in San Francisco, I joined him there and we got a little too sure of ourselves. I had come on pretext of visiting a couple of great-aunts I hadn't seen in decades and whom it was suddenly imperative I see before they upped and died, you understand. The thought of having to actually sit through these visits made me seize up with boredom in advance, so I hit upon the brilliant idea (after a couple of whiskies, I must admit) of spicing them up by taking Juan along with me, posing as my husband. Juan didn't object — to him this was merely another proof of how creative I was, as imaginative in my life as in my books.

The great-aunts were enthusiastic. They found him charming, worldly and handsome, all of which was true. They served us tea and crumpets with a little sherry on the side. I was sure they'd content themselves with exclaiming at how good Juan's English was, and be incapable of telling a Danish from a Spanish accent. Unfortunately, they bombarded him with questions about the Queen of Denmark and were made suspicious by his systematic changing of the subject. Word got back . . . Wasn't Nadia's husband *blond*?

I thought it ungrateful of them to tattle on me. Hadn't I given them one of the jolliest afternoons they'd had in ages? Hadn't they peed in their drawers laughing at his jokes? Okay, so the person I'd brought along wasn't *the* man — still, he was *a* man, wasn't he? I mean, it was close, right? Why should it have to be precisely *such and such* a man? I call that spitting in the soup.

I'm making this sound like a joke whereas what happened wasn't funny at all.

I lost Per.

We lived together two more years after that, two heartbreaking years during which he was — obstinately? angrily? sadistically? masochistically? — impotent, and in the end we were forced to acknowledge it was hopeless.

This was a very different thing from Jonas's impotence . . . Well no, not that different, come to think of it. Per, like Jonas, couldn't make love to me because he loved his wife, the problem was that *I was* his wife. It was to me he could no longer make love, only declare it (he loved me he loved me he loved me, he must have said it ten thousand times, weeping, and he trusted me, yes, he believed me when I said I was sorry, it was just his goddamn body that would not obey, would not go forth, could not enter me anymore, all of him tense and hard except the one part that needed to be, and that part shrank away from me, retreating in terror like a child from the dark mouth of a cavern filled with wolves) . . . I was dumbfounded. How could I have known, after years of happiness in bed with dozens of lovers, after all the porno movies and newspaper horror stories in which the male member is shown to be imperiously, irresistibly driving and pounding and thumping its way to its ends, how could I have known that the erection is such a fragile miracle and can wilt like a violet, shrivel to nothingness, to worse than nothingness, a poor sad handful of flesh with no more willpower than a jellyfish stranded on the beach . . .

Oh, Per! how we wept together!

. . . And of course I lost Juan, too.

Shit.

Feel utterly defeated, deflated, flat.

Let's hightail it out of here.

The Resurrection Sonata

VIII - Remedies

More years go by and then another of the dreaded "mortalities," as the peasants call them, rolls around. For the second time in a row it takes the form of famine rather than war or plague — a cruel winter frost kills the seed in the furrow and the infernal sequence starts up again. It is just as in Barbe's early childhood, only this time she observes and understands it all, follows the disaster step by step, watches as the colour fades from Marguerite's cheeks and Donat's face closes down. Everyone knows what the future holds in store — a mediocre harvest, the price of bread leaping sky-high, incomes plummeting, people resorting to the foulest of foods, their bodies weakening, fresh epidemics of dysentery and pneumonia breaking out, to say nothing of the various diseases carried by pedlars, pilgrims, prostitutes and parasites — anything goes: the infections will prosper and make merry, the corpses will stack up, the death-wagons will make their rounds; before long, the graveyards will be filled to overflowing.

Barbe works on in silence, eating almost nothing; her master has forgotten her existence.

The villagers bristle up in generalized distrust. Those women who do not die lose so much weight that their monthly bleeding stops, banishing all hope of new life from their bodies. People pray, weep, and curse; they spy on each other, trying to figure out whose fault the whole thing is, who can have brought this disaster upon them, what they can do to overcome it, to punish the culprit, to survive — they pray and weep; their bones ache with the cold. Winter lasts so long that the hedgerows no longer suffice to heat their homes — they steal firewood from the forests owned by the lords; many are caught in the act and hung. To make things worse, the priest of Sainte-Solange is turning into a demonic madman before the very eyes of his parishioners. A woman with a broken arm says he struck her with the pastoral staff as she was leaving church one Sunday after Mass; another claims he threw himself upon her, clutching his privy parts in one hand; still others maintain they have seen him sneaking into the meadows in the middle of the night and beating the cows with a shovel; the children say he terrorizes them at catechism with his oaths and blasphemies . . . How can they confess to such a rogue? How rid themselves of their sins? The world pitches and slides, the very air seems to seethe with evil spirits and omens; crushed beneath the weight of guilt and fear, the peasants entrench themselves in their homes and tremble.

Barnabé, plunged in shadow, is accustomed to fasting — hunger affects him virtually not at all.

As is often the case with the blind, he is considered by the local population to be something of a clairvoyant, endowed with exceptional interior vision. He is solicited to preside over inhumations, sometimes as many as six or seven in the same day, mostly children — abandoned, wandering beggar boys and girls. His mother forbids him to elude this painful task, for it was only by the grace of God that he had not suffered the same fate as theirs. He does not see the little cadavers, but each time he buries one, he feels he is entering the earth with it. He grows serious. Worse than serious. Solemn.

His voice is unaltered, but he sings less often than before — never outside of church, never for the sheer joy of it — and he has long since given up imitations, which he now considers to be frivolous nonsense that estranges one from God.

Having been ordained as a priest and authorized to hear confession, he listens to the unending complaints of the poor and they do not leave him unscathed; they nibble and gnaw at his soul; he gradually becomes infected, obsessed with the prevailing tension and unhappiness. Even his conversations with Marthe no longer suffice to appease his anguish. Why does God allow such misery to exist? Dismayed by his own doubts and interrogations, Barnabé decides that his faith needs fortification. He resolves to wear a hair shirt, deprive himself of sleep and walk barefoot in the snow, taking as his example the founder of the order, Robert d'Arbrissel.

All that can be said in favour of this year is that it ends.

In March of the following year, dazed and
sore, dizzy with hunger, the peasants watch as the
world greens around them. They sow the spring
wheat mistrustfully — dreading another frost,
another catastrophe. But no. The fine weather has
indeed returned, irrefutable, inebriating — and in
spite of their hunger, almost in spite of themselves,
people start to hope again. The birds seem to be
chirping beneath their skin, beneath their scalps.
The first, pale-green, pointy shoots of crocus and
daffodil dive into their hearts, stinging and stimu-
lating them to sensuality, petals of bright pink,
vaginal corollas, dew drops, buds bursting into
bloom, sublime tension, yes, the sap flowing
upward, spurting forth once more, all this in
silence, wordlessly, and yet the reawakening of the
senses is like a vast celebration.

Not only does it not snow — it rains! Once the
seeds have been sown, a lovely spring rain falls for
two full days without stopping, after which the sun
scatters armloads of diamonds over the green
sprouts of wheat.

It is in the mud, the thick rich after-rain mud
at the entrance to the barn, that Donat takes Barbe
for the third time. She has just finished sowing the
hemp and, passing in front of the barn where her
master is repairing a ploughshare, she brushes a
few seeds of hemp from her apronfront and this is
enough, seeing this flitting movement of the
woman's hands at her chest and stomach is enough
to make Donat's member stiffen and rise, the blood
throb at his temples, oh it has been so long, so very

long, he grabs Barbe and drags her towards the barn, his plan is to take her inside but when they reach the puddle her clog skids and she falls sprawling to the ground, her twisted skirt revealing a few inches of naked thigh and it is too much, it is too much, within seconds he is inside of her, huge, hard, shoving, and within a few more seconds he has emptied himself with a great boar's grunt, then, hastily disengaging himself, he stands up and readjusts his clothing, glancing around nervously — but Marguerite, thank God, is nowhere to be seen. Turning his back on the maidservant still wallowing in the filth, he picks up his repair job where he left it.

This time Barbe feels sullied, humiliated. She is hurt, confused, furious at the way Donat brutally rubbed her face and body in the muck, taking his pleasure so rapidly that she herself had the time to feel nothing.

Though she doesn't know it yet, it is this contact, worthless and awful as it was, that is about to change the course of the young woman's destiny.

When she realizes that the seed sown inside her has sprouted, that it has not been frozen in the furrow, that a tiny life has hooked on to her innermost recesses with the firm intention of getting bigger, she is deeply troubled.

Mother. She scarcely knows the meaning of the word.

Barbe, mother — two so very different things.

She blushes, listening to Marguerite's confessions by the washing-place. Her mind wanders. She moons and daydreams — about nothing. Then shakes herself awake. Something is happening. It is real, it is serious. It must be stopped.

She rubs and scrubs the clothes on the washboard — and then, just as she is lifting up one of Donat's heavy, dripping shirts to wring it out, an abominable image enters her mind — the *washerwomen*, the condemned souls of mothers who murdered their own children and must wash their little bodies forever and ever . . . It is said that if you go out walking at night and happen to pass by a stagnant pond, or even a clear fountain, they can be seen furiously thumping the little corpses on their washboards, wringing them out, plunging them back into the water and rinsing them, then starting all over again, thumping, wringing, rinsing . . . It is also said that these macabre laundresses lay ambush to anyone who ventures too close to them at night, breaking their arms or even drowning them . . .

Barbe's stomach turns over.

"Forgive me, Madam — I've never asked you for anything for myself, but . . . "

She stops, her face reddening.

"What is it, little Barbe? You have a sweetheart, is that it? You want to take an afternoon off? Go ahead! Go out walking with him one of these days — you can take the evening, too! It's springtime, after all!

"Thank you, Madam, you're very kind. But . . . what I'd really like, with your permission . . . "

"Go ahead, girl! Out with it!"

"Well, I'd like to walk to Torchay and visit my friends there. You know, the fat innkeeper I told you about . . . "

"Hmm. I don't remember. "

"Well, it's been nearly ten years since I saw them last . . . But I'd need the whole day to make the trip there and back."

"A whole day! Oh no, that wouldn't make my Simon happy, if he heard tell of it . . . Why don't you wait until haying-time, when he leaves home at dawn and doesn't get home till midnight? Otherwise he might lose his temper with me. At haying-time, all right? Can it wait? And then we'll keep it a secret between the two of us."

"I'm sorry, Madam — it can't wait. You see . . . my friend the innkeeper appeared to me last night in a dream — she was mortally ill, wasting away . . . Now my mind won't be at rest until I'm certain it was only an idle fancy."

Barbe winces: she knows that telling a lie like this could do actual harm to Hélène's health, but she can think of no other solution. The conversation goes on, punctuated by the thumping and scrubbing and rinsing of clothes — and in the end, by virtue of her gentle, courteous, and submissive manner, Barbe has won her point.

She is terrified at the thought that the people of Torchay might recognize her. But ten years have passed, and she has tied a scarf around her head, gypsy-fashion, to ward off suspicion: people aim hostile stares at her as she walks down the street, but they do not recognize her.

She trembles with emotion as she approaches the little church, then crosses the square towards the inn. Nothing has changed! Is it possible that Jeanne will not come rushing out to meet her, a smile on her lips, breasts and blond hair bouncing?

As for Hélène, she recognizes Barbe the instant she walks in the door. Throwing her arms wide as if she had been expecting her, she crushes the young woman's head to her voluminous bosom.

"Sweet one! My darling child! Here you are at last!"

The famine has spared no one. Barbe realizes with a shock that Hélène is an old woman now. Well into her forties. Lots of grey hair. Wrinkles that indicate she has done much laughing, and much worrying.

"Come — you're just in time for lunch, I've got a nice pot of beans and lard simmering on the stove . . . "

Barbe, going livid, sinks onto a bench, and Hélène understands at once.

"I see," she says.

Barbe nods. Her eyes are dry. She waits. She hopes. She is counting on the witch.

"You taught me certain things when I was young," she says, staring at Hélène unwaveringly. "But you never got around to teaching me this."

"Yes, I remember. Was it your master?"

Barbe's eyelids flicker in assent.

"Naturally. And it's been. . .?"

"I'm not quite sure. My moons had stopped during the famine last year; they hadn't gotten back to normal yet."

"Yes, but . . . the day it happened?"

"It was just after the great rain, you know . . .?"

"Ah yes. It rained here, too — two days without stopping — is that when you mean?"

"Yes."

"Well, my dear, that was on Palm Sunday, nearly a month ago already. Why have you waited so long?"

Without taking her eyes off Hélène, Barbe shrugs very slightly.

"Can you help me?" she says.

"I can try," says the innkeeper, taking Barbe's puny hands in her fat fists and squeezing them hard.

Barbe's lesson lasts more than two hours. Hélène teaches her the remedies as if they were a poem, making her recite them until she has them down by heart. First the simples — mugwort, birthwort, colocynth and setterwort, wild cucumber, fernseed, fennelseed and dill. Then the more powerful substances — ammoniac juice, ox gall, liquid pitch, asafœtida, galbanum. Then, if these have not yet produced the desired effect: nettle pessaries to be slipped deep up inside (where the young woman has never touched herself before); baths of camomile ("But however shall I take a *bath?*"); fumigations with native sulphur and sandarac ("Be careful," Hélène warns her, "these are poisons. Your

measurements *must* be accurate, do you hear?").
Finally, but only as a last resort, white violets ("These
will extract the child if it's dead, and corrupt it if it is
living."); and the smoke of a just-extinguished lamp
or candle ("Breathe in the smoke — but not too
much! It could damage your brain") . . .

When she is certain Barbe has committed the
list to memory, Hélène gives her further advice. "Be
sure you try only one thing at a time," she says.
"Mixing remedies can be dangerous. Also, dear
heart, you must act swiftly. If it is a boy, the infusion
of the soul could happen any day now. And once
you get past that point . . . if someone finds out
what you're up to, you'll be in bad trouble, I can't
tell you how bad . . . You've told no one, I trust?"

"No one."

"Good. You always were a careful girl . . .
Anyway — don't forget to *move*, too! Dance, jump,
sneeze, spit, vomit, shake yourself up, do whatever
comes to mind — even lifting heavy objects — but
be careful not to hurt yourself, you hear? No silli-
ness! No throwing yourself downstairs, no knit-
ting-needles — all right, my pretty one? Promise
me that much — your brother and I would never
forgive you . . . "

"My brother! Barnabé! Have you heard from
him?"

Hélène deems it best not to add to Barbe's worries by telling her of the little monk's mutilation.

"He has been ordained, he's a priest now.
Father Thomas says the Orsan dames refuse to confess their sins to anyone else."

"Oh . . . my dear Barnabé! I wonder when I'll see him again . . . "

"You must be off now," says Hélène softly, "if you want to get home before twilight. Take a bit of bread to eat as you walk — otherwise you're liable to get dizzy. I wish you lots of luck, little Barbe . . . You'll come back and see me when it's all over, won't you?"

It is like a dream.

On the one hand, Barbe does what Hélène instructed her to do. Obediently, methodically, day after day, choosing her hour carefully, out of sight of her masters, she essays the remedies and essays them thoroughly, gulping down foul-tasting liquids, breathing in smoke, slipping substances that burn, sting or tear into her most intimate recesses . . . Everything bubbles and gurgles inside her — her organs heave, her temples pound — her entire body seems on the verge of turning inside-out. She sticks her fingers down her throat, leaps off tables and chairs, lands on her feet as heavily as possible, then lets her knees buckle under her and falls backward or sideways, rolling on the floor like a disjointed puppet . . .

On the other hand, she does all this somewhat as if it were a game of make-believe — as if she didn't really intend for her attempts at murder to succeed. And indeed, when she wakes up each morning and feels the other little being still stubbornly hanging on inside of her, refusing to give up and let go, undiscouraged by the hot liquids, the godawful odours and poisons, the violent jerks and shocks she has inflicted upon it, she cannot help feeling proud — of it, and of herself. It is strange; it is almost incredible; but for the first time in her life she enjoys touching and looking at her body. One day, glancing down, she sees that her stomach, which has always been as flat and hard as a bread-board, has a faint, nearly imperceptible curve to it. Tears start from her eyes and she must bite her lips so as not to cry aloud in sheer delight.

Things continue in this manner.

She tries not to be pregnant; she knows that in being pregnant she is heading for disaster — and yet, in her heart of hearts, *she wants it*, and her secret wanting is more powerful still than the most powerful remedies of Hélène Denis.

She counts the days. When she reaches the for-tieth day and realizes that, if it is a boy, it now has a soul, she begins to talk to it, deep inside herself. She is proud, moved, proud. She puts a stop to the reme-dies. Whenever she finds herself alone, she passes her hands slowly over her mysterious stomach and her swollen, sensitive nipples. At night, she caresses herself in bed, conjuring up beneath closed eyelids images of horses coupling, dogs coupling, Donat coupling with Marie the miller's wife when she was still alive — and she moans, weeps with happiness.

One morning, she has just pulled off her nightgown and is contemplating, in secret delight, the just-visible yet firm roundness of her naked stomach, when she senses someone watching her — in all the years since her flight through the countryside, this instinct has never left her. Turning to look out the window, she sees Little Robert the simpleton standing motionless in the middle of the road, staring at her openly and grinning from ear to ear, his two pigs grunting and routing next to him. As usual, he waves to her enthusiastically.

Barbe hesitates. She should step back at once, move out of sight. Hide, cover herself. And yet, somehow, she feels that this man is not really a man — an innocent, rather; a child. Didn't Jesus say we must become as little children if we wish to enter the kingdom of heaven? Might Little Robert not be Christ Himself in disguise, come to test her kindness and compassion? Moreover, was it not God who had wanted this new life to grow inside of her? Every child in the world is the child of God — even the simpleton, even the child of rape. Barbe's son may one day be mocked and ridiculed like Little Robert, but the two of them are brothers . . .

Thus, instead of withdrawing, Barbe does just the opposite. She turns slowly so that Little Robert can see her in full profile. Then, gently moving her hands over her breasts and stomach, she glances at him out of the corner of her eye. Little Robert's eyes bulge and his grin widens still further. He jumps up and down, clutching his crotch with one hand.

Gradually, without Barbe ever feeling she has made it so on purpose, this becomes a ritual between the two of them. She simply happens to be at the window every day when Little Robert goes by with his pigs; and he stops and waves to her, drinking in the vision of her nakedness. If one of them is a few moments late, the other lingers, waiting without appearing to do so. Each day it is the same thing. And each day Barbe's stomach is very slightly rounder. Her heart beats wildly at the thought that she is sharing her mortal secret with an idiot.

The *Scordatura* Notebook

Lake House, April 20th

Writing this — much like orgasm — the sensation that something is spilling out of one — and yet just the opposite of loss, depletion — the more it spills, the richer one feels . . .

Advancing blindly. Such a strange, elusive process. Extreme heat and extreme cold in alternation. The book a bronze statue gradually emerging from writhing garbage. And, in advance, one has only the vaguest notion of the statue's ultimate shape. (I had not expected Barbe's pregnancy to go that way.)

It's better this way, huh?

I suppose so. As a general rule, what you do is better than what I intended to do. But it's so very different from . . . you know . . .

The truth?

Well, yes.

Ha! Don't make me laugh.

Well, all right, not the truth but . . . that thing. The story I tell myself about my own . . . No, I can't set it down here in black and white, not yet. Next time, perhaps. Don't ask it of me.

You're the one who asks things of me, Nada. Let's not get the roles reversed here.

Perry Street, 6 p.m.

Just came back from the country and got stuck for half an hour on the front steps making small talk with Mike and Leonora. Little Sonya kept running up and down the staircase, hopping and skipping on the sidewalk — both her parents were distracted from the conversation, keeping an eye on her lest she should dash into the street — she's so quick now, they said, so impetuous and unpredictable — it's the most dangerous age, they added, the age at which they can do everything and understand nothing. And I felt them searching my face, as young parents often do, for signs of envy. It must be tough to be an old maid, a barren aging scribbling spinster; her looks may still be passable for the time being but before long the neighbourhood kids will start whispering about her . . . The witch . . . did you see the witch? Long straight hair, skinny body, glasses sliding down her nose, darty beady eyes? Hey, did you see her looking out the window at us? I bet she was casting a spell on us . . .

The desire for magic so powerful — true fear so exhilarating — the taste of it acting on the soul like strong liquor, taking your breath away, belting you in the gut, oh yes, hit me again!

Joanna and I staring out our bedroom window at the special star, long after Father had come and gone, leaving our bottoms burning . . . Almost every night he would barge in and spank us for talking after lights out, we were inured to it, indifferent, we would pull down our pyjamas afterwards and compare the redness of our bums to see which of us he'd hit the hardest this time, and then, lowering our voices to a whisper, we would part the curtains . . . "There! That one, look at it! Can you see? There's a special aura, it's trying to communicate with us . . . " Our expectancy so intense that after a while the star did indeed begin to throb and glow — as if some cosmic princess being held prisoner there were trying to send us a message . . . Our hearts thumped, our stomachs leaped — thrilled and terrified, we clasped each other tightly and vowed to keep it a secret . . .

Secrets. Word gems. Memory diamonds, stashed away in the treasure chests of our souls, safe from the gaze of reality.

Or else we'd try to faint. Each of us in turn. Crouching head between thighs, taking twenty deep breaths, then — quickly — standing up straight and rigid, fists clenched at side, eyes squeezed shut, breath held — ah, the fabulous dizzying rush of blood away from the brain . . .

Yes! Take me to another world! Let me plummet into the divine dreamless sleep of Snow White! Sleeping Beauty! Rip Van Winkle!

Once Joanna actually did faint; falling she banged her head on the chest of drawers and came to instantly, but Ronald slammed in to see what was going on and I got the thrashing of my life . . .

Give us another world, another world!

Whence: the Kingdom of Lies. Discovering it when I was twelve or thirteen and rejoicing. The same high, heart-fluttering pleasure as theft. I lied to parents, teachers, priests — and they believed me! I made up stories — I was at the movies, I was with a friend, we lost our bus tickets, the teacher kept us after school — and they replied yes, well all right, go ahead, okay, I understand, fine, and my pulse would speed up, race with excitement. That was when I left home forever, left my family, left the surface of the earth, though in appearance I continued to eat and sleep and do my homework in the house on Morris Avenue with my mundane, truth-fettered siblings and parents.

When Father found out about my lying it got even better. When I was fifteen, for example, and he discovered I hadn't spent the night sleeping over at my friend Donna's but rather listening to jazz and smoking cigarettes and drinking beer with a man at the Village Vanguard, it got much more interesting. There was drama, there was outrage, there was violence. Not that I enjoyed being whammed across the face with the back of his hand, no — I still remember the instant nausea, the ringing in my ears — but afterwards, there was the challenge. How to disobey *more perfectly* the next time. How to organize everything impeccably so as not to get caught. How to bribe Jimbo and Joanna into helping me, covering for me, lying with me, so that they, too, would be gradually infected with the pleasure. And when Joanna started getting whacked across the face, she too caught on to the challenge, yes, the excitement. We became increasingly conspiratorial and duplicitous. Our alibis grew more plausible as our adventures grew more reckless. My little sister . . .

1 a.m.

Stella just left. She came over for dinner and we both drank a great deal, I'm rather fuddled but I want to call Long Island in two hours to make sure she's gotten home safely so I'm going to write to stay awake — also to get down at least a little bit of what we said.

As I prepared the barbecued spare ribs this evening — plunging my bare hands into the bowl filled with bones and blood-coloured sauce, I kept thinking of all the witches' recipes I'm reading about in the library. Those of the famous poisoner La Voisin, for example, who was beheaded for having helped Madame de Montespan eliminate her rivals and regain the favours of the Sun King.

La Voisin's own daughter Marie-Marguerite testified against her, describing the sinister "Masses" held at her mother's place on Madame de Montespan's behalf. At one of these ceremonies, said Marie-Marguerite, she saw an "infant, which appeared to be premature, presented to [the abbot] Guibourg, the knife slitting its throat, the blood flowing onto the host in the chalice, the words of consecration to Astaroth and Asmodeus, "*princes of love and friendship*" pronounced over the hideous mixture, which was distilled the following day and taken away in a vial by Madame de Montespan . . . " (Arlette Lebigre, *L'Affaire des poisons*, p. 116)

The witches' recipes in *Macbeth* are equally gruesome —

> *Finger of birth-strangl'd babe, ditch-deliver'd by a drab . . .*
> *Pour in sow's blood, that hath eaten Her nine farrow . . .*

— to say nothing of the witch who fattens up poor little Hansel until Gretel comes along and tumbles her into the oven in which she was planning to roast him! These obsessively recurring images of women killing and eating children . . . is it I who am mad, I who am morbid? Or were not the witches' cauldrons filled to overflowing, burning and bubbling, toiling and troubling with our fears about what *all* mothers might be concocting in their kitchens — *there but for the grace of God go we?*

The spare ribs were delicious.

"You don't mind my making pork, do you?" I asked Stella when she arrived.

"Heavens no," she chuckled. "That taboo is only for *Muslim* Jews! I'm a *Protestant* Jew."

"The only ribs I can bear to look at," she added a while later, gnawing on them voraciously.

As a young woman she was, if not exactly willowy, at least of normal build. She started putting on weight in 1945, when she learned that all the French side of her family had been deported to Bergen-

Belsen, and saw the first photos of the concentration camp survivors with their ribcages sticking out, bone by pitiful bone. Ever since then, skinniness has been connected in her mind with horror and she has done everything in her power to avoid it, for herself and for her family. Never that. Never ever that again, or anything that resembles it. Eat, eat. *Bon appétit!*

We kept sucking on our spare ribs and drinking the terrific Bulgarian wine she had brought over. Then the spare ribs came to an end and we started in on the second bottle of wine. Waxing a bit too garrulous as I often do with wine (though I know it's dangerous, know I should remain dead silent on the subject), I told her a little bit about my *Resurrection Sonata*: among other things, that some of my characters are ghosts. She laughed. Then she thought it over for a while.

Then she said, in effect, "It's really weird, isn't it? We tell our children, come off it, grow up, there's no such thing as ghosts, witches, hobgoblins, we just invented all that to help you get to sleep. In fact, there's nothing to be afraid of at all!"

I laughed.

"Whereas *in fact*," Stella went on, sighing and dabbing at her lips with a napkin, "there's a helluva a *lot* to be afraid of in this world . . . If they had any *idea* how much there is to be afraid of . . . Bullets, bombs, clinical depression, nuclear fallout, pornography, spiders, mice, the list is endless . . . "

"Sometimes," I said between sips of wine, "I'm afraid to get out of bed in the morning."

"I know you are, dear," Stella said immediately.

"I'm afraid of other people, all their different worlds . . . When I walk past them in the street I can see the suffering in their eyes and it invades me, I can't protect myself against it — it's as if I had no skin; their pain keeps entering me like an electric charge and I can't ground it; all I can do is quiver and quake and wait to be alone again. The idea that every single one of them contains a world of fear and pain and anger drives me mad! There's too much, too much, there's not only Manhattan but Brooklyn, the Bronx, Detroit, Chicago, to say nothing of Tokyo, Manchester, Calcutta, Rio, Kinshasa, Moscow, billions of people rushing in and out of stores and offices and factories and nuclear plants with problems in their heads . . . I'm sounding perfectly maudlin, aren't I?"

"Yes you are, dear, but I don't mind. Besides, you're quite right. Life is appalling. If any single human being were required to know the full extent of what there is to be afraid of in this world, they would drop dead on the spot."

"Suicide or heart attack?"

"Take your pick."

"Heart attack."

"Me too," nodded Stella. "And how silly we were when I was young, how absurdly wrong we were with our Marxism. It was the same thing, really. Getting rid of illusions. Ghosts and hobgoblins do not exist and religion is the opiate of the people. Nobody up there. Nobody down there, either. Nothing anywhere — nothing but reality. We thought it was so *brave* of us to insist on looking reality in the face! It was like going on a spiritual diet, you see. Attacking all forms of mental self-indulgence, softness, pleasure — mercilessly cutting off excess dreams and fantasies like so much fat and sewing up the mess with the needle of dialectics and the thread of materialism! Oh yes, by the time Marx got through with us, our minds were very skinny, very narrow indeed! "

"Then my generation came along and expanded theirs with drugs. My little sister expanded hers so much it was like the Big Bang."

Stella laughed gently; she knows this is not an amusing story. I was quite drunk by this time and I felt lousy. Head heavy. The past weighing on me. Dark thoughts. Joanna's madhouse.

There was a long silence. Looking at Stella, I could tell that she, too, in her memories, was traipsing down the road to hell — a different one. Some days all roads lead to hell.

"I could definitely have used some illusions when my Andrew was killed," she said at last.

I took her fat hand and patted it drunkenly. Thought of quoting to her my favourite pagan French proverb, "*Les morts sont les invisibles, mais ils ne sont pas les absents*", but decided against it. In certain contexts, even profundity is trite.

"Jack's dying was different," she went on after a moment. "I mean, of course I would have appreciated his keeping me company for another decade or two. But the death of a son is . . . unthinkable. Literally. You *cannot think your way through it*. It just keeps driving a knife into your heart, over and over again. Yup. Reality. *That's the way it is.* You brought your son up day after day until he was twenty-one years old, and now he no longer exists. He has *truly* been reduced to nothingness, and you will *not* meet up with him again in Heaven and, moreover, *no* superior being endowed with a wisdom that surpasseth all understanding decreed that he had to die, and he has *not* gone to sit "at the right hand of Allah" as the heroic martyr of a just cause — no, he is simply, irrevocably *gone*, for no reason whatever, and all forms of comfort and consolation are illusory . . . "

Stella lapsed into silence. Then she added, "That's MUCH more terrifying than vampires and werewolves, don't you think, Nadia? I'd be perfectly overjoyed to see my Andrew again in the form of a vampire, or any other form he might choose to take . . . "

"Do you dream about him sometimes?"

"It's been years. No."

"Ah . . . Because dreams are everyone's last little acre of illusion, aren't they? Even Marx couldn't get rid of them."

"For sure. That's why dear Father Freud chose to set up camp there."

"I've dreamt about Sabina. Maybe half a dozen times . . . I feel lucky; at least she visits me."

"You *are* lucky, dear . . . How long has it been now?"

"Nearly a year."

"Is that possible?"

Now it was Stella's turn to pat my hand, and

my turn to go traipsing down *another* road to hell: the phone call from Sabina's husband last May in the middle of the night . . . Every time someone breaks this sort of news to me, I think they must be joking, or at least exaggerating . . . *Dead?* Come come, no need to go so far — hurt perhaps; sick perhaps; unconscious if you insist; in a coma, screaming, bleeding — all right, I can handle that — but *dead? Sabina?* The friend with whom I shared a million cups of coffee, a million phone calls (no, that's false — tell me, Witness, what was the exact number?), the woman I visited in hospital every time she had a baby, just for the pleasure of seeing her *glow?* So what was the point of my following her through the vicissitudes of divorce and marriage and divorce, success and failure and success in her career as a poet, if it was all to come to *this?* Oh, shit, what were we talking about . . .

And I tried to push away the image of Sabina crushed and mangled at the wheel of her car, using the idea of having visited her in hospital to switch over to yet another road to hell — my recent visit to Elisa in Vermont.

"Do you remember that countertenor from the Ensemble?" I asked Stella suddenly. "Edmund, his name was?"

"Of course. Edmund Welch. British. A wonderful singer. He was only with the group for a couple of years."

"Was he in love with Elisa?"

"He most certainly was."

"And she . . .?"

"Yes, she too. But she never let anything happen."

"You're sure?"

"Oh, absolutely! Edmund left the country because of it — went back to London heartbroken, poor dear. I never knew what became of him."

"I must have sensed something, when I saw them together . . . "

"You're right. They were very much in love. But — I don't know whom she feared more, Ronald or God — your mother never once cheated on your father. Despite all my encouraging nudges . . . "

"Really?"

"Well, I thought she deserved a little fun in life."

There was a longish pause, as both of us mused about Elisa's pathological fidelity. And then, I'm not sure why, I asked, "And yourself?"

"Same thing. Faithful as a dog. Ridiculous, isn't it?"

"Not necessarily," I said. "It depends how much you were in love with Jack."

"Oh, but it was the same thing, you see. Jack would have girlfriends, and I'd learn about them. I'd hear he was taking other women with him on his business trips, and I'd be so *humiliated* . . . "

Stella had never talked to me about this before. There was one woman in particular. It's one of *her* formaldehyde images, dating from over forty years ago — the day on which she "screwed up her courage to go see who her husband was screwing" on the Upper West Side.

"I had to *see* her, you understand. It was a very dignified visit, I asked the doorman to announce me and I behaved with great courtesy; I did not go there to scratch her eyes out with my fingernails; I simply needed to know what kind of a person my husband was betraying me for . . . "

"And?"

"Well, I was floored. Her name, I remember, was Ann Driscoll. A society lady, for heaven's sake! You know, Jack and I were both card-carrying communists, I'd always thought his overriding passion was the class struggle, and here he was carrying on with a dolled-up West Side *shikse!* Reeking of expensive perfume, long painted fingernails, make-up a foot thick, hair perfectly styled, smoking with an elegant cigarette-holder, walking around in spike heels and this tight slinky thousand-dollar dress in the middle of the afternoon, and when she looked at me — well, I just felt like a Jewish *worm*. One couldn't be anything but frumpy next to a woman like that — even *you* would have become frumpy, Nadia. You might even have become Jewish! Ha! I can laugh about it now . . . But you know, it still hurts. Because I couldn't help thinking, well, if Jack likes that sort of woman, what in heaven's name is he doing with *me*?"

Their son Andrew was only three at the time; their daughters weren't born yet. Crisis in the marriage, tears, recriminations, promises made and broken, threats of divorce. The girls would not have been born.

Now Andrew's splattered flesh and blood are fertilizing some anonymous ricefield in North

Korea, the girls have grown up and moved out and had kids and crises of their own, Jack and the slinky society lady have both been rotting in their graves for twenty years but the betrayal *still hurts*. Their ghosts haunt Stella. She still has nightmares in which they gleefully reject her and hop on a plane together, headed for San Francisco.

Human existence is so bizarre. How can it seem bizarre, when it's all there is? It's not as if we had another intelligent species with which we could compare ourselves — a nice, straightforward species in which behaviour is sublimely rational, to whom love means love and happiness happiness and death death — whereas we crazed creatures systematically damage those we love, seek out our own misery, revive our dead . . . and tell lies.

Despite the late hour, and despite all the Bulgarian wine in her veins, Stella insisted on driving back out to Long Island. She enjoys waking up in her own bed, she said. I hate the thought of her driving at night — she's not a fantastic driver even in the daytime. But when she makes up her mind about something, there is no unmaking it. So I gave her a cup of strong coffee and a hard hug and she was gone.

Sunday morning

Whether it was the supernatural conversation or the wine, an eerie dream this morning . . . I was over at Jonas and Moira's place — the two of them had worked out some sort of alchemy, a stupefying process thanks to which, by carrying out a series of increasingly abstract calculations, one could engender homunculi — tiny embryonal creatures, actually more like baby gnomes or imps than baby people, black hairless wiggling things — the problems were handed out to us and we had to endure spectacular mathematical throes, cogitating at length on the powers of a thousand, until our efforts were rewarded by the arrival of these strange slippery bits of flesh endowed with heads and limbs . . .

No doubt about it, my mind is not in good shape these days. Why are you forcing me to write about lives smothered in mud and blood and viscerae, blind violence, bloody orbs?

You must trust me, my dear. I know where I am going.

The Resurrection Sonata

IX - Expectancy

Since her visit to Hélène, Barbe has been counting the days of her pregnancy by scratching tiny crosses on the windowsill with her thumbnail. Shortly after Midsummer, she reaches the eightieth cross. There is nothing more to be done — even if the child is a girl, its soul has now entered the body and it is too late.

She can feel the baby. She who has never had flesh on her bones, never paid attention to her appearance, never even noticed when she was hungry, gradually begins to listen to her body. And though she continues to conceal her state from everyone but Little Robert, binding her breasts and stomach tightly with strips of cloth when she dresses in the morning and wearing only baggy garments, her body has begun to seem lovely and sensuous to her. Her face is lit up from the inside by her secret, and when she happens to catch a glimpse of her reflection in the water, she cannot help staring tenderly into her own eyes. She is happy. At last she feels that someone needs her — *her* in particular, and not merely a servant or a sex. Nature has chosen not just anyone's body, but *hers*, Barbe's, for the making of this child, and the child is curled up inside of her, at once vulnerable and imperious . . .

At night, running her hands over her body, the sensation of her rounded stomach, tight swollen breasts and tender nipples makes her entire being arch up in a throb of pure life, and she fairly swoons beneath the sheets. In the daytime, now that there is *someone else* who needs to be fed, Barbe discovers the pleasure of hunger pangs. She eats with relish, while doing her best to conceal her new appetite from Marguerite. Once, walking past the goatshed in the middle of the afternoon, she slips beneath a she-goat and drinks avidly from its dug.

She considers her situation. She knows she should do something now, decide on some course of action. But what? Perhaps she could give the child to Mrs. Guersant, who has always longed to have one? And then their lives could go on as before?

She decides, in any case, that the time has come to tell her.

It is sheep-shearing day. Marguerite holds the animals firmly between her knees and Barbe wields the shears. They enjoy this early-summer job, they've been doing it together for years now and they've got the rhythm down pat — even the baby lambs no longer struggle to break free when they feel the cold blade of the clippers pressed to their skin.

"Madam . . . "

It is difficult.

When the words have been pronounced, a fat ewe escapes half-sheared from Marguerite's hands and goes bounding across the field, bleating absurdly.

For once, Marguerite Guersant has nothing to say. She sits on her stool, staring straight in front of her, and weeps. The tears fill her eyes, overflow and run down her cheeks, and she simply sits there, making no effort to wipe them away or to hide her face. She weeps.

Barbe lets the clippers drop into the grass and kneels down next to her mistress.

"Oh, Madam," she murmurs, ill at ease. "I never wanted to make you unhappy."

But Marguerite does not reply. She goes on weeping in silence, her hands limply abandoned on her thighs, palms upturned.

The two women remain thus for a long while.

When the sun nears its zenith, telling them the man will soon be home for his midday meal, Marguerite turns slowly toward Barbe, her eyes red and sad.

"You'll have to leave, my little Barbe," she says in a husky voice. "I really like you — you know that, I've always been fond of you, and I know it's not your fault . . . In fact it's not the first time, you probably know that . . . But you see — I couldn't bear to have you here beside me every day . . . I'm sorry, believe me . . . I'll miss you . . . But you'll have to go away."

"But Madam," stammers Barbe, totally taken by surprise, so far were her daydreams from reality, "but Madam . . . go away . . . where?"

"I have cousins in Montrémy. The Meillats, Jacques and Sylvain. They own a small estate and I know they were looking for a scullery-maid . . . "

"But . . . in my condition?"

"Oh, I won't say anything to them of your condition. You're so thin it doesn't even show, and so far it hasn't slowed you down in your work . . . They won't notice a thing. You know that some women conceal their pregnancies to the end, don't you? And then, when the child is born . . . well, you'll manage, I'm sure."

"Manage. . .?"

"It's not my problem," says Marguerite irritatedly. "What had you planned on doing with it?"

Troubled, Barbe averts her eyes. She dares not admit she had hoped to bestow the child on her mistress as a gift.

"You haven't told Father Jean about it, I hope?" asks Marguerite, suddenly anxious.

"Oh, no . . . "

"Ah! You see, my little Barbe," — Marguerite cannot repress a slight sigh of relief — "you're managing already! It's a mortal sin not to declare a pregnancy."

"Yes I know, but . . . "

"Oh, I understand quite well. Telling that vile rogue would have been tantamount to shouting it from the rooftops. And the people of Sainte-Solange must never, ever hear about it."

"What will you tell them . . . to explain my leaving . . .?"

"Oh, I'll come up with something. Don't worry."

Barbe is in her room collecting her meagre belongings when Donat comes home. He has no sooner set foot in the kitchen than Marguerite flies at him.

Crouching, Barbe cautiously lifts a corner of the blanket to watch the scene. Marguerite has decided to unleash her rage at last, she has discovered unsuspected strengths within herself, it is a pleasure to see her like this. Railing and hollering, she grabs a long stick and clobbers Donat with it, beating him about the shoulders, back and legs — he fends off the blows as best he can, grumbling and swearing all the while, has he so much as grasped what the problem is, doubtless he has because Marguerite keeps repeating that this is the fifth time, the fifth maidservant she will have to get rid of because of him — and so it is that Barbe departs from the Guersants' home just as she had arrived there ten years earlier, in the midst of a marital quarrel.

She does not even wish them farewell.

Montrémy is a few leagues distant from Sainte-Solange, in the opposite direction from Torchay. Barbe finds herself on the road again, walking in the stifling heat of mid-July. Her pregnant stomach is cumbersome and uncomfortable — the child dislikes being jounced and bounced like this; it squirms inside of her, hurts her, slows her down. By the time she arrives at the Meillat brothers' estate, Barbe is panting and drenched in sweat, parched and famished, and when two great black hounds meet her at the gate, barking and snapping, she all but collapses in a faint.

The Meillat brothers are taken aback, and also annoyed. This woman is still young — how can a day's walk have been such a strain on her? Is she ill? Has she the pox? Their cousin hasn't palmed off a former harlot on them, has she? Well, they shall find out soon enough . . .

Sylvain and Jacques Meillat are not only the proud owners of their farm and chattel, they are also cocks of the walk in town — mayor and notary public, respectively. Stout, arrogant bachelors imbued with a sense of their own importance, they employ some twenty individuals in all — shepherdesses, ploughmen, farmhands and chambermaids. They run the household with a double iron fist — each day of the week has its unvarying schedule; grace and Mass are compulsory; minutes are counted; idleness is chastised; meals are dispatched speedily and in silence.

Mrs. Roger the cook, a robust woman in her fifties, is in charge of the other female servants, who respectfully defer to her age and authority. At first, perhaps because she bears a vague resemblance to Hélène, Barbe wonders whether this woman might not become her confidante, but it is soon clear this will not happen. Like the others, Mrs. Roger keeps her firmly at a distance — she is new, a stranger, possibly a soldiers' girl. Moreover, her behaviour is suspicious — she is too quiet, there is always a sly little smile on her face, and she is unduly secretive, never washing or undressing in front of the girls with whom she shares a room.

After a few weeks of this ostracism, Barbe begins to waver. Perhaps she should simply go to the priest of Montrémy, declare her pregnancy to him and put herself in the hands of God? But this is unthinkable. No one knows her around here; the townspeople would cast her out as an unmarried mother, a sinner — and she would find herself on the road again, with no way of feeding her little one — it would be hell.

She speaks to her baby in a low voice, and she is convinced that it can hear her. Its presence is a comfort to her through the long days of hard work in the kitchen and garden.

"You see, little poppet, you have to eat. And if I told the priest the truth, we'd be driven out of town. It seems I noticed you weren't too keen on life on the road . . . Am I right? So you see, you'll just have to wait, be patient for a while. I'm here, I'm your mamma, and the Good Lord is here too, so you've nothing to fear. He knows we've done nothing wrong . . . Right, little one? You've done nothing wrong, have you? He wouldn't allow a lambkin like you to be punished, that's impossible . . . What's your name, anyway? Maybe . . . maybe . . . Barnabé, like my twin brother! He's the finest man on earth, as sweet and warm as sunshine in the month of May. You'll meet him some day, I promise. He knows how to imitate everything! Baby lambs, big bad wolves, beggars, fancy ladies — he'll make you scream with laughter! Not only that, but he sings like an angel. Oh yes, you'll get to meet everyone I love. Hélène, the innkeeper at Torchay, who was like a mother to me . . . And good Father Thomas, too, if he's still alive. I can't believe how the years have flown, I'm an old maid — already twenty-five years old! — no one will want to marry me now, that's for sure — but you'll keep me company, won't you, my poppet? I'll never be alone again, now that you're here. I hope you don't feel too squashed in there! It can't be much fun with all those bandages holding you in . . . When I bend over in the garden to thin the carrots, I can tell you're not too happy about it. But things will get better soon, believe me — we'll pull through, we'll find some place to live together and I'll make you a wonderful life . . . "

All day long as she goes about her work, a stream of tender, reassuring words flows through Barbe from head to womb, always the same and always different. The stream of words protects her from the wrathful eyes of her masters, and from the subtle harassment of the other maidservants.

Though she is dead tired every night at bedtime, Barbe cannot settle onto her palliasse just any way. Lying on her stomach has become impossible — her swollen breasts are too tender — and she must avoid lying on her back for fear of betraying her secret, so she sleeps on her side, curled protectively around her child, her marvel, her innocence. She sleeps like a log, like a stone — never has she known such depthless slumber.

In the daytime, she is obsessed with food — her hunger seems unappeasable. She dares not filch eggs from the chicken coop or plums from the plum tree for fear of being caught red-handed, but once in a while she sneaks around to the compost heap behind the barn and stuffs herself with refuse — quickly, quickly — munching peapods, radish leaves, moldy old breadcrusts, chicken fat — anything, anything. She needs to eat.

At table, she does her best to keep her voracious appetite in check. She is careful, as well, never to fold her hands over her stomach as she has seen pregnant women do. Sometimes, in order to appear young and carefree, she even crosses her legs, though this position is atrociously uncomfortable.

In church, too, she finds it excruciating to kneel on the icy flagstones for long minutes at a stretch, but at least the pain is made up for by the music. Barbe imagines her little Barnabé listening to the psalmodized prayers and wriggling with delight inside her womb — she likes to think that he will inherit his uncle's gift for song.

Harvest time, at July's end, is an ordeal. As a scullery-maid, Barbe had not expected to have to work in the fields, but it is an absolute obligation at this time of year. Wheat, in these parts, bears no resemblance to what went by that name in the hamlets Barbe has known since childhood — a few miserable stalks that sprouted willy-nilly and were as likely as not to be destroyed by frost, blight or wild beasts before reaching maturity. Here on the Meillat brothers' estate, wheat is cultivated for the lord of La Chaume in person, in fields extending over several acres — and when harvest time comes round, not only are men hired especially for the occasion, but every available hand is put to the task.

A row of men moves forward, rhythmically slicing the spikes with scythes; behind come the women, who pick them up and tie them into sheaves. By mid-morning Barbe is already dizzy with the effort of bending and straightening in the punishing heat; she staggers in the endless merciless rush of yellow light; thorns bite her hands again and again; particles of straw burn her eyes and nostrils; she sneezes, sweats, and weeps, stopping every few seconds to wipe her nose and forehead. Finally her distress so irritates the other girls that Mrs. Roger, in a fury, orders her to go back to the house and make lunch for everyone.

Vintaging, at mid-September, all but kills her.

Again she is forced to work with the others from dawn to dusk — but this time she has not even the right to straighten up. Bent double, she moves down the vineyard row by row, picking tens, hundreds, thousands of purple bunches — and whenever she pauses to rub her aching loins, one of the Meillat brothers materializes next to her and viciously berates her for her laziness. She sits down only twice in the entire day, to gobble a handful of walnuts and a piece of goat's cheese, gulp down some water — and then she must take up the same cruel position and resume detaching the purple bunches from their stems.

Towards mid-afternoon, her baby's small, reassuring movements come to a halt and Barbe's stomach grows frighteningly hard. It is as if it were no longer a part of her — as if it had suddenly become a foreign, hostile entity, a block of stone. Her back aches, she is dizzy and nauseous — and yet she must hold out at all costs, for if she faints someone will rush over to her, untie her corset laces and bandages, examine her closely — and this would mean disaster, banishment, death . . .

She must hold out.

Michaelmas arrives — the archangel stabbing the demon marks the beginning of autumn, the season of death and decay, when the whole world seems to wither and fall into ruin. The hunting season. Day after day, the sharp barking of dogs and the sharp report of guns ring out from the nearby woods — wealthy men exercising their macabre prerogative.

Barbe has a strange dream. She dreams she is with Sylvain Meillat in a clearing in the woods. Dozens of rabbits are dashing about and Sylvain is shooting them one after the other, all the while showing off the prowess of his dogs. As soon as a rabbit is hit, the two dogs leap on it and skin it alive, first tearing off the skin in a single piece, then severing one of its hind paws with a snap of their jaws, so that all the animal's blood flows out into the grass. "There!" says Sylvain, proudly. "Ready for the stewpan!"

Barbe wakes up in a sweat, with Mrs. Roger snoring next to her.

By contrast with their summer chores, the women's activities in the autumn are fairly easy. They spin hemp and wool, crack, sort and crush walnuts to extract the oil, stack apples, pears and quinces in baskets for storage in the attic, cover windows with oiled paper, clean out the fireplaces for the winter . . . But Barbe senses that, since vintaging-day, something has changed inside her; something is wrong. She worries — it is all she can do not to panic. The baby's movements haven't stopped altogether but they are less frequent, more erratic than they used to be; and when she speaks to it, she does not feel the same sense of intimate communion as before. Mother and child have somehow been disconnected — Barnabé is *there*, but his presence no longer chimes with Barbe's breathing and her heartbeat. Frightened, Barbe loses sleep, loses her appetite; at table, and as she goes about her chores, Mrs. Roger scolds her for "daydreaming" . . .

If only she could ask Hélène's advice! But the Meillat brothers would never consent to give her a day off, as Marguerite did, to make the trip to Torchay. Besides, in her present condition, she would be unable to cover the distance on foot .

The reassuring stream of words dries up.

The days grow shorter.

On All Saints' Day, though none of her dead are in the Montrémy graveyard, Barbe goes there alone, just before dawn. She needs to talk to someone. Drawing her grey drugget cape closely about her, she pushes open the gate and advances toward the tombstones. The sun has not yet risen, a dark, heavy fog weighs on the earth, an icy drizzle begins to fall and Barbe allows the droplets to catch on her eye-lashes. Walking up and down the rows of tomb-stones, shivering with the cold, she begs Marthe and Jeanne to help her, explaining her predicament to her dead mother and her dead friend, telling them everything that has happened, pouring out to them her intolerable fears. At last, to her relief, she feels warm tears begin to mingle with the cold rain on her cheeks. When was the last time she wept? She cannot remember. But day is breaking — she must hurry back to the house. If anyone were to remark her absence, she could be beaten.

The days grow shorter still. Mute and tense, Barbe awaits her deliverance.

The *Scordatura* Notebook

June 12th

Dream in which my father, wretched and cantan-
kerous (he looked like one of those crazy, bleary-
eyed, foul-mouthed homeless men who lurch
down the street hectoring everyone they pass), was
counting his remaining pennies. It came to a ridiculous sum — something like a dollar and seventeen
cents — and with this he intended to go to Paris,
alone. I reasoned with him gently, explaining that
Paris was an expensive city and suggesting that
perhaps he could use a little extra, but he ran-
corously rejected my offer of financial aid. "Miss
Know-it-all!" he snarled. "If you're so smart, could
you please tell me why the Parisians call their
prison Health and their hospital Pity?" (His voice
still burns in my head, as one's throat burns when
one has vomited or screamed, a voice of bile and
hatred.) I, meanwhile, was frantically packing — I
had a plane to catch (where was I going? nowhere,
anywhere, in my dreams I'm always trying to leave
and something is always stopping me) — I kept
reopening my suitcases to remove large, cumbersome objects which, deep down, I didn't really
need, tossing in clothes at random . . . Then I was
playing the violin but the notes kept disintegrating
— the music decayed and crumbled until there was

only one note left, and little cherry tomatoes went rolling about derisively amidst the strings . . .

Bleak black brain this morning. What am I supposed to glean from a dream like that? In my *Resurrection Sonata*, too, the music keeps threatening to stop. What is my one remaining note? And what in heaven's name do the cherry tomatoes mean? Oh, I don't want to know, I don't want to know, I'm not a violinist . . .

Okay, so I'm a violinist. Is the dream saying I'm trying to take over where Elisa left off?

It was Schumann whose madness consisted in the progressive ruin of harmony and interval. At the end, when all he could hear was a single note resounding unstoppably in his head, AAAAAAAA-AAAAA, he begged to be committed to an asylum.

A single note is meaningless, therefore innocent. Was Schumann striving to retrieve his lost innocence? *Paradise regained.* (Again: the mono/tony of heaven. Milton has always put me to sleep.) It takes two to tango/tangle. Only a *combination* of notes — an interval — can be deemed beautiful, or strange, or disturbing. Even diabolical.

Ah. I was wondering when you'd get around to that.

Yes. The tritone, the interval of three whole tones was known for centuries as *diabolus in musica* because of its "instability." C is innocent, F-sharp is innocent, but C combined with F-sharp — horror and damnation! Sin and excommunication! The "devil's

chord" was classified in the thirteenth century as a
discordantia perfecta, and its use was prohibited in
liturgical music. (Even much later, in Romantic
opera, it was systematically used to connote omi-
nousness and evil. I'll bet Thelonius uses it all the
time, unholy "Monk" that he is . . .)

My parents were *diabolus in musica* personi-
fied. And I am the product of that dissonance.
Scordatura. No kidding. No wonder.

And if Martin's and my child had lived?

There. I have written it.

Perhaps I had this dream — Father's destitu-
tion, Mother's disintegration — because I ran into
Martin last night, for the first time in years.

A depressing literary do at R. Centre, to wind up
the equally depressing book fair, and why did I
agree to go when I knew in advance what it would
be like, why do I still allow myself to be sucked
into these things by fast-talking agents and editors
and publicity people who assure me that my presence is indispensable, and that it will be an intimate, select group, only fine writers, no hangers-
on, no journalists, and so I finally relented, though
I knew it was a mistake, knew I was going to spend
a miserable lonely evening, knew there would be
three hundred of us elegant snobs milling hysteri-
cally about, playing the same game, vying for status, testing our fame, has it gone up or down since
the last cocktail party, X pretending not to recognize Y because he's outgrown *that* category, but

hoping now to be recognized by Z who's in the category above. Sabina and I used to wander around this sort of event arm in arm and get sloshed together and point at people with our eyes crossed and ostentatiously jot down quotes in our notebooks from the asinine conversations we overheard. But since her death I have no one to go with so there is no longer any point in going, I knew it would be wiser to sit at home and sip white wine and listen to Telemann's *Fantasias for Violin Solo* . . .

What I would have wanted to share with Sabina this time, though, had she been with me, was how unutterably poignant the whole thing was. I know she would have understood . . . *there we were*. A few hours earlier, we had all been in the process of choosing our clothes, combing our hair, shaving or putting on make-up in front of a mirror, pulling on socks or panty-hose, zipping up skirts or trousers, buttoning shirts or blouses, selecting ties, necklaces, perfume, going to the bathroom one last time and . . . *there we were*. We were all our respective ages, some young, some middling-young and some no longer young at all . . . We had been on this earth a specific number of days and we looked exactly the way we looked. Every man who was balding had lost just so many individual hairs and not one more, not until tomorrow, and some of the older women looked younger than they had at cocktail parties ten years ago, and *there we were*, three hundred discrete human entities of different shapes and sizes, reunited for a moment, looking our best for the occasion, and in just a few hours the occasion would explode, sending us flying our separate ways, never to look or feel quite the same again as we had, with such extreme fragility, on this particular evening in June — yet no one was noticing this, no one was marvelling at it . . .

You do know what I mean, don't you Sabina? — how *human* we were, and how comical our self-importance, as if there had been no yesterday and would be no tomorrow, as if we had not all been crazy little kids caroming around corners and would not soon be doddering elders staring into the void . . . Oh it was sad, sad and odd, to see all these people who write books, who ostensibly know all there is to know about the human species, yet who were clearly quite oblivious to what made them beautiful . . .

and, it the midst of it all, Martin.

Martin Schuller with whom I lived for more than two years of my life (crucial years, twenty-one to twenty-three), with whom I shared a bed, shopped, cooked, joked and made love for over seven hundred days and nights of my precious existence . . . Martin Schuller was the last person to whom I could have confided my emotion about the evening.

It had been at least six or seven years since we'd last run into each other, though I read his work sometimes, standing up in bookstores. He has continued his spectacular ascension as a literary critic, the very worst sort of literary critic, preening, fawning, flattering . . . oh he was positively *greasy* last night; I found him repulsive. Getting fat but not

a good fat, not the nice middle-aged general thick-
ening of someone like Per — no, an unpleasant,
unhealthy fat, which he denies with tight clothes
and holds in with belt and bow-tie so that it seems
even more obtrusive — bulgy, bulbous, ugly. He has
wined and dined too many authors, consumed too
many French meals with thick cream sauces, wines,
liqueurs, desserts . . . He even smokes cigars now,
waving them in the air with ludicrous arrogance,
bragging loudly about the famous people he's inter-
viewed, the compliments and honours he's
received, and it made me want to weep. How is it
possible that I once loved this man and that he
loved me? What was it like when he came — did he
shout, collapse, groan, whimper? I can't remember
— *scordare* — nor can I recall the shape of the shoulders, back and buttocks I caressed so fervently, the
texture of his skin beneath my palms — yes *I*, yes
him — and here he was, "coming on" to me as he
had and would to every pretty woman in the room,
"playing Don Juan", the smooth urbane seducer,
making it ostentatiously a role — just as the influ-
ential cigar-waving critic was a role — but when did
the quotation marks come off? Where was the real
Martin? Conveniently, he has read so much sophis-
ticated French theory, Lacan, Barthes, Derrida *et al*,
that he no longer believes in reality — everything is
Discourse. I remember him telling me one night
over dinner that Camus and Beckett were the true
founders of modern literature because on the first
page of both *The Stranger* and *Molloy* was the declaration: My mother just died and I don't give a shit.

In other words, abandon all hope of reality, ye who enter here; this is a purely verbal universe, a world of signifiers with no signifieds, a world of arbitrary juxtaposition and formal experimentation. "But in real life," I protested, "Beckett and Camus were both deeply affected by their mothers' deaths!" "Humph!" said Martin, shrugging his shoulders and pushing his plate away as if I had spoiled his appetite, whereas in fact the T-bone steak on it had already been gnawed clean. "Real life!"

Whereas you, my dear, turned to me as soon as you understood that it was the other way around: that just because real life exists, and is meaningless, it is essential that art, which revolves around the non-existent, have meaning.

Yes, right. Only, you see, what I'm beginning to wonder is . . . well, to put it plainly, how can I care about Barbe's dead baby if I don't care about my own?

Now, now. You're not going to get sentimental on me in your old age, are you?

No, of course not . . . Where was I? Ah yes. Try as I might, last night, I could not recall what our happiness had been like, what had made the specific colour and flavour of our days, what I had loved about Martin Schuller . . . apart from the fact that when we went on long car drives he used to sing to me in a terrific deep voice, Paul Robeson songs, old trade union songs from the Thirties, Broadway musicals, *If Moses Supposes* — but that was acting, too, he was pretending to have a "terrific deep voice"; perhaps the only real thing he ever did in his life was to get me pregnant.

And there I was at the cocktail party, staring at this perfect prick, this overweight dandy, and wondering what on earth would have become of our child had we not killed it. *Our child* — the combination of that person and myself? A monster! Another *scordatura*! Ah yes, I know we would have divorced eventually, and the child would have been mine to raise; still, he would have had the genes of that lamentable individual and, assuming I had come to despise Martin as I do now, how could I have refrained from despising every sign of the father in the son?

Had we stayed together, on the other hand, I would have become someone else. I'd have met neither Per nor Juan, both of whom changed me radically, taught me to take myself seriously, as a person and as a writer . . . But then, had I stayed with Martin, perhaps he himself would not have turned so rancid? *Who are we, oh my God?*

Later

I know it was a boy.

I have always known it. I lived with him, knew him, as I have lived with and known no other human being. He inhabited me for three full months. My son.

Words I have never committed to paper before, outside of novels. My son.

It's been so long since you came to see me. You used to come, my darling, my tiny baby boy, my Tom Thumb. You would come and visit me at night, it would be raining in my dreams, always pouring rain, and you would be at the window, shivering, tiny boy, drenched to the bone, knocking desperately on the glass, "Mother! Mother! Let me in! Please! I'm freezing to death! Mother, please let me in!" Over and over. I could hear you but I could not go to you. *Could not allow you to enter my life, enter human history, have a story of your own.* Darling. Your words are chiselled into my heart. I'd wake up with a shout, the blood pounding in my head. If I went back to sleep, the persistent tapping at the pane, at the pain, would start up again — "Let me in! Please! Please! I'm freezing to death!"

I have never stopped hearing those words. I'm trembling as I write this. And yet, secretly, I yearned for the nightmare to return, because at least it let me see you . . .

The other babies I got rid of quickly, when they were but tadpoles. But this one was before Roe vs. Wade. It grew. You grew, Tom Thumb. First it was *it*, then it was *you*. Martin and I had no intention of becoming parents (this is perhaps the only issue on which we still agree today). Days and weeks went by. Gradually rising panic. Gradually swelling stomach. Nervous phone calls. Appointments in seedy apartments — how many? Five? Ten? I would go alone. The *faiseurs d'ange*, the angel-makers, as the French call them (are you an angel now, my love?) were a filthy lot. First they would take my money, then feel me up, running their hairy hands over my breasts and stomach, shoving them up my vagina, then ask for more money . . . and I would go home sweating, jittery, broke. Broken.

Martin could not fathom why everything was so complicated. A mistake had been made and needed to be unmade; it was as simple as that. You were the mistake, darling. You kept growing. It was in June that, like Barbe, I reached the stage at which you would have had a soul. "Even if you had been a girl." Which you weren't. And, suddenly, Elisa came.

My mother. Your grandmother.

I hadn't seen her in fully four years, since I was eighteen, since the day I had kidnapped Joanna from the psychiatric hospital to which Ronald had committed her to "protect" her from her drugged-out hippie boyfriend. (That whole mess. Joanna and I sharing a basement studio on the Bowery, hungry angry dirty drop-outs, keeping ourselves alive through stints as dishwashers or waitresses but both of us too bummed out on hash to hold down anything like a real job — a wonder we didn't turn to whoredom, perhaps we did and I've simply forgotten it, *scordare*, those eighteen months are a single grey blur in my brain, we spent almost every evening smoking hash and talking about how much we hated Ronald, what a supreme asshole he was, how we would murder him if we could get away with it . . . Poor Father, so bewildered as he watched his daughters becoming women, fearing for our bodies and our souls in the upheaval of those days, — Vietnam War days, flower power days, LSD days, SDS days — everything wild and uncontrollable, threatening to pulverize the very foundations of his existence, work, family, marriage; poor Father had resorted to the old alchemical recipe by which fear is magically transubstantiated into anger . . . But after a year and a half of this Joanna got fed up and, promising not to reveal my whereabouts to our parents, went home to the Bronx. I hung onto the Bowery basement for a while and then met a handsome eloquent young grad student in modern French Lit named Martin Schuller, fell head over heels in love with him, moved into his cruddy little apartment on Saint Mark's Place that stank of incense from the Intergalactic Trading-Post downstairs, registered in French at City College so I'd be able to read the books he raved to me about, and started writing furiously experimental short stories inspired by my sister's hellish dealings with hallucinogens and loony-bins.)

And then you came, Tom Thumb. And then Elisa came.

It was like seeing a ghost, an apparition. I could hardly believe she was really there, she had really found me. I had come to think of the East Village and the West Bronx as two different dimensions of the universe — how was it possible for a being who belonged to that dimension to suddenly be incarnate in this?

I fell into her arms.

"Mother!"

I wept and wept, and as she hugged me, pressing me to the stomach that was once my home, you were between us, little one, we both felt you, and when we finally drew apart Elisa's eyes were moist, too. She nodded.

"I sensed you needed me," she said.

I was nonplussed. I had never heard her say a thing like that. No one in our family believed in telepathy — we scarcely believed in empathy! Every man for himself . . . Then I grew suspicious. My body stiffened against her and I felt you stir in response, Tom Thumb. What was she doing here? Had Joanna dared to betray my whereabouts? But no, she must have done her own research, for I hadn't been in touch with Joanna since leaving the Bowery.

Mother. Lots more grey in her hair. (She was five years younger then than I am now . . .) But only softness in her eyes. I relaxed . . . then stiffened again: *too much* softness? *Grandmotherly* softness, perchance? Cloying, frilly, smelling of talcum powder and prayer? Was she intimating that she would help me through the pregnancy, then adopt the child once it was born? Was she suggesting that I allow God to go through with His plans?

No.

We sat down together at the purple plastic coffee table, the only table Martin and I owned, and had tea. Conversation was awkward but I was inexplicably glad to see her. Glad and relieved. I told her about the three short stories I had published; she beamed and said, "I know." I flushed with pleasure.

"Does Ronald know you're here?" I had to ask.

"No. I swear it."

"You don't need to swear . . . How's Joanna? How are Jimbo and the boys?"

(Even now, whereas they're pushing forty, we still call Sammy and Stevie "the boys".)

"Everyone's fine, we're all fine . . . apart from Ronald's drinking, of course."

Elisa actually winked at me. Again I was staggered. When I was living at home, she had never so much as acknowledged that Ronald had a drinking problem. Was it because I'd become a woman in the meantime?

"How did you find me?"

She named the magazine in which my short stories had appeared. A friend of hers had seen my name (with the *i* still in it) on the cover. Elisa had looked up the magazine in the phone book and claimed — yes, lying! Elisa! telling a deliberate untruth! — to be a photographer interested in doing my portrait. They had given her my address.

We laughed like schoolgirls at her clever trick.

Then Mother suddenly grew serious.

"How far along are you?" she asked — and, without warning, I burst into tears again.

"Nearly three months. I've been trying . . . "

I could not finish my sentence.

"To get an abortion?"

A fresh shock. It was the first time the word had been pronounced, and to think it was Elisa who had pronounced it — devout, all-suffering, self-abnegating Elisa! Martin and I used certain euphemisms and the sordid angel-makers used others, but no one said *abortion*, which means, literally, to compel that which was rising to set. From *ab + oriri*. To force the Orient to Occident, the East to West, to push people off the edge of this world, into the other world, the netherworld. *Occire*. To kill.

"Yes, Mother."

Crossing my arms over my protruding stomach, I bit my lower lip and repressed a sob. Suddenly I was four years old. I felt as if I hadn't seen my mother, been alone with her, really looked at her since the day she had mocked my bowing of the violin.

I will never forget what she did next. Reaching across the purple coffee table, detaching my hands from my stomach and pressing them to her cheeks, she looked gravely into my eyes and said, "Nadia, don't worry. I'll help you."

The Resurrection Sonata

X - The Miracle

Hélène is worried. She has heard nothing from Barbe since her anguished April visit. It is now late November. This silence cannot be a good sign.

Barnabé, who has devoted himself to fasting and vigil with ever-increasing ardour this winter, can now feel his physical strength beginning to wane. At the same time, his love of God intensifies, clarifies and sharpens. He allows his flesh to be invaded by the pure bliss of weakness, frequently kneeling all night long in prayer on his palliasse, forehead bent over clasped hands, unable to determine whether the tremors that run through him are of a spiritual or a corporeal nature. The dormitory is unheated and an icy wind whistles through the roof-tiles, but Barnabé, engrossed in prayer, his body trembling, is happy.

Christmas draws near.

One night in mid-December, as Barnabé is singing matins with the other monks — in a voice which, while still sweet, is thinner than it used to be — a diffuse blue light begins to seep and spread across the red wall of his eyelids. It has been months since his mother last appeared to him. Moved, he smiles and goes on singing. But this time the light does not rearrange itself, is not transmogrified as usual into the familiar maternal features; rather, it slides over him and into him like a warm liquid. And when it speaks he hears it, not with his ears, but with every pore of his skin.

"Your shadow is coming now — beware! Beware!"

It is Christmas Eve, the night on which cows converse together, foretelling the future — and human beings must avoid listening to them, on pain of hearing an evil fate predicted for themselves.

Jacques Meillat, in a better mood than usual, tells Barbe to go out and check the stables.

"Go see the doors are closed up tightly," he tells her, playfully whacking her on the behind as if to push her in the direction of the barn. "We must make sure the devil can't get in!"

Barbe goes out into the night — it is cold and diamond-hard; she has not taken her cape, and walking across the courtyard she shudders violently. She does not raise her eyes to the starry sky but keeps them trained upon the ground, for fear of stumbling on a stone or a dead branch and falling flat on her face. Her feet carry her with difficulty, her entire body hurts; she feels compressed and cramped, on the verge of exploding.

When she reaches the stable, one of the cows bellows in surprise, making her start in turn. And, immediately afterwards, she feels the first pain. She freezes in the dark, eyes wide. The thing pulls, pulls at her entrails, then gradually releases its grip.

So this is it. So it is to be tonight — her child will arrive on Christmas Eve, just like the Baby Jesus. Suddenly Barbe's heart stops beating and she is submerged by a naked, icy, unspeakable fear. Where can she go? How will she ever elude the obligation to attend midnight Mass? The whole household is going off to church together, in several carriages . . . Panic-stricken, she drops to her knees on the frozen ground.

"Please, dear Lord — help me!" she murmurs, clenching her teeth to keep them from chattering. "Answer me, I beg You! I can't bear it any longer. Protect me and my child. Take us into Your hands."

And at last God deigns to answer her. At last Barbe hears His voice. He explains to her that, far from overlooking her predicament, He has arranged things this way on purpose, so that the child could be born while the others were off at church.

"Trust Me," He tells her. "I am here. I shall not abandon you, either you or your son."

Relieved, Barbe crosses herself and stands up. Stops, stiffens — the second pain. Waits for it to end.

"You certainly took your time," says Jacques Meillat, still jocundly, when she returns. "I hope you weren't chatting with the black ox, now, were you, my girl? That one sure knows how to talk up young ladies, and he doesn't always choose the prettiest ones, either — not by any means! My

word, you look as if you *had* just seen the devil —
you're white as a sheet!"

"Yes, Sir . . . Excuse me, Sir," stammers Barbe.
"I went out without my cape, I think I must have
caught cold . . . Please may I keep to my bed
tonight? I feel all whichways."

"People don't catch cold just like that, in a
matter of seconds!"

Third pain. Meillat sees the young woman's
features distorted by the inner agony. He frowns,
puts a hand on her forehead . . .

"Hm! You do seem to have a bit of a fever.
Well, all right. You can go lie down for a while. But
it would be nice if you'd lay the midnight supper
table for our return."

"Yes, Sir."

Curled up on her palliasse in a corner of the bedroom, eyes closed, Barbe listens to the other maidservants getting ready for church. Tittle-tattle,
mocking compliments on dresses and hairdos,
bursts of laughter. Even Mrs. Roger's voice, repeatedly admonishing the girls to hurry up, is more
jovial than usual. Barbe listens to all this as if from
a great distance. The thing pulls, pulls at her
entrails, a little harder every time. A moan escapes
her lips, but no one notices. No one is paying her
any attention.

Finally they leave the room. They descend the
staircase, still jabbering, and Barbe hears the large
front door of the house swing shut. Silence. She is
alone. Her terror returns. Drops of sweat stand out

on her forehead. But she has God's word. How could God not keep His word?

Not here.

It must not take place here.

Though she has never attended the delivery of a woman, she has seen cows, sows and she-goats giving birth: she knows there is blood, sometimes a lot of blood.

Wait, little Barnabé, wait for your mamma. Everything will be all right.

The pain takes hold of her, serious and inexorable. Each time it returns, its clench is longer and deeper.

Did the Virgin Mary endure these same pangs? Why does the Gospel never mention them? This can't be much less painful than what Jesus went through on the cross . . . Oh, it's a mortal sin to think such thoughts. Forgive me, God, forgive me, don't be angry . . .

Her thoughts spin in her head, she feels sick, she must get hold of herself, go downstairs.

She ties on her shoes, then, rising to her feet with difficulty, undoes her bandages, laying bare her stomach and looking at it at last — white, swaying, enormous, impressive. At the idea that, whatever happens, a human being must come out of there within the next few hours, fresh waves of nausea wash over her. Her knees shake uncontrollably.

Come, little Barnabé, she says to herself, perspiring. We must get out of the house. I know it's cold as death outside, but we'll go into the stable, it'll be just like Baby Jesus, we'll have the animals to keep us warm and everything will be all right, you'll see . . . Come now, off we go.

She talks to give herself courage. Carrying the released weight of her stomach in both hands, she goes down the hall in spurts, lurching forward a few steps, stopping when the pain seizes her and hanging onto the balustrade, head thrown back, eyes squinting at the ceiling, all her features screwed up in a spasm of pain. In the staircase, she loses her footing and nearly falls. Recovers her balance with a cry of fear that echoes across the empty vestibule.

The dogs, lying next to the kitchen stove, bark twice or thrice in their sleep and relapse into silence.

At the door, another flash of panic — the doorknob sticks. Horror — have they locked her in? But no — suddenly she is outside. Set free, in the free air — like her stomach just now — like her baby, soon, soon.

Yes, Barnabé, let me set you free . . .

She hurtles across the courtyard — unkempt, reeling, wild. Yes, I know the stables are supposed to stay closed tonight, but God will protect me, God will protect us both, little one — look, we'll go all the way to the back, there, against the wall, where there's a beautiful ray of moonlight, come quickly now!

Letting out a loud groan, almost a sob, she falls to her knees on the hard earth, carrying her stomach full of pain.

"Please, God, give me a sign! Only let me sense Your presence and I promise to be strong!"

And once again, God assents. He allows Barbe to hear the sublime *Vespers to the Virgin* which the monks of Orsan priory are singing at this very moment, to the accompaniment of organs and trumpets.

Barbe listens, transfixed, and is suddenly suffused by a strange calm.

"Thank you, dear God," she murmurs in relief.

Dixit Dominus, Domino meo — sede a dextris meis. Donec ponam inimico, tuos, scabellum pedum tuorum — the voices transpierce her, transport her, they are angels' voices and Barbe is wafted up with them into the sky, she is weightless, her back pressed up against the rough boards of the stall, her knees bent and spread apart, she looks upward and strains, strains to hear — *Laudate, pueri, Dominum: laudate nomen Domini. Sit nomen Domini benedictum, ex hoc nunc et usque in sæculum* — the pain transpierces her, the lightning-bolt transpierces her, the voices transpierce her, she is torn apart with happiness, weeping with happiness, soon she will go to meet her Maker with little Barnabé in her arms, yes the twins, Barnabé and Barbe, one baby in each arm, she is larger than herself, larger than the barn, larger than the village, she is the Earth itself, quaking, splitting, heaving, burning, exploding, disgorging its boiling lava, now the water sac has burst, a boiling geyser spews forth from her innards and Barbe listens to the angels' trumpets, straining and ecstatic, head thrown back, hands squeezing her knees, she grunts with joy, at her side the cows have wakened, they are talking amongst themselves and Barbe can make out what they are saying, at last she understands their language — *Nisi Dominus ædificaverit domum, in vanum labouraverunt qui ædificant eam* — yes, at last she understands all, all, and even were the black ox to appear it would make no difference, no, for there is nothing left to fear, the devil is none other than God Himself — all, all, is God, and so is she, yes, she is part of this same irrepressible, tumultuous energy and nothing can ever do her harm again, she is omnipotent with these golden notes resounding in her breast, her stomach rolling and thundering, her blood dripping out onto the straw, her hair bathed in sweat, she cries out for joy and the cows low softly in response, yes, for they too know that they are all, that they are God, that the Divine Child is born — ah! Barbe understands at long last, how can it have taken her so long to understand — *Lauda Jerusalem, Dominum: lauda Deum tuum, Sion. Quoniam confortavit seras portarum tuarum: benedixit filiis tuis in te* — all women are Mary . . .

At the final extravagant ecstatic heave, all resistance yields, a black mass of flesh is projected from between her legs, Barbe catches it just in time with both hands, the mass is slippery, she clasps it against her and collapses in the straw, annihilated with bliss.

"Thank you, dear God," she repeats.

For a while, the heavenly vaults continue to wheel wildly in her head. Then she feels the sticky mass stir against her chest.

"My darling boy . . . "

She holds it up a little distance away from her and tries to see it. A cloud must have partially covered the moon, for she can make out almost nothing in the weak gleam that filters through the crack between the planks . . .

Sees, however, that it is a boy. Tiny, strangely twisted, nearly hunch-backed, shoulders raised, head wobbling.

Sees that it is breathing unevenly.

Sees the bloodstains on her own hands, holding it.

They are still attached to one another. Grasping the cord between her lips — quickly, so as not to have time to be afraid — she sinks her teeth into it. To her own astonishment, she severs it in a single bite.

"You see, love?" she says proudly to the child. "Your mamma can do just about anything, can't she?"

A new pain takes her unawares. At first, feeling the wrenching upheaval begin all over again, she thinks it must indeed be twins, and that she will die.

But no. It is only the afterbirth.

"There, angel. The worst is over now. Listen darling, could you wait here for me — I'll only be a moment."

Setting the child in the straw, stomach-down on the placenta so it will not be cold, she rises to her feet, totters — no, this won't work, she cannot stand up yet — gets down on all fours, then, like a beast — yes, all of us are beasts — the Virgin Mary too, God too — come on, God, let's go — and crawls away . . .

Finds, at the entrance to the barn, a pointed stone.

Returns to the child's side, still on all fours, and starts scratching at the earth. Barnabé, his skin mottled in the moonlight, shudders and lets out a tiny moan.

"Don't worry, angel!" says Barbe in a soothing, maternal voice. "I know it's chilly but this won't take long. Be patient! You're always in such a hurry! I'm your mamma, you should trust me, I know what's best . . . "

The stream of words has started to flow again. Barbe is happy. She digs feverishly, joyfully.

"Almost ready, sweet one. I'm making up your bed. You'll see, my poppet. Sheets embroidered with my own hands, cushions soft as clouds, curtains of pure tulle — it'll be the loveliest cradle in the world, a cradle worthy of a prince — and it's all for you, all for you . . . "

The earth is hard but Barbe is still omnipotent, she knows exactly the depth and shape of the hole she needs, her fingers scrabble in the dirt, wielding the sharp stone with dexterity, one would think she had worked all her life as a gravedigger, her eyes widen in contentment as the hole grows larger, and at last she announces,

"There. It's ready. You see? It didn't take that long."

When she picks the child up again, its tiny body is limp.

"Ah! So you've already fallen asleep, have you? You little rascal! Couldn't even wait to see the nice bed Mamma made for you? Well, come then, come . . . Oh yes, love, I know you must be tired. You go ahead and take a nap now — and then, as soon as you wake up, we'll go pay a visit to your uncle. All right, my little Barnabé?"

Very gently, Barbe lays the infant on the flat bottom of the hole. It remains inert when she removes her hands from its body. Its head falls to one side. She leans forward and kisses the odd, bulging forehead, then sets about covering it with earth, beginning with the knobby feet and legs. Yes — without for an instant ceasing to speak to it, she buries her baby.

"There, you see? This way you won't be cold anymore. That's better, now, isn't it? They're real woollen blankets, son — I spun the wool myself, all winter long, thinking of you, dreaming of you . . . "

She scatters the last handful of earth on the baby's head. Sees one of its ears sticking out. Covers it with straw. Wipes her hands on a flap of skirt. Then drags herself over to the door, grabbing onto the choir stalls for balance, bowing to the Three Wise Men as she passes them, accepting their homage with a gracious, modest nod of her head — yes, the miracle has taken place, yes, the Divine Child is born . . .

She bursts out into the courtyard.

The sweet seraphic voices of the monks in Orsan Chapel continue to resound, vibrating against one another, weaving and intertwining in the air beneath the dome of her skull before they rise, floating, up to Heaven . . .

"Thank you, dear God," says Barbe for the third time.

Pulling off the bloody rags that still hang about her body, she drops them in a heap in a corner of the garden, then reenters the house at last, naked as a worm, her skin streaked with mud and dung.

She hears the clatter of the carriages bringing the others home — masters and servants who have communicated together, celebrated the birth of the Messiah together, yet understood nothing . . . while she, Barbe, knows all, understands all, *ex hoc nunc et usque in sæculum* . . .

But she has not the strength to climb the staircase.

So she waits in the drawing-room — naked, neutral, absent, leaning against the mantelpiece. In the hearth, tiny flames are still licking at the embers of last night's fire.

The *Scordatura* Notebook

Lake House, July 13th

Thank you, dear dæmon.

Oh, don't mention it.

I came up here to try to write about the abortion and . . . got side-tracked. Seriously side-tracked.

Can't believe it actually happened. But then, there's no valid reason it should not have.

Mr. Harley. I know his first name is Peter but I've been calling him Mr. Harley for so many years that Peter is impossible. He's never been anything more than a good neighbour, someone I could count on to lend me a fuse or a pair of hedge-clippers, and to keep an eye on the house when I'm away in the city. One winter a few years ago we ran into each other on the lake — both of us had gone out for a walk at sunrise, before the snowmobiles arrived, and that was the only time we ever talked. I learned he was a retired post office employee. Wife long dead, kids scattered across the continent, I don't remember where. (I usually don't listen too closely anymore, to new people. I've heard too many life stories and I tend to avoid them now, lest they invade me like rats, nibbling at my few remaining brain cells, drinking off the dregs of my

emotional energy . . .) You must be lonesome, I probably said to him, distractedly.

He is seventy at least. A good prospect for
Stella, not for me. But why must I be ironic — what
does "good prospect" mean? He's alive and I'm
alive, for as long as our bodies hold out. That's
what it's all about.

you do the hoochie-coochie
and you turn yourself around,
that's what it's all about — hey!

So we did the hoochie-coochie.

It was the first really hot day of the year and
our houses were stifling, he was sitting out on his
porch after lunch and I was sitting out on mine,
our porches are about seventy-five yards apart but
we started a conversation anyway, yelling back
and forth about the vacationers' motorboats which
we hate as much as the snowmobiles, and then he
came over to tell me about this pick-up truck that
went through the ice last winter. A large and rather
grungy Massachusetts crowd had parked it plunk
in the middle of the lake, then set up a picnic table
and chairs and built a nice bonfire and cooked a
whole pig over it and spent the afternoon guzzling
beer and gorging themselves on roast pig, but as
luck would have it their fire was just a bit too close
to the truck and the temperature had not quite
gone down to freezing the night before . . . Cracks,
screams, shifting blocks of ice — the revellers managed to scramble to safety but their truck and table

and chairs and pig-bones all sank in a slow whirling whoosh to the bottom of the lake.

Mr. Harley told me the story with one foot propped up on my deck steps; he told it so well that by the end my stomach hurt from laughing so I felt I should invite him in for a glass of iced tea. Then somehow one thing led to another, and I still can hardly believe it, and he actually apologized when he left and promised it would never happen again.

He was scared. I could sense it the minute his hand grazed my cheek, my lips — scared that I would reject him, make fun of him, or that his body might refuse to obey. (Whereas *we* used to be so scared of *them*! Joanna and I in the streets of Lower Manhattan, a couple of skinny frivolous teenagers continually being approached by forty- and forty-five-year-old men with angry erections in their pants, desperate to get laid. It is all a matter of time. Those men are now Mr. Harley's age . . . Ah, the disconcerting rapidity with which frightening older men turn into frightened old men!)

I was moved almost to tears. The same emotion as at the cocktail party last month — that we're all alive, and all dying. So strange to see fragility, awkwardness and self-consciousness introduced into the world of eroticism, which one had always thought of as the world of wild abandon and wild invention. His gnarled fingers shakily undoing the buttons of my shirt. Embarrassed by his clumsiness, or by his arousal, he blushed and I could see his whole pate reddening through his sparse white hair, even the age-spots turning ruddy.

There was also my own boniness, my incipient sagginess, the scars on my back and stomach where dubious-looking moles used to sit — we carry our histories with us . . . so I closed my eyes. What was happening between Mr. Harley and myself, I thought, was not intended to be seen, not even by ourselves. Sex, perhaps, is a visual thing only for young bodies.

Sheer amazing sensation, on the living room rug, as the afternoon light gradually smouldered and intensified.

It was nearly six by the time I finally made our iced tea, spiking it with whisky to facilitate the return of language. But we really didn't know what to say to each other — and so, shortly afterwards, still blushing, apologizing, Mr. Harley returned home.

The subject at hand.

Yes. Sorry The subject at hand. Oh, it's not that earth-shaking, really. It hardly even makes a story. It can by no means be construed as the climax of my existence. Simply, by whatever miracle, my mother walked into my life at exactly the right moment and took charge of the murder of my son.

She phoned her cousin Charlotte, who was an obstetrician in Chicago. Explained the situation to her in the firmest of voices. Set up an appointment for the following week. Made plane reservations for the two of us. I had never seen her behave this way before — like an autonomous adult. It was as if she had suddenly reverted to her pre-marital personality, recovered her ability to take initiatives, make decisions, look after logistics . . . But what about God? I couldn't help asking myself. Wasn't Elisa worried about abetting a mortal sin?

We had to wait nearly a week. I remember our departure was scheduled for a Wednesday, and in the interval Elisa displayed an astonishing capacity for deceit. She would come down to Saint Mark's Place every day and we'd spend hours talking, walking, not only catching up on each other's news but discovering one another as women for the first time. Towards the end of the afternoon she'd take the subway back up to the Bronx, get supper ready for Stevie and Sammy and Ronald ("It's lonesome, being the only woman in the household," she confessed), and welcome them home as if she'd spent the whole day ironing and watching television.

On Tuesday, she let me in on her plan. My Martin was to call that evening, pretending to be Charlotte's husband Bill. Ronald always answered the phone (he insisted on monitoring everyone else's calls), but as he'd never heard Martin's voice there should be no problem. He would call Elisa to the phone and "Bill" would inform her that Charlotte had had a heart attack, she might not pull through, she was begging to see her favourite cousin one last time . . . could Elisa come to Chicago?

Thus it was that we found ourselves in a taxi headed for La Guardia Airport, the first and last trip we ever took together, just the two of us.

Chicago was murderously hot and muggy, it was by now the beginning of July and when we emerged from O'Hare into the blasting heat and humidity I thought I would faint. You didn't like it either, did you, Tom Thumb? You squirmed inside of me and I grabbed onto my mother's arm . . . Oh, she took such good care of me that day! Until then I'd never been fully convinced that she loved me, but now there was no room left for doubt. "Relax, dear," she said as we hailed another taxi. "It'll all be over in a few hours, you needn't worry anymore." And she gave the driver the address of her cousin's clinic in one of the cushier suburbs of the city.

At the clinic she continued to behave calmly and, as it were, professionally. I could not stop staring at her, open-mouthed. Charlotte met us in the lobby — a woman of about her age, brisk, crisp, yet warm — and the two cousins embraced. Then Charlotte took both my hands in hers. Then we were in the elevator, the three of us, the four of us. And then at last, at last, we were in a tiny stuffy room with the Venetian blinds pulled down — the room of your demise, little Tom.

Mercifully, Charlotte extinguished the light in my brain. (Into what netherworld did my self then slide? If I have a soul, where did it go? Did it join you, little one, outside of life, outside of consciousness? Did it descend into my entrails and await your destruction with you there?) While I was gone, the two cousins, the two witches, deployed their know-how — bravely, serenely transgressing a sacred tenet of their own religion and a sacred law of the United States of America. Elisa handed

Charlotte the instruments she needed as she went along and regularly checked to see if I was still bleeding, I mean still breathing, they did not cut me open with a scalpel, I sustained no scars from this operation, at least not on my body, they were extremely deft at extracting my quasi-son, my proto-son, my would-be son, my wouldn't-be son from his abode, his dark cave, gently cutting off his supply of oxygen-giving blood, then wrapping him in tissue-paper and flushing him down the toilet — an inglorious burial for you indeed, Tom Thumb, Elisa's first grandchild, tumbling head over heels amidst excrement and dishwater through the pipes of the Chicago sewage system, to be unceremoniously spat a few hours later into Lake Michigan — yes, such was the outcome of the inadvertent encounter in New York City of one of Martin Schuller's hyperactive spermatozoids with one of my fat eggs.

I read in the paper the other day that Pope John Paul II, who has been holding back his spermatozoids so long that they must have gone to his brain, decrees you should have been given Christian baptism and burial.

What do you think of that, Tom Thumb?

The seventeenth-century French witch-hunter Pierre de Lancre explained that "God often allows Satan to kill [non-baptised babies] . . . because, having foreseen the enormous sins they were destined to commit had they lived, God did not wish them to acquire a more serious damnation, and thus we have not the right to complain that God is cruel or unjust, as for Original Sin alone they merited death" (*Tableau de l'inconstance des mauvais anges et démons*, p. 139).

What do you think of that, Tom Thumb? Do you believe that Satan asked God's permission to kill you and God said "Sure!" Would you really have become such a dreadful sinner?

Nowadays people tend to claim just the opposite: "That baby you nipped in the bud might have become a great artist, a genius, a messiah!" Either Hitler or Mozart — is that our choice? Of course not. Aborted babies are just plain folks. Who don't "merit death" any more or any less than the rest of us. Who get it, though. Smack in the face. Real early.

Yes, Tom Thumb, I admit it. I took away your chances — for happiness, for unhappiness. *That's the way it is.* (Sorry, sweetheart. But your death was far less tragic than that of Stella's Andrew.)

You'd be twenty-seven years old by now, had I let you live. A dizzying thought.

When I came to, Charlotte had left the room and Elisa was sitting next to my bed, holding my hand and stroking my forehead.

"How do you feel?" she asked in a very tender voice.

"Like hell," I whispered.

It was true. I was nauseous, and there was an ache that ran from one end to the other of my innermost being.

The dream did not begin until after my return to New York.

Martin wanted me to be stoical. I found it obscene to be stoical about the elimination of another human life.

"For heaven's sake, Nada," he said, "God does it all the time!" Martin was a militant atheist, but he suspected I'd regressed to the superstitions of my childhood and was writhing in Catholic guilt. "What's more, He does it cavalierly, nonchalantly, without batting an eyelash! He snuffs out human lives every second of every day, for no reason whatsoever. Embryos, infants, toddlers, men and women in their prime — He doesn't give a shit!"

"But we have to be *better* than God," I insisted between clenched teeth. "We have to *justify* our murders. God is a crazed, immoral serial killer who answers to no one."

When you started appearing to me at night, I told Martin about it and he simply scoffed. "How can you be so upset about a person who doesn't exist?" He did not believe it was really *you*, Tom Thumb, tapping at the window of my life. Why didn't you appear to him, too? Why didn't you torture him, too? After all, he was your father — exactly as responsible for your creation and your annihilation as I was. Several months passed before we began to quarrel seriously, another year before we had gone through enough ripping and reconciling to become indifferent . . . But his flippant dismissal of your nocturnal visits was the beginning of the end.

Of *course* you don't exist! You're a ghost, and ghosts don't exist, I know that, everybody knows that. But the greater part of human passions has always revolved around non-existent beings — Jehovah, Beelzebub, Shiva, Isis, Damballah, the Virgin Mary, Hercules, the Great Gatsby, Madame Bovary, the Blue Fairy, my twin brother, my angel son, Sabina my dearest friend, Stella's son Andrew and her husband Jack . . . All these imaginary entities thrive and throb within us, act upon us, influence our moods and our behaviour . . . *Les morts sont les invisibles, mais ils ne sont pas les absents* . . . How can anyone be so stupid as to think they don't *matter*? (Pardon me for saying so, Tom Thumb, but your father was truly, spectacularly stupid. Imagine believing in Discourse but not in ghosts!)

One need not *be* matter to matter. You matter a great deal to me, my darling. And I apologize for calling you a beetle, in the first pages of this notebook.

The Resurrection Sonata

XI - The Trial

The music has stopped. A vast white silence blooms and spreads throughout Barbe's head.

The women reenter the house before the men, who are putting the horses and carriages away — Mrs. Roger the cook is the first to glance into the drawing-room, and to see.

A cry escapes her. Her hands go up to her cheeks, slide together and press hard against her lips.

The other maidservants come running — then, braking suddenly, jostle one another at the door of the room. After a moment of baffled silence, they start to giggle nervously at the sight of this thing, this Barbe who is not the Barbe they had left a few hours before — this naked, filthy, incomprehensible body with its slack sagging stomach, its blood-stained legs, its gaunt and staring face . . . it is too much.

Mrs. Roger, to whom the body is not incomprehensible, rushes to the young woman's side.

"Where is the child?" she asks in a low, urgent voice.

Very slowly, Barbe turns to look at her. Recognizes her. Someone from here below. Her eyes light up; a shy smile parts her lips.

"I . . . I left it in the garden," she murmurs. "Over in the corner, next to the wall, to protect it from the wind. You see, it wanted to be out of doors for the twelfth stroke of midnight — when the stones rise up, revealing hidden treasures."

"But . . . "

Hearing the Meillat brothers come in, Mrs. Roger hastily removes her own coat and throws it over the young woman's shoulders.

"Was it stillborn?" she asks in a whisper.

"No, no, it gave a cry — it's a nice, strapping boy! Everything's fine, only it didn't feel like coming into the house right away. There were so many stars in the sky — and such beautiful music playing, too — we listened to it together. Never in my life have I heard anything so beautiful . . . "

Mrs. Roger pales.

"Poor girl," she breathes.

Frowning, she turns to the other maidservants and motions fiercely for them to be gone. The girls scuttle off. Their excited babbling can still be heard in the staircase when the Meillat brothers enter the drawing-room.

"What's going on?" demands Jacques. He is hungry and angry — the table, he sees, has not been laid.

He receives no answer. Seeing the young woman dishevelled and trembling in the cook's arms, he repeats threateningly, "What's going on?" Still no answer. Sylvain has an idea.

"Was someone here while we were out? Has she been violated?"

"No," says Mrs. Roger, jaws clenched, eyes on the floor. "No. What happened is, she . . . she had . . . a baby."

The final word all but inaudible.

The men are astonished; but following hard on the heels of their astonishment is indignation — their cousin Marguerite has hoodwinked them but well. They grind their teeth in rage.

"So she was a harlot after all. Ha! I'm not surprised. I even suspected as much. And where's her bastard?"

"She says . . . she left it outside, in the garden."

"*In the garden?* In this cold? Good God, she's not only a harlot — she's off her head as well!"

Each of them seizes a candle and one of Barbe's arms, and they yank her out of the house with them, into the courtyard.

"Where? Where is it? Where did you leave it?"

"Over there, over there . . . "

Both her arms being gripped by the infuriated men, Barbe can only motion with her head. Her teeth clatter with the cold, but otherwise she is calm. Swearing under their breath, Jacques and Sylvain drag the young woman over to the garden wall, throw her to the ground in disgust and start rummaging about in the heap of bloody clothes.

Nothing.

"*Where is it?*"

"I left it right there, I swear . . . It wanted to look at the stars."

Barbe pulls Mrs. Roger's rough cloak more closely around her body, she is trembling but her voice is low and her eyes are dry. She will never weep again. She is with God.

"What did you do with your goddamn bastard, you whore?"

They pick Barbe up and shake her.

"She's a crazy drab, I told you so from the start."

"You didn't tell me a bloody thing."

"What in God's name has she done with her bastard, damn her to hell?"

The Meillat brothers are terrified. Unbaptized dead babies are dangerous, everyone knows that. Their souls are impure, tainted by their mother's original sin, and since they have not been buried in holy ground they can find no rest — they wander ceaselessly around the place of their birth, attacking the living . . . It is a calamity.

"Where did you put it, bitch? Did you eat it or what?"

"No, I'll bet you she cut it into little pieces, to use it for making philtres and unguents. Didn't you, you bloody witch?"

The moon casts ghastly shadows on the men's faces, distorted by fear.

"Where did you put it?"

Christmas is a day of dazzling light and freezing cold. Barbe spends the entire day sleeping, alone in her corner of the maidservants' bedroom. The other girls avoid her as if she had the plague. The Meillat brothers let her sleep at the insistence of Mrs. Roger — who, though her own three sons are already grown, has not forgotten what it is like to give birth.

There is no longer any question of Christmas dinner — the baby must be found. The whole village takes part in the search, masters and servants alike, to say nothing of the dogs. They look everywhere — scouring not only the house and grounds but the surrounding fields, vineyards, orchards, riverbanks.

They do not find Barbe's baby. Neither that day nor the next, nor any other day. As dogs are not allowed inside the stables, for fear they might sour or dry up the cows' milk, and as Barbe's grave-digging job was impeccably neat and clean, no one will ever discover the little straw-covered tomb.

The accusations of witchcraft rise and sharpen. The day after Christmas, Jacques Meillat goes to the lord's estate and denounces the young woman for concealment of pregnancy and infanticide.

Barbe is in prison in La Chaume, locked up with thieves and prostitutes in the women's common cell. Rapidly brought up to date on the affair, the good people of La Chaume resent this unnatural mother for bringing danger into their midst — they throng about the prison, shouting insults at her, venting their rage and fear.

Barbe remains serene. She is filled with confidence because little Barnabé is with her, he lives nestled up against her skin — like Tom Thumb hidden away in the ogre's wife's pocket — Barbe talks to him continually and God watches over them both.

Everyone else, however, interprets Barbe's serenity as sinister indifference, not to say diabolical cynicism. The judge recalls famous cases of witches who concocted taciturnity powders by burning in their ovens, among other unspeakable things, upbaptized newborn boys: criminals who had rubbed even the tiniest quantity of this powder into their skins would refuse to confess, remaining miraculously silent even when put to the Extraordinary Question.

From morning to night, Barbe is interrogated with brutality by men she has never seen before, men who can understand nothing of her experience, ventripotent bearded men in black robes: prosecutor, priest, doctor, lawyer — and, last but not least, the judge. Day after day, she is asked the same questions, and she frames her answers so as to protect the life of her son.

"What did you do with your child?"

"Oh! It can scarcely be called a child, it was no longer than a finger . . . "

"Is it true you left it outside in the cold?"

"Yes, Milord, but only long enough to run and search for help . . . "

"Did you pour water on it at birth?"

"No, Milord, for it was dead."

"And yet you told Mrs. Roger it had cried out?"

"I didn't know what I was saying . . . I was beside myself . . . When I saw that it was dead . . . "

"Why had you not made your pregnancy known?"

" . . . "

"You do attend Mass every Sunday?"

"Yes, Milord."

"Then four times yearly ever since you learned the use of speech, you have heard the priest read from the pulpit the decree of Henry II concerning the concealment of pregnancy and childbirth?"

" . . . "

"Where is the child?"

"I don't know."

The interrogations are annoying, repetitive, interminable — and yet Barbe remains calm. She prays to God and God hears her, accedes to her every request. She feels strong — so much stronger than ten years earlier, when the inhabitants of Torchay had turned upon her in hatred. The questions surround and penetrate her, they are like moles digging tunnels into her heart, into the depths of her past. Despite the affection she still feels for Marguerite, she finally consents to name the child's father — Simon Guersant, known as Donat. In a dry, even tone of voice, giving as few details as possible, she describes the circumstances in which the latter thrice abused her — first the marital bed, then the goatshed, and finally the mud puddle in front of the barn. She describes the day of her departure, the couple's quarrel, Marguerite beating her husband over the head with a stick. She quotes the figure five, five maidservants whom this same man had gotten with child over the past twenty years. Then she falls silent. Prays to God. Begs Him to keep Marguerite from despising her as the others do.

The trial drags on. The Guersants, husband and wife, are summoned and questioned. Deeply affected, Marguerite confirms Barbe's version of the facts, but Simon Guersant calmly and smilingly denies the whole thing. Never has he touched this woman or even been tempted to do so; never once have any of his maidservants been pregnant, either by his doing or by that of another man — one need only question those who know him well. Donat's friends and neighbours are brought in, men with whom he has been working and drinking for years. All remember his love affair with Marie Bourdeaux, the little miller's wife, and all are careful to avoid mentioning it — including Marie's own widower André, who has just remarried. All testify to Donat's good conduct — the more praiseworthy that his wife never gave him a child, and it would not have been surprising to see him fickle. Several, on the other hand, remember the suspicious behaviour of Barbe Durand — the way she used to get up before sunrise and go off to gather herbs in the woods, most likely for the fabrication of poisons . . . Oh, yes, it had not taken them long to guess she was a witch . . . Indeed, amongst themselves, they'd always thought Marguerite's persistent barrenness must be due to her servant's evil eye . . . And then there was the story of little Philippe — yes, yes, you remember, two or three years ago — a perfectly healthy little boy who had upped and died after seeing a mouse — even then, they had figured the mouse must have been a witch's familiar — and who else if not that strange, skinny silent girl who worked for the Guersants? Yes, she must have been trying her hand at infanticide already, they'd thought as much at the time but they hadn't had sufficient proof . . . No, they hadn't mentioned it to the village priest, either, for the latter was a thoroughgoing scoundrel who kept the whole parish in a thrall of fear; it had been months since anyone dared confess to him . . .

The witnesses get carried away by the sound of their own voices. As the trial proceeds and Barbe's subterranean history ramifies, one mole-tunnel leading to another, more and more clues are unearthed that point to the twisted, evil nature of the accused. What was she doing in Sainte-Solange in the first place? They had warned Marguerite not to take a perfect stranger into the house — but Marguerite was Marguerite; she did whatever came into her head, and she had refused to listen when they told her to beware of this Barbe. Where had she come from, anyway? They'd never been able to find out.

"Do *you* know, Mrs. Guersant? Where did the prisoner reside before her arrival in Sainte-Solange?"

Without daring to look in Barbe's direction, Marguerite blushes and murmurs that the young woman once mentioned having friends in the town of Torchay.

An inquiry is carried out in Torchay and fresh witnesses are brought to the stand. Hélène, when she hears of Barbe Durand's trial, fairly suffocates with rage — with fear, too, for the young woman she cherishes — but, being ill and bedridden, it is out of the question for her to make the voyage to La Chaume. Despite the absence of this key witness, numerous other members of the parish, both male and female, are more than willing to appear before the judge. They describe to him the day the young girl first appeared in their midst — out of nowhere, like something not quite human . . . Ah, yes, well do they remember her eccentric ways, her habit of going to church alone early in the morning — what was she up to? Some sort of blasphemy, that's for sure, since God's wrath was eventually visited upon her.

Proofs accumulate, feelings rise, the inhabitants of Torchay recall that something happened in the woods at the edge of town, one day when Barbe Durand and Jeanne Denis were out picking strawberries together — they don't know exactly what it was, but it had something to do with spells — perhaps the stranger had made a first attempt on young Jeanne's life that day — "the very daughter of the woman who'd taken her into her home!" exclaim the witnesses, glad that Hélène is not there to contradict them.

The people of Saint-Solange listen and nod their heads. Yes, they had always suspected as much . . .

And when the new witnesses get to the story of how the witch provoked a thunderstorm, and how Jeanne's body was found struck down by lightning, naked and brainless, cries of terror and anger ring out in the courtroom.

Finally, shortly after Carnival, Mrs. Raffinat, Little Robert's mother, comes to testify. Cheeks aflame with indignation, she recounts what her son has finally confessed to her, after an entire year of shame and silence — namely, that all last spring the hussy had shown herself naked to him at the window in her pregnant state, and caressed her own body in front of him, thus inciting him to fornicate with her, but Robert had remained virtuous depite all the sorceress's wiles, and despite the secret formulas she had pronounced to magically seal his lips, making him incapable of telling this to any human being, but only to his pigs, the magic having been so powerful that only yesterday had he succeeded in overcoming it, opening his heart to his mother — and she, the mother, had resolved to come and testify in lieu of her son, who, having not all his wits about him, Milord, would doubtless have gotten the tale all jimble-jumbled and confused.

Silence ensues; then an undescribable uproar breaks out in the courtroom. "Death! Death to the witch!" People jostle and trample one another in an effort to lay hands on the accused, strike her, spit in her face.

Barbe remains motionless, eyes closed, a sweet smile playing on her lips.

"Did you hear Mrs. Raffinat's testimony?"

"Yes, Milord."

"What have you to say in your defence?"

" . . . "

"Is it true that you bewitched her son the simpleton, doing all you could to entice him into lechery and sin?"

" . . . "

"I must warn you that every refusal to reply on your part will be recorded as an acquiescence."

Barbe nods, still smiling. She does not know what the word acquiescence means, but she is eager for all this to be done with; it is tiring and unpleasant for her little Tom Thumb to have to sleep in a cold cell, amidst the stench of bodies and excrement, and then spend long hours in this crowded, tumultuous courtroom . . . It is time the two of them recovered their freedom and set off together down the road. Barbe is convinced that her son will enjoy travelling, now that he has left her body. She wants to show him the wheat fields and the woods, teach him the names of flowers, mushrooms and birds — she is filled with joy at the prospect of sharing with him everything Hélène once taught her, and everything she has discovered, little by little, on her own.

Ah, yes! It's time to break away from this stifling atmosphere and get some fresh air! Spring is here, little one! Soon we'll be celebrating Easter — the death and resurrection of Our Lord Jesus Christ . . . Everything dies and everything is reborn — yes, you'll see! I'll take you to Hélène's inn at Torchay and her daughter Jeanne will be there, I want her to be your godmother, and the two of us will teach you how to dye Easter eggs using onion peels for yellow, violets for purple and sorrel for green — it's great fun, you'll see! We'll have a huge feast to celebrate our reunion, we'll stuff ourselves with roast kid and eggrolls, and then we'll all go dancing under the trees — they must be in blossom by now! Apple trees, pear trees, plum, quince, blackthorn — yes! tossing handfuls of petals into the air — come, come with me, my son! Let's get away from here!

A few days elapse. Finally, at the end of April, after an unusually long and dramatic trial, the verdict is handed down.

Simon Guersant, known as Donat, is sent away absolved. Applause breaks out in the courtroom; the atmosphere is festive.

As for Barbe Durand, her physical penalty is mentioned first, before the money penalty, whereas of course the opposite order will need to be respected in the actual unfolding of events — for, once hanged, strangled and burned, she would find it hard to pay the fine of two hundred pounds to the judge. The execution is to take place right here in La Chaume, on a market- or a fair-day. The exact date will be set in the near future.

To Barbe's ears, the words of her sentence are cumbersome and opaque. Only her ashes, which are to be scattered on the wind, enter her mind and mingle there with the flower blossoms, floating and fluttering beneath the trees. The rest remains at a distance and does not disturb her, does not impinge in the least on her certainty and joy.

The *Scordatura* Notebook

Perry Street, July 26

The first edition of Perrault's fairy tales was published in 1697, when Barbe was eleven years old. It contained the story of Tom Thumb, and as Perrault collected only the oldest and best-known tales of the oral tradition there is little doubt but that Barbe, though illiterate, would have been familiar with the story of the thumb-sized child. At her trial, she repeatedly insisted that her dead baby was no longer than a finger . . .

Come to think of it, the folk figures of Tom Thumb, Thumbelina and the like may have been no more nor less than the popular symbolization of all the little fetuses peasant women rid themselves of before they were ripe, and who returned to haunt them, taking up lodgings in their pockets and following them everywhere they went . . .

An amazing thing happened when I got home this afternoon. Little Sonya was playing on the stoop, throwing a ball up and down the steps. When she saw me her face lit up and she said, "Play with me." I almost looked back over my shoulder to make sure she didn't mean someone else. Me? Play with her? *Play?* How does one play? Plunking down my suitcase and portable computer on the walk, I bravely said, "Okay," and we started tossing the ball back and forth. I looked at her. Her eyes were absolutely blazing with excitement — just because I'd said okay, we could play ball together for a minute! She was standing at the top of the stairs. I'd throw the ball up to her; she'd miss it every single time and it would come bouncing back down the stairs and roll into the bushes; I'd climb over the little wire fence and bend down and scrabble around under the bushes looking for it, scratching my arms on the prickly branches; she'd scream with laughter; and then we'd start all over again. "Again! Again!" She was so happy she could scarcely contain herself. I asked her how old she was and she said, "Two and a half." Ah. So at two and a half one can already say one is two and a half? Then she asked me my name. We've been living in the same building since she was born and she didn't know my name. So I told her. "My name is Nadia," I said.

I decided to drive back to Manhattan today because I sensed that the worst was over, for Barbe and for myself, and that I could handle things from here on in.

Mustn't get too cocksure, my dear. You never know what I might have up my sleeve.

Hm! Haven't heard from you in a long time.

What on earth do you mean? I've been dictating to you for months!

Have you, now? How strange. I didn't sense that while I was writing. At least not all the time. Not even most of the time, these past weeks.

Don't forget I'm in charge of your sensations, too — the true ones and the false, illusion and accuracy, clairvoyance and ignorance — all this and more comes under my dominion. I am omnipotent.

Yeah, right. You know what, dæmon?

What?

I think you're about as omnipotent as one of my mother's Odd Socks.

Go ahead — joke, mock, insult me, I don't mind! Even your sense of humour comes from me; I am the supreme master of jokery as well. Nothing can hurt me.

You know what, dæmon?

What?

I need you about as much as I need an Odd Sock.

That is actually correct, because if you get rid of me you won't have a leg to stand on. You won't need socks or even shoes. What you'll need is a wheelchair.

Are you by any chance threatening me, dæmon?

How could I be bothered with such a piddly little activity as threatening human beings?

You know what, dæmon?

This dialogue is getting tedious. For the last time, what?

I think you need me more than I need you, that's what.

Later

Just had a long conversation with Stella. I called her because Hélène is ill and bedridden in the novel and . . . well . . . I thought I'd check up on her. She's fine. That is, she sounded a bit tense, anxious, depressed, harassed, whatever it is that all of us are most of the time and some of us are all of the time in this day and age — but her health is all right. She hasn't been taking more nitroglycerine tablets than usual.

Let me write it down here and have done with it: I'm afraid that if I kill Hélène in my *Resurrection Sonata*, Stella might die. It sounds preposterous, but it is true. And I wouldn't admit it to anyone alive.

What happened to Elisa after our trip to Chicago? She was so fresh and energetic and wide-awake during that whole period, as we plotted and carried out the murder of Tom Thumb. But the minute it was over, I relapsed into incommunication. I needed silence, solitude, difficulty. I felt that in order to write, I had to be cut off from my family (that age-old illusion of self-engendering).

I can't help wondering . . .

Go ahead, get it over with.

I can't help wondering — if I'd stayed in touch with her, would her destiny have changed? Would she have managed to stay awake? Would we have done things and gone places together? Might I have been able to bring her back to music, give her the courage to pick up her instrument and play again — *play, Mother, play?* Or did our unique, unprecedented intimacy at the time of Tom Thumb hinge entirely on our complicity in crime?

When Elisa went back to the Bronx and resumed her lifelong habits of prayer, confession and Communion, she must have been over-whelmed with guilt about the role she'd played in my abortion. And I left her to deal with it alone. So . . . the worst question of all: was it this intolerable, undigestible memory that gradually led my mother to blot out memory *per se?*

The thing was, I still hadn't forgiven Ronald for putting Joanna in the madhouse and cutting off our funds, and I wanted everything from the past to die.

Nada. Nothingness. A clean slate. It was then that I changed my name.

God knows there were times, especially around Christmas, when I missed the younger children, longed to know what was happening with Sammy and Stevie and dear little caught-in-the-middle Jimbo . . . It hurt to think they were living in the same city, growing up and changing and turning into real adults unbeknownst to me . . . They must have thought their older sister was cruel, stuck-up, indifferent, strung out on drugs . . . some combination of the above.

Of course I could have called Elisa and continued to see her on the sly. But I needed to stay out of touch. Only Joanna had my new phone number. When she got small parts off-off Broadway, I'd go see her on stage and we'd meet for a drink afterwards at the White Horse Tavern; I'd ask her about Elisa and the kids; she'd show me photos and tell me stories . . . It was painful, yes, given that they were all living only ten miles north, at the far end of the asphalt jungle . . . but that was the way it was.

Stella, too, gave me scrips and scraps of Mother's news whenever she was in New York and we could find time for a meal together. But she herself was out of touch, always travelling, either abroad for concerts or hither and thither to the various states where her daughters set up housekeeping. She sent me tickets to the Ensemble's concerts in the city and I attended them fanatically, alone or accompanied, drunk or sober, no matter what was happening in my life. Stella introduced me to a hundred baroque composers — at home I'd fight with my boyfriends over whether to listen to Gesualdo or the Rolling Stones . . . and whenever I moved out, which was often, my unwieldy collection of baroque LP's was the first thing I took with me.

When I finally left Martin there was another rough period, lots of penises and drugs in my body, lots of beetles and tadpoles disposed of in various clinics around the world, lots of pages torn up or crumpled and hurled into wastebaskets, lots of death wishes, and then suddenly everything cleared up at once (this does happen sometimes, I must admit, though one can't help wondering in an Eyore-like manner what the point of going up is if one must necessarily come back down) — Per entered my life at almost exactly the same time as my first novel was accepted, and then it was Copenhagen, love, more novels, each grimmer and more successful than the last, and then it was Juan, that marvel, that mess, the slow collapse of my marriage, more death wishes, one of them acted upon, and then recuperating at Laura's place in central France, patiently gluing together the pieces of my shattered self, a summer unexpectedly stretching into two long years as I grew engrossed in the research, fell more and more deeply under the spell of the language and the lore . . . And then back to New York, more novels, and so on, and so forth, blah, blah, blah, and why am I writing this utterly uninteresting crap in my *Scordatura Notebook* when it is not at all what I wanted to get at?

What I wanted to get at was the "meanwhile".

What was happening meanwhile? How did I think of Elisa during those years? How did I imagine her existence? This is what I just can't fathom, can't get back to, can't forgive myself for. After the gesture she had made, the way she had walked into my living room at Saint Mark's Place and taken my life in hand and saved it . . . had I really just dropped her? Let her sink back into the scummy stagnant waters of her everyday martyrdom — written her off, forgotten about her? It seems incredible, but that's exactly what I did.

Oh, Mother. I let the years go by . . . and then there was a day . . .

    — there are years, and then there are days —

    Why do I feel like weeping?

    Why is it so hard for me to write this?

    A stifling smoggy Manhattan-summer evening, July, almost exactly eight years ago. I was giving a reading from my novel-in-progress at the Y. Open to the public. A charge for admission. Posters plastered all over the neighbourhood, with my face on them. (A rather old face, that is, a rather young one. It's weird to see one of your former faces staring out at you from every lamppost.)

    The hall was packed to bursting. Somewhere between two and three hundred people sitting on uncomfortable folding chairs, looking sweaty and expectant, full of imbecilic hope. The accoustics were atrocious, there was no air to breathe, I was feeling premenopausal and bitchy, I didn't want to be there, I wanted to be out at Lake House going for a swim before my solitary supper on the deck. Moreover, I am superstitiously leery of reading from a work that isn't finished, and I was angry with myself for having accepted this invitation in the first place. It was a bad evening and all it did was get worse: the microphone kept acting up, producing that unbearable shrill ring that makes everyone want to cover their ears and run; finally I turned it off and tried to shout out my sentences but they felt so frail, so breakable that shouting them was agony, yet when I lowered my voice the people in the back rows complained they couldn't hear, they'd paid good money for this event and they intended to hear what was being read, so I turned the mike back on, it pretended to be nice but as soon as I opened my mouth it recommenced its strident angry ring, I went on reading but I could feel my blood pressure rising by the second, I wanted to banish to inferno the audience, the hall, the whole island of Manhattan . . . and, just at that moment . . .

— there are days, and then there are moments —

who should come staggering up the aisle but . . .

I broke off in the middle of a sentence, set the pages down on the table, and stared. At first I wasn't even sure it was Ronald — it had been more than twenty years since I'd seen him, he had aged terribly and I thought I must be hallucinating, the heat had gone to my head and I was probably forcing some anonymous drunkard's features to coincide with those of my father. But no. It was really him. When I realized this, an icy calm came over me.

Oh yes, I said to myself. This is perfect. You've chosen the ideal moment, Father, for your remake of the Riverside Church concert of 1948. Well, that's not the way it's going to happen this time round. You may have succeeded in destroying my mother but if you think you're going to destroy me too, you've got another think coming, Buster . . .

The problem was how to get rid of him. Should I allow the organizers to pounce on him, carry him off and toss him into the street like a bum? But that bum's blood was in my veins, his genes explained the colour of my eyes, the shape of my feet, and my inordinate love for Scotch whisky. I couldn't simply . . .

Ronald continued advancing towards the stage. Nervously, the organizers rose to restrain him. I sat there, mesmerized — as if this scene had occurred before many times, as if it were part of a film I knew by heart, as if all I could do was to watch helplessly as it unfolded once again before my eyes. Then, all of a sudden, Ronald beckoned to me. Pronounced my name. And I snapped out of it. I signalled the organizers not to touch him.

A deathly silence came over the hall. The audience was spellbound. All motion suspended, as in *Sleeping Beauty* . . .

Ronald came up and leaned against the stage.

"Nadia," he repeated. And I saw that he was crying.

The microphone recommenced its angry ring. I turned it off and rose to my feet. Shakily crossed the stage to where my father waited.

"Nadia." He reached out a hand to me, tears rolling down his cheeks. Without leaving the stage, I crouched down next to him and looked into his eyes. Said nothing. Speechless.

"I'm sorry," were his first words. He snuffled, blew his nose loudly (Ah! That familiar honk! The handkerchiefs I used to iron!) and began again.

"I'm sorry. I'm really sorry, believe me, Nadia. I'm *really really* sorry to barge in on your reading like this. I would never have done such a thing, I swear it. Don't be mad at me, Nadia. *Please* stop being mad at me. I had to get in touch with you. I didn't know where you were, I didn't even know if you were in New York, it's been years since I even knew if you were on the goddamn planet. I'm sorry. But anyway, I saw the posters — and, well, when I saw the posters, it seemed like the only way . . . Nadia, your mother isn't well. Please come and see her."

My stomach turned over.

"Is she . . . dying?" I whispered.

"No. No, it's not that, don't worry. No, she isn't sick, she isn't dying. It's something else. I . . . I just wanted to give you our new address, you know? In case you didn't have it. I wasn't sure you had it. We figured the old place was too big for us, you know? After the boys moved out. So we're here now, this is the address, see? Still in the same neighbourhood. Please — come and see Elisa. Will you do that much for her? I won't keep you any longer, I apologize — believe me, Nadia, I wouldn't have barged in on you like this if I'd been able to think of any other way . . . "

Yes. In his desperation, Ronald had come to me. Not to any of the other children, the ones who had lived with him until they finished college, the ones who continued to call several times a month and to come home at Christmas and Easter. No, he had come to me. Because I was the oldest? The richest? The one he judged most capable of steering them through the terrifying labyrinth of doctors, hospitals, clinics, homes?

"It's all right, Father," I mumbled. "Don't apologize." I hadn't pronounced the word Father since the mid-Sixties. "You did the right thing. I'm glad you did. I'll come soon. Very soon. I promise."

He lurched away and I somehow managed to get through the rest of the evening. I remember nothing about it — what I read, how I read, whether the microphone finally calmed down, whether the applause was polite or thunderous — nothing.

Something was wrong with Elisa. Oh God. Oh God. Oh God.

Of course by the time I got there, it had been going wrong for so long it was irreversible.

I stood at the door to her room in an unfamiliar apartment, and there she was. Her hair so white it took my breath away. I couldn't speak. Glancing up at me, she rose and took me in her arms, and though she breathed my name, "Nadia," there was uncertainty in her embrace. Then, drawing back, she asked me, and I had to steady myself against the door frame, "How's your little boy, dear?"

"You see?" Ronald whispered, shrugging. "She's completely out of her mind."

Indeed. Out of her mind. This expression seems to me more fitting than any other — senile, crazy, mentally deranged, and so forth. She had not "lost her mind," either. She had simply, gradually, gone out of it. As one leaves a room or a house one does not wish to live in any longer.

Once, Ronald told me, pouring me a cup of coffee a few moments later in the kitchen (he'd learned to make coffee, I noticed — my hands still trembling, making the cup rattle in the saucer), Elisa had dashed out of the house in her nightgown and slippers and curlers at six in the morning and gone tearing down the Grand Concourse screaming his name at the top of her lungs — "Ronald! Ronald! Where is my husband? They've taken my husband away from me!" But when the police finally brought her home, Ronald was still fast asleep in his own bed.

Had she forgotten they'd been sleeping in separate bedrooms since the last, hideous, near-fatal miscarriage, thirty years before? *Scordare:* to mistune. To forget.

She could remember nothing, hold onto nothing, control nothing, not even her bladder. For the first time in his life, Father had learned to use a washing machine and to fold sheets. As Elisa tended to mislay things and could no longer follow a recipe, he'd even taken over most of the shopping and cooking. Perhaps it had finally dawned on him how much he loved his wife, how much he needed her.

But it was too late. Elisa was losing it. Worst of all, she knew she was losing it, and was desperately attempting to hang on, put some order into the flotsam and jetsam at the surface of her thoughts, keep tabs on who she was, where she came from and where she intended to go. She incessantly wrote reminders to herself, and then reminders of the reminders — recording in her fine, meticulous hand the people she planned to call or write — (*Nadia* — my name cropped up several times among the others), her family tree, Ronald's family tree, apparently random dates and place names, the names of composers, conductors and performers she had frequented in her youth, a list of the cities in which she had given concerts, to say nothing of shopping lists (oh Mother, how I loved to watch you draw up shopping lists when I was little! How serious and pretty you looked, chewing on your pencil and frowning, mentally checking the contents of the pantry and fridge) . . . Now these notes were multiplying in all directions, proliferating across her desktop like a cancer of paper — do this, look for that, in order to get here you must turn right, it's just across from Yankee Stadium, don't forget to turn out the light, flush the toilet, ask R. for a new checkbook, I put the chicken in the freezer . . .

There was still anguish in her then — now it is gone. One day something snapped inside her and, relinquishing once and for all her grip on the world of human affairs (and sacred affairs, too, so far as it is possible to tell from the outside), she entered the same state of affable absence as Barbe.

Mother. My little girl.

The Resurrection Sonata

XII - The Visit

Hélène Denis is writhing in the ignoble throes of dysentery, probably picked up from some Parisian passing through. Everything has been tried — remedies, cups, even formulas uttered regularly at a distance by her great friend the bone-setter from Ronzay — but to no avail. She can eat nothing; she is losing her substance; worst of all, she is reduced to passivity and impotence, forced to remain in bed and allow the neighbour women to attend to her. As they go about changing her sheets several times a day, these biddies take a perverse delight in bringing her up to date on the trial of Barbe Durand at La Chaume.

When at last they report the verdict handed down by the judge, interspersing their tale with excited chirps and yelps, Hélène lets out a horrendous cry of rage — and, from that moment onward, seems to lose all desire for recovery. She lapses into silence and prostration, relinquishing her enormous body to the illness, allowing her generous female flesh to be reduced to foul squelching liquids. In her brief hours of respite between colic attacks, she puts the inn's affairs in order, knowing full well that the place will fall back into the hands of the lord of L... the minute she gives up the ghost.

Towards mid-May, sensing that the end is imminent, Hélène sends for Father Thomas. Quite bald now, arthritic, presbyopic and dyspeptic, worn down by the years yet as kind and charitable as ever, the priest rushes to his friend's bedside, bringing everything he needs for the administration of the last rites.

"Yes, yes, little Father," says Hélène. Her voice is weak, but she smiles at him with her usual ironic affection. "We'll take care of that in a minute, if you like, but just now it's something else I'm after. You must promise me . . . "

A stomach spasm forces her to break off.

"Promise you what, my dear Hélène? Oh, how it pains me to see you suffer like this! Tell me what I can do for you. I'll do anything you ask, so long as it doesn't involve the Evil One."

"Can your legs still carry you, you old idiot?"

"Oh, not too badly, not too badly — though I must admit I've learned to whip horses, too."

"Well, good."

Again, Hélène grimaces in pain and has to wait for her entrails to calm down.

"Now listen carefully, little Father. I want you to go and warn Barnabé of the fate that awaits his sister."

The priest starts.

"Oh dear, that's not a good idea. You haven't seen Barnabé in years, my friend. He has changed. He has become, in a manner of speaking, otherworldly. I'm certain his days among us are numbered. He does nothing but pray and sing, sing and pray, with an angelic smile on his face. His skin is diaphanous — and he's so thin you can almost see through his body, you'd think he were about to evaporate, instead of passing away like a normal human being . . . There's no point in disturbing him, sister. He'd be able to do nothing, it would only upset and oppress him, poor soul . . . "

"Do you know if they've set the execution date yet?"

"Yes, I do know," sighs Father Thomas. "They finally decided on Whit Monday, because it's a fair-day in La Chaume. The judge insists on making Barbe an example for the other women . . . "

"He wants to be sure there's the biggest possible crowd for her hanging, is that it?"

"I'm afraid so," admits the priest sadly, his head drooping.

"Well, you listen to me, little Father. I don't know what Barnabé will do, but I do know it's not fair to let them murder his sister in the next town without his even knowing about it. Either send someone else or go yourself, I don't care which — but do it quickly! That's an order, do you hear? We've known each other forty years, Thomas, and this is my last will and testament — you can't wriggle out of it!"

The good father hesitates, resists a moment longer — but then, shaken by the sallowness of his friend's complexion, he gives in.

"I'll go myself, Hélène. You can put your heart at rest."

"All right. Then I give you permission to take out your magic potions."

The priest signs himself precipitately. "My Heavens, what are you saying? Calling the sacred oils magic potions — that's blasphemy!"

"Come, come," says Hélène, in an all but inaudible whisper. "This is no time for us to squabble. I've got my concoctions and you've got yours. Mine tend to reach the soul through the body and yours do the opposite, but it's up to God to decide whose work best in the long run. Come, now, you're not going to sulk about such a little thing, are you? Go ahead, put some on me — where do you put yours, anyway? Ah, on the forehead . . . the hands . . . Yes, that's nice . . . it feels good . . . Thank you, dear Thomas. I've always been fond of you, you know."

Only as he is closing his friend's eyelids a few moments later does the good priest realize he quite forgot to ask her what sins she had committed since her last confession.

The priory of Notre-Dame d'Orsan is in a sorry state. If the truth be told, it has never fully recovered from the depredations inflicted on it one and a half centuries ago by the Duke of Two-Bridges and his reiters — never reascended to its former level of prosperity and influence. Moreover, these past few years, local lords have been nipping up the ecclesiastic properties one after the other — watermills, ironworks, wheat fields, vineyards — so that at the present moment Orsan's financial situation is precarious not to say desperate. The prioress Marie de Lagrange, after making a careful calculation of the monastery's revenues and expenses, has reached the sobering conclusion that the latter outweigh the former to such an extent that the good sisters will soon be in need of dowries or donations to survive.

The monks eat badly.

Barnabé eats virtually not at all.

He prays.

Father Thomas keeps his promise. On the very evening of Hélène Denis's death, Barnabé learns that his twin sister is sentenced to be hanged and burned in public. Lips pressed tightly together, eyebrows knotted over his empty eye sockets, he listens to the whole dreadful tale in silence.

He spends the following night weeping for Barbe, reminiscing about their first encounter in the farmyard, their caresses and confessions — and suddenly, already swooping over their heads, the bats. Such is life. After happiness comes misery; death's shadow follows hard on the heels of life's light. So few meetings between brother and sister! So very few! They managed to see each other only four or five times before that Midsummer's Eve bonfire behind the Torchay inn. And then there was the anguished, secret rendezvous in the Orsan Chapel. And then — nothing. For so many years — nothing. And now this. His poor, poor sister . . .

Barnabé feels the days seeping away, the last days of May, the final days of Barbe upon this earth. He prays God to save his sister's soul; on the offchance, he also asks his mother's advice, but

Marthe has not appeared to him in ages — not since her last, mysterious admonition to *"Beware!"* Barnabé finds it increasingly difficult to see what Barbe's luck consists in, in what way the caul she wore at birth has improved her fate. Unless, that is, their mother meant to say: blessed are those who, like herself, the little singing shepherdess, die young, leaving this vale of tears the sooner to be reunited with their Maker. Yes, in the final analysis, perhaps this was all there was to understand.

I only hope . . . I only hope Barbe gets to heaven, says Barnabé to himself, ill at ease.

Every year at Orsan, Whitsuntide is the particular feast day of Mister Holy-Heart. Tens of thousands of pilgrims pour into the priory from all over the kingdom to render homage to the relic, benefit from its soothing presence, and request — if such be the will of God — that it heal their various ills (Mister Holy-Heart is reputed especially efficacious in the area of stomach ailments). Moreoever, as the priory is celebrating its six hundredth anniversary this year, Marie de Lagrange and the good sisters are looking forward to Whitsuntide with the utmost impatience. They hope to get even more generous gifts than usual out of the pilgrims — not only food but hard cash, which will enable them to repay the interest on their debts and perhaps even begin to rebuild the sacristy.

Barnabé loathes crowds. Increasingly, he prefers to avoid all contact with other human beings so as to remain receptive to the voice of God. This evening, desirous of spending a moment of silent inward contemplation in the presence of Mister Holy-Heart, undistracted by the sight of the ill, lame, destitute, pestiferous and otherwise abject pilgrims who have been congregating around the monastery for days, he has asked for and obtained Sister Marie's permission to remain alone in the chapel after matins. Thus, at three hours past midnight on the morning of Whitsuntide, Barnabé kneels in front of the chest that holds the relic's pitiful remains, bows his head and sinks into prayer.

And, lo and behold, a miracle occurs. Five hundred and ninety-six years after the death of the famous founder of the Double Order of Fontevraud, Robert d'Arbrissel's Heart answers the blind monk. It says, "Go see your sister."

The voice is soft and deep. It resonates in the little chapel with a clear, echoless timbre. Barnabé starts violently.

"What?"

"You heard me, Barnabé. Yes, it really is my voice speaking to you. Go to La Chaume immediately, this very day, and pay a visit to your sister in prison. You can tell the wardens you were sent by Sister Marie de Lagrange herself, to hear the poor sinner's confession."

"But that would be a lie!"

"Oh, don't worry about that — I'll let her in on it, too. I'll convince her this trip is of the utmost importance, the only thing to be done under the circumstances — and that, moreover, she will be giving *me* great pleasure by letting you go. After all, today is my personal feast day, and I've always had a weakness for fallen women, unhappily married women — the ones who'd *lived* a bit, you know what I mean? At least when they renounced the world, they knew what they were renouncing!"

Barnabé cannot believe his ears.

"Virgins and noble widows," the Heart goes on, "always bored me to tears. They had seen and done nothing, they understood nothing of human existence — which meant they had no sense of humour, no culture, no philosophy . . . Oh, they were a bunch of dumb dames, I can tell you! I couldn't help wanting to slap them around a bit. Sometimes after listening for hours to their insipid confessions and namby-pamby prayers, it was all I could do to refrain from kicking them in the butt. I *had* to make them suffer a little, you understand — from hunger, cold, silence, a few strokes of the whip every now and then — so that at least *something* would happen in their narrow little brains and bodies before they went on to the next world. Oh, yes . . . I far preferred the company of the unhappy whores and miserable mammas. They were so much more interesting to be around! That's why I set up my palliasse in their dormitory — and boy, did we have a good time! We'd sit up together, talking and laughing, telling stories until the break of dawn . . . Your sister's pretty terrific, too, Barnabé. She knows a hell of a lot about this world, I can tell you. No, seriously, I really like her. She's got spunk."

Barnabé clears his throat.

"Will she go to Heaven?" he asks, embarrassed.

"Now, don't you worry your little head about that. Just do what I tell you. Go visit her in jail this afternoon; I'll open the way for you. And don't tell anyone you're her brother, tell them you're her confessor . . . "

"But that would be a lie!" Barnabé repeats.

"A lie, a lie, is that the only word you know? Don't you trust me or what? Do you dare to challenge my orders?"

Mister Holy-Heart's voice grows suddenly ominous.

"No, no, of course not," says Barnabé hastily, wondering if this might not in fact be the Evil One, imitating the voice of Robert d'Arbrissel. Come to think of it, how would he recognize d'Arbrissel's voice? He has never heard it before . . .

The Heart becomes mellifluous again.

"That's all you have to do. Go talk to her, find some way of seeing her alone, and God will take care of the rest."

"Well!" mutters the young monk in amazement.

"Yes, well! Now hightail it out of here! Off to bed with you! And as soon as the sun rises, go ask the prioress for an outing permission. I should catch forty winks myself — I'll be needing all my strength to put up with the lamentations of those plaguy pilgrims out there."

Sister Marie de Lagrange instantly agrees to Barnabé's request for a final interview with his condemned sister — indeed, she admits she was surprised he had not asked this favour of her long ago. Though already overwhelmed with preparations for the long day ahead, she rapidly organizes the young monk's expedition, hiring a local driver to take him to La Chaume, putting the priory's best carriage at his disposal, and slipping a chunk of bread into his hand for lunch.

"Be sure to be back by nightfall, won't you?"

"Of course, Mother," says Barnabé, cheeks aflame. "Thank you, Mother."

He has not ventured beyond the reassuring walls of the priory in several years — not, in fact, since his accident. The instant the carriage trundles out of the large central courtyard and starts down the road, his skin seizes up in fear. He feels naked, exposed, afloat in an unknown world, at the mercy of one and all.

The driver drops him unceremoniously in front of La Chaume prison. Barnabé quakes and shakes uncontrollably as he announces the purpose of his visit to the prison wardens.

"It will only take . . . a . . . a few minutes," he stammers. "But I must be left alone with her, to . . . well, to hear her confession . . . and give her the last rites."

"She's had 'em already," retorts one of the wardens in a rough gruff voice. "The local priest came yesterday — because today's Whitsuntide, in case you didn't know, and he's got better things to do."

"But I've been sent by the abbess in person!"

insists Barnabé nervously, assuaging his bad conscience with the thought that this is more of an
exaggeration than an outright lie.

"Well," pipes up another, apparently younger
warden, with a lewd little laugh, "could be she's
committed some more sins since yesterday and she
needs to confess all over again. You never know
with harlot bitches like her."

Everyone laughs uproariously. The discussion
goes on in this manner for several minutes, punctuated by great bursts of laughter, now at the
young woman's expense, and now at the blind
monk's. Barnabé is utterly at a loss. It has been ages
since he had intercourse with anyone but nuns and
angels, and he no longer knows how to talk to ordinary people. He is terrified by the cruel, narrow-
minded vulgarity of these individuals — but no
doubt it is he who should attempt to appeal to their
nobler instincts. They, too, are creatures of God, after
all . . .

At last he feels himself being grabbed by the
arm and jerked out of the room.

"Are you turning down my request?" he asks,
blushing crimson.

"On the contrary!" answers the other jubilant-
ly. "We're satisfying it, brother, we're satisfying it!
The only problem is, we didn't know where to put
you and the harlot bitch so you could have a nice
chit-chat together. And then we figured there was
only one place that'd really be *private*, if you know
what I mean . . . Ha! ha! ha! . . . But p'raps you're
too holy to know about that sort of thing, huh? Do

monks shit?"

With a guffaw and a nudge, the man continues dragging Barnabé down a long corridor, and the poor monk is too obsessed with the fear of tripping and falling to listen. Suddenly, he feels soft earth and grass beneath his feet, hears a door open and finds himself hurtling forward . . . His forehead bangs up against a wall of moist wood, a revolting smell assails his nostrils, and he realizes that his final moments on this earth with his sister are to be spent in an outhouse.

"Here you are, bitch," growls the other man, addressing Barbe. "Your final confessional. Now's the time to get rid of the last little bits of filth you have weighing on your conscience. Ha! ha! ha! You did stuff your conscience up your arsehole too, didn't you?"

Barbe, in turn, is shoved into the shadow and stench.

"Barnabé!" she murmurs incredulously, recognizing her brother.

The twins embrace tenderly in the latrine.

A few rays of yellow June sun manage to slip through the chinks between the boards, and Barbe gradually makes out her brother's features in the obscurity.

"Barnabé!" she repeats — but this time her voice is filled with horror.

"My sister, my little sister," says the monk. "I must be a dreadful sight, forgive me. Of course, you didn't know . . . But it is *you*, not I, who deserve to be pitied, sweet Barbe . . . Oh . . . dear God!" he exclaims suddenly, running his hands over his sister's face and head. "What have they done to you, my poor angel? They've shaven your head?"

"Not only my head, but every hair on my body," laughs Barbe. "I'm as bald as you are! It's to prepare for tomorrow's ceremony."

Tears well up in the monk's empty eye sockets and slide down his smooth cheeks.

"Don't cry, brother dear," murmurs Barbe. "Everything will be all right. Really, I assure you. And you know why? Because I've kept the baby with me!"

"You . . . you . . .?"

Barnabé is disconcerted, but the young woman can scarcely repress her excitement.

"Not only that," she goes on, "but his name is Barnabé too! I named him after you, dear brother! And I promised he'd get to meet you some day, only I had no idea how to go about it . . . And now look — God has answered my prayers once again! Oh, you can't imagine how close I feel to God these days, Barnabé. Ever since Christmas, ever since my son was born on the same day as His, He's been at my side, we talk together all the time, I've never been so happy in my life . . . "

"How strange," says the monk slowly, as if to himself. "I have just the opposite impression . . . Whereas I spend the better part of my time in prayer, God seems to have withdrawn from me. I feel His presence less and less often . . . As for our mother, she hasn't come to see me in months . . . And, this morning, I must admit that for a moment I feared it was . . .

the Evil One who told me to come and visit you here."

"What a silly idea! How funny you are, brother! Oh, my poor dear . . . "

"There's something else I should tell you, Barbe . . . Father Thomas came to Orsan last month, to bring me news of the outside world . . . Sad news, all of it. He was the one who told me . . . about you . . . And he also informed me that . . . Hélène Denis departed this earth, just after Easter."

"Oh!"

"She died of dysentery . . . but she went on wisecracking up to the end — he swore it!"

Brother and sister remain silent for a moment, each of them lost in their own thoughts.

The idea occurs to both of them at exactly the same instant. They jump, so abrupt and astonishing is its simultaneous arrival in their respective brains. From this moment onward, they speak only in whispers.

"Are you sure, Barnabé?"

"Of course. It's obvious. That's why I was sent here."

"You'd do that for me?"

"For you . . . and for your little one."

"Yes. For His Majesty Barnabé the Second."

They clamp their hands over their mouths to keep from laughing.

"Tell me," Barbe goes on. "What must I do?"

"Well, my habit has a hood; you can use it to hide your face. It's not difficult to play blind — all you have to do is close your eyes and allow yourself to be led out to the carriage. The wardens don't exactly have a velvet touch, but you're used to that."

"And then?"

"And then, once you're settled into the back seat, keep your face well in the shadow of the hood but look sharp. Just as you're leaving the city, the carriage has to stop to make a left turn. The driver will have spent the afternoon in the tavern, so at that point he'll likely be either singing his head off or yelling at the horses — anyhow, the second he comes to a halt at the crossroads, you slip down and take yourself off. Do you still know how to run like a hare and vanish like a lizard?"

"I think so, yes."

There is a brief silence. Then Barnabé asks, "What about me?"

"Oh, they won't do much more to you. This is the hanging dress . . . pretty scratchy, isn't it? Wait, let me adjust it for you . . . there! It's a perfect fit. You have no more hair on your legs than I do, brother!"

"And you have no more breasts than I do, sister!"

"True, true," says Barbe, shaking her head. "Donat always used to call me the weasel."

"Who is Donat?"

"Oh, it doesn't matter now. That was a long time ago . . . Anyhow, when they come and get you, they'll throw you into a cell — it's a black hole, I can't see any more in there than you can . . . And then tomorrow morning, before you leave for the gallows, they'll put a blindfold over your eyes and tie your hands together . . . So you see, you've nothing to fear — someone will be there to guide you just as usual!"

"Fine. As far as tomorrow goes, that's fine. But what about now, when they come to take me out of here? What if someone notices my eyes?"

"Oh, they don't look at me very closely, you know — I'm an object of horror. But here — take this scrap of cloth, it's my little boy's blanket but I'll find him another one . . . That way when you go back out, you can cover your eyes with it, as if you were weeping. It's not far from here to the dungeon — they won't notice a thing."

"You're wonderful, Barbe. I adore you."

"Me too, Barnabé. I've always adored you and now I'll adore you always. Do you still know how to imitate my voice?"

After a brief hesitation, Barnabé clears his throats and says, in a perfect echo, "Do you still know how to imitate my voice?"

They embrace, smothering their laughter in each other's necks.

"I thank you, little sister," says Barnabé at last. "For years now, my dearest wish has been to die."

"I thank you, too. There's no doubt this is what God wanted, is there?"

"None. Absolutely none at all."

The *Scordatura* Notebook

August 9th

WHAT ARE YOU DOING?

I'm having the time of my life, that's what I'm doing.

You can't get away with it! The Resurrection Sonata *ends with Barbe's hanging — you know that! You've known it from the beginning. It's a tragedy!*

Not anymore, it isn't.

Yes, it is! It's a tragedy based on an actual historical event!

Jesus, just listen to you. Now *you're* the one who wants me to stick to the facts. I thought that was God's job! Barbe is right — you and He are six of one and half a dozen of the other.

How dare you turn it into slapstick?

Ah . . . I'm learning to catch laughter like glittering fish in the running water of language, the flowing river of language . . . Who knows? Maybe Sol will like it this time! Maybe it'll make him laugh so hard that he'll have no choice but to get down on his knees and ask me to marry him.

Do you want to marry Sol?

Nope!

Come on, stop fooling around. Just look how your style has gone to the dogs since you kicked me out!

Ah! At least you admit I *kicked* you out, whereas you said I wouldn't have a leg to stand on . . .

Nada, you can't just twist things any whichway. Your new idea is perfectly ludicrous and implausible. Believe me, you can't get away with it! No one will take you seriously!

The name is Nadia.

Besides, what was the point of my bringing your twin brother into existence if you were just going to kill him in the end anyway?

Ask God. He did the same with His son. There *is* a point, dear dæmon. I have a very good reason for doing what I am doing. At last, at long last, thanks to *The Resurrection Sonata*, I can relinquish the fantasy of my twin brother as perfect Witness, accept his death — oh, it hurts! it really hurts! How wonderful to feel the pain at last! — and be myself. Now alone, now in the company of

others — others real and imaginary, living and
dead . . .

I won't stand for it!

You're next in line, pal. Don't forget, you're
neither more nor less than one of my characters —
I brought you to life, and I can get rid of you whenever I see fit. It seems to me you're starting to out-
live your usefulness. A devil playing a violin isn't
bad, I grant you, but just think — a violin playing
itself! Striking sharp chords of memory and imagi-
nation from its own depths! Now, *that* is magic!
Diabolus in musica is nothing — wait till you hear
my new intervals! . . . lapsing from harmony into
dissonance and back again . . . Listen, seriously. I
intend to stop the nevers and forevers, the alls and
nothings. I intend to embrace mixtures and mitiga-
tions, content myself with pieces of perfection (as
in: pieces of music). Hell and Heaven are both right
here on earth, you know. Nowhere else. Nowhere
else. Oh, dæmon, can't you see? You'll never win.
Every decision to despair is instantly annulled by
the face of a child, the smile of a friend, the beauty
of a poem or a painting or a flower. . .

No, I'm dreaming!

. . . not because these things are reason to hope
(don't worry, I'm not that far gone yet!); only
because they *are*. Period. No future. I believe in the
characters of my novel in the same way supersti-

tious peasants believe in ghosts, or mothers in their children — not because I hope for something good to come of them, but because they're *there*, infrangibly miraculously *there*. It's just as silly to despair as it is to hope, don't you see? The truth is neither permanent blazing light nor eternal gloom and doom but *flashes* of love, beauty and laughter on a seething background of shadow; the gleam and glint of instruments in darkness — yes — like music against silence, rhythm against flatness — like the rays of sun filtering through the putrid boards of the latrine in which Barbe and Barnabé have just embraced for the last time . . .

You are making yourself ridiculous.

Can't scare me with that word anymore! . . . In the second part of the book, Barbe will find her way to Paris, she'll learn to read and write, Louis XIV will die and be replaced by Louis XV, Barbe will become famous throughout the capital as a healer, consoler, spell-lifter, angel-maker and broken-heart-repairer; around the middle of the century she'll have an affair with Jean-Jacques Rousseau who is twenty-six years her junior — ah, Stella will love that! — she'll tell him the story of her life, he'll teach her to read music and to sing, she'll live to be very very old, Louis XV will die and be replaced by Louis XVI, perhaps Barbe will end up doing so much business as a witch that she'll get herself arrested and imprisoned in the horrible Salpétrière General Hospital — but if she does she'll foment an uprising there, inciting the beggars and prostitutes and lepers and syphilitics and madwomen to revolt . . . Anything is possible; everything is possible — she'll only be a hundred years old in 1786 and she can very well have had a premonition of the French Revolution — she's bright, you know.

. . .

Oh, come on, dæmon, don't look so glum! Remember Goethe's Mephistopheles — "Nothing in the whole world is more absurd than a despairing devil!" Really, you mustn't worry. There are plenty of people who will be delighted to welcome you into their hearts. My own is full up now, overcrowded, reservations made in advance well into the twenty-first century. No room left, no room for hatred.

What about . . . hydrangea?

Oh. Glad you asked. Mr. Harley just called and invited me to come up next weekend and see his hydrangea.

Do you want to live with Mr. Harley?

Nope. But they're all in bloom, he said. Just gorgeous, unbelievably gorgeous, the bubbling burst shape, the full-cumulus cloud shape — and the colours, my God! Pink, white, lavender, but especially the blues, every shade of blue from pale morning sky to summer night indigo — come and see them, he said! And you know, he added, the loveliest hydrangea of all are the ones I have in the house, from last year. I dried them hanging upside down, and the result is quite extraordinary. Sweet winey rust colour, pearl and heather. You must come, really. You've never been inside my house. I'd love to have you over for dinner, if you have time.

This edition was typeset using a customized compressed Palatino font variation, and composed at Moons of Jupiter, 134 Eastbourne Ave., Toronto, (416) 481 4470.

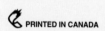
PRINTED IN CANADA